ABOUT THE AUTHOR

Pamela Hart is an award-winning, bestselling author of more than 35 books. She writes the Poppy McGowan mystery series and also historical novels; *The Charleston Scandal* is her most recent historical story, set in 1920s London.

As Pamela Freeman, she is well-known as a beloved children's author and fantasy writer. Her most recent children's book is a non-fiction picture book, *Dry to Dry: The Seasons of Kakadu*. Her adult fantasy series, The Castings Trilogy, ended with the award-winning *Ember and Ash*.

To be kept up to date about the next Poppy McGowan story, you can subscribe to her newsletter at pamela-hart.com/newsletter; you even get a free story!

DIGGING UP DIRT

Pamela Hart

FICTION

LEVEL
BEST BOOKS

First Published 2021
First Australian Paperback Edition 2021
ISBN 9781867201878

ISBN 978-1685128371 US Edition | Level Best Books August 2024

This is a work of fiction. Names, characters, places, and incidents are either the product of the author's imagination or are used fictitiously, and any resemblance to actual persons, living or dead, business establishments, events, or locales is entirely coincidental.

Published by
HQ Fiction & Level Best Books
An imprint of Harlequin Enterprises (Australia) Pty Limited (ABN 47 001 180 918), a subsidiary of HarperCollins Publishers Australia Pty Limited (ABN 36 009 913 517)
Level 13, 201 Elizabeth St
SYDNEY NSW 2000
AUSTRALIA

® and TM (apart from those relating to FSC®) are trademarks of Harlequin Enterprises (Australia) Pty Limited or its corporate affiliates. Trademarks indicated with ® are registered in Australia, New Zealand and in other countries.

A catalogue record for this book is available from the National Library of Australia
www.librariesaustralia.nla.gov.au

 Australia by McPherson's Printing Group

For Ron,
whose idea this was,
with much love

CHAPTER ONE

Monday

'Hello, miss?' It was Boris, my carpenter, and he sounded worried. 'Miss, I found something.'

'Something? What? Where?'

'I dug the hole for the post. I found ...' His voice dropped. '... body.'

'What?'

'A *body*, miss.'

'What kind of body?' I was thinking, for some reason, of an old car body—a Valiant or a Ford or something, and wondering how they'd got it in the door.

'You know, bones. Skellington.'

'A *skeleton*?' I almost dropped the phone. And I'm ashamed to admit it, but my first thought was, *This is going to completely stuff up my renovations.*

The day had started like almost every day did, with me at my little house, talking to a tradie about their day's work on my renovations. All I wanted to do was get agreement on the task for the day and head off to my own work. But no.

'They're all so far away, miss …'

My carpenter was telling me the story of his life. Of course.

Boris was bemoaning the fact that all his family were thousands of kilometres away in Croatia and he missed them so much and there was this girl … I nodded and smiled sympathetically, but in the meantime, I had a chipboard floor that needed to be pulled up before the electricians could come in and rewire.

Why not tell him to get back to business, you ask? It just doesn't work that way. Trust me, I've been through this before.

Boris is short and stocky, but his face has the long lines and the deep, sad eyes of a hound dog, and he was never sadder than when he was talking about his family. With other people, he has a reputation for never saying more than two words at a time. With me, he rambles.

Don't ask me why it happens. Maybe it's my face. Maybe my background in interviewing makes me put on an interested look automatically. Me, I think that character is destiny, and my fate is to go through life having people tell me their problems, their sorrows, their disappointments—and sometimes their triumphs. And I admit—it *is* interesting. People always are, if you listen long enough.

'So, maybe, I get permanent residency …' Boris concluded hopefully. I patted him on the shoulder.

'I'm sure you will.' I shifted my gaze to the floor. The plasterers had finished, thank God, which meant the chipboard, already a bit damp and mouldy, was now festooned with drying lumps of plaster. Next to my beautiful clean walls it looked even more disgusting than it had before.

'The electricians will be here on Thursday to do the power points,' I said, slightly plaintive. My big brother the builder says that the best way to get help from tradesmen is to simply state the problem and let them come up with the solution. They don't like amateurs telling them what to do. This is true of female tradies as well.

Boris patted my shoulder.

'Don't you worry about that, miss,' he said. 'Them floors'll be gone by then. I'll pull 'em up and put in the newel post.'

The freestanding staircase in one corner was held up structurally by a square metal column underneath the half-landing, but the balustrade needed a newel post at the bottom to hold it steady. The old one had simply rested on top of the chipboard floors, but Boris was going to put in a proper post that went down to ground level and had a solid concrete footing.

He hefted a big crowbar and grinned, showing one gold tooth and one gap among otherwise blindingly white teeth. I grinned back. I like Boris. He's a good carpenter, and I could trust him to look after my house. I felt it needed looking after, even though there's nothing there yet, except the bricks and, now, the beautiful old-fashioned proper plaster walls. My tiny little worker's cottage, only twelve feet wide, had been emptied out completely—plaster scraped from the walls, carpet gone, new damp course, new ceilings, and soon the floors themselves would go, at least on the ground floor. I was redoing that from the dirt up, because it had been *really disgusting* when I bought it (only reason I could afford it). The only snag was that I had to live with my parents for the duration.

I looked around, at the morning sunlight coming in through the back window, the high ceilings complete with ceiling roses and rose-patterned cornices, the Victorian mouldings around the doors, and sighed. It was worth it. I loved this house. It was the kind of house I'd walked by as a uni student, when I lived in a block of flats around the corner, and imagined living in one day.

I left Boris to it and drove to work, past the statues of World War One soldiers on Anzac Bridge, past the Fish Market where the tourists were taking pictures of the fishing fleet, over the Sydney Harbour Bridge and up the freeway to Artarmon. I technically work at the Children's and Education Department of the ABC in the city, in Ultimo, but my day-to-day work is at Artarmon.

The Australian Broadcasting Corporation is what an American friend of mine calls 'PBS on steroids' but it's probably more accurate to compare it to the BBC. We don't have the BBC's budget, but we are government funded and apolitical. 'Innovative and comprehensive broadcasting services' is our charter, and we use TV, radio and the digital universe to deliver them.

The program I was currently a researcher for was what is known in the trade as a 'co-production', which means that we worked with an outside contractor, Star Shots, who had the rights to sell the show overseas, and that was where I was based. I had to organise the week's shooting schedule and make sure I had delivered all the recce information the camera crews needed to find and shoot the footage we wanted.

The show was called *Stage 1: Launchpad*, and was an education program aimed at littlies in the first three years of school. Heavily linked to the curriculum, we made programs about things like 'Where does milk come from?' and 'How do fish come from the sea to the table?' and 'What happens at the zoo after closing time?'

I was the researcher and scriptwriter, which meant I was given a topic by the director/producer, Jennifer Jay, and then I found the information, locations, people to interview, anything we needed, really, and put it into a script.

By the time I got to Star Shots in Artarmon it was raining hard. Not one of those Sydney squalls which dumps buckets on you and passes in a few moments, but a solid, long-lasting rain that would probably go on all day. So much for my camera shoot at Luna Park. We were making a show about what happens at the amusement park behind the scenes.

As I walked in, shaking off my umbrella and my unruly mop of hair, Jennifer Jay hurried out of the office. Jennifer Jay (everyone uses her full name, like a character in a picture book) hurries everywhere. She's a slight woman with the nervous mannerisms of an ex-smoker trying not to reach for a fag. Sharp brown eyes, pale skin, dull brown hair that always seems to be showing a strip of grey at her centre parting—and how is that possible, unless she does it deliberately, which I wouldn't put past her? You don't much notice how she looks because she is very *intense*, very concentrated on you or the job or both.

'So,' she said as I walked in, 'which tradesman have you been charming this morning?'

This was what she always asked if she thought I'd been wasting time on the house. I wasn't *technically* late. I work public service hours, because I'm an ABC employee. Jennifer Jay was, too. But the other people at Star Shots were private contractors, which means they worked all the hours God sent, so they'd been here since before breakfast. Jennifer Jay liked to work along with them, clocking up flexi hours which she never took. I don't think she has a life outside the show. She's divorced with no children and the only reason she goes home is to feed her cat and swap her library books. Which makes her sound pitiful, and that is *so* wrong.

'The carpenter wanted to tell me the story of his life,' I said defensively.

She laughed, and so did the receptionist, Cherie. It was an ongoing joke. Mind you, both Jennifer Jay and Cherie had told me the story of *their* lives on different occasions, so I didn't feel they should laugh too loud. Particularly as Cherie's story about how and why she got her many piercings had needed a very strong stomach to listen to.

Jennifer Jay looked out the window to the parking lot.

'That shoot at Luna Park has been called off. Weather Bureau says this'll go on all day.' She scowled. She resents wasting camera time. 'Do we have anything else we can send them to? Indoors?'

I went through my to-do list in my head, but couldn't think of anything. We'd done the indoors shooting at Luna Park last week, on another wet day.

'Not on this program,' I said. 'I could have a try at setting something up for the next one.'

'The archaeology one?'

'No, the one on recycling. Archaeology's the one after that. There are sections of the recycling centre that are under cover.'

Jennifer Jay nodded.

'Have a try.'

She walked off to Editing and I went to the production office, which was, as always, full of people, whiteboards, old digital tapes, paper, and fraying posters from past productions sticky-taped to the walls.

People always think that working in television is glamorous. Maybe if you're interviewing starlets on the red carpet at the Oscars, but not in our production office, and not when you're knee deep in cow dung in the middle of a milking yard at five o'clock on a cold morning, trying to write down the *exact* sequence of moves the dairy farmer makes so the camera crew will film *everything* they need to. Not glamorous. But quite a lot of fun, all the same.

And I like the fact I learn stuff—the behind closed doors stuff, the trade secret stuff. It's surprising, the amount of information I have tucked away. I started out writing video scripts for the Museum of New South Wales, so all in all I've learnt some esoteric facts in the last few years.

On that particular morning, I had dumped my bag on the desk and was looking at my emails when my mobile rang.

'Hello, miss? Miss, I found something,' said Boris.

And that's when it all went pear-shaped.

CHAPTER TWO

'A *skeleton*?'

While I clutched my phone, I also clutched at the faint hope that Boris might be wrong. When I worked at the museum, people were always calling up to say they'd found ancient Aboriginal remains, but when the archaeologists got there it was usually dog or sheep bones. Once, it had been a kangaroo and they'd got all excited about pre-European settlement middens until they did the carbon dating and found that the bones were from the 1950s, when the owner's father used to go spotlighting in his ute. So I was hoping that Boris's 'skellington' was some long-ago family pet, buried in the garden of the big house down the road, whose grounds had been subdivided into building lots in 1894, when my house was built.

So, 'Are you sure it's a person?' I asked.

Terry, the camera operator, looked up from his fishing magazine. I tried to pretend nothing exciting was going on. Terry used to be a news cameraman until he got a bit too old and a bit too stout to run away from riots and fires, but he can still smell a story. He nudged Dave, the sound guy, and they began collecting their equipment. Terry and Dave look like your standard Australian blokes, and cultivate a 'nothing to see here' demeanour, but they're both as sharp as needles.

'Just some bones, sticking out of the ground,' Boris said. 'Looks like a leg.'

One of the esoteric things I know from my time at the museum is that the long bones of the leg are in fact a good way to identify humans, but also that a lot of mammal leg bones look alike. It might just be a cow or something. I pushed away the question of why someone would bury a cow under my house.

'I'll be right there,' I said soothingly. 'Go make yourself a cup of tea.'

'I call the police, miss?'

'No!' I said quickly. 'Not until we're sure it's a human body. I'll—I'll get an expert in.'

'Okey dokey, miss.' Boris sounded more cheerful.

Jennifer Jay also has an unerring instinct for news from her days as a current affairs producer. She perched on the edge of my desk. 'What's up?'

'Boris has found bones under the house.'

That took even her aback. 'Human bones?'

'Not sure. So …' I thought fast. It was imperative that I got this sorted out in time for the electricians on Thursday. Booking an electrician was like arranging an audience with the Pope: miss it and I'd never get another.

I'd done a lot of the work on the archaeology program already. 'Why don't we kill two birds with one stone? I'll see if Annie can scare up an archaeologist to check out the bones, and the boys can come and film him—her, them—working. Then at least we won't have wasted a shooting day, and we'll have some footage up our sleeve for the archaeology program.'

Jennifer Jay nodded. 'Okay.'

My friend Annie Southey was the reason we were doing the archaeology program in the first place. She was Director of Gallery Operations at the Museum of New South Wales and she had run a very successful open dig at a site in The Rocks all through the previous school holidays. So successful that Jennifer Jay had heard about it. She knew that Annie and I were friends, so she'd announced that archaeology fitted in with the curriculum theme 'people who help us' and we would do a program. I personally thought it was stretching the curriculum a bit, but it looked like being an interesting show, so what the hell.

I rang Annie in a bit of a fluster. 'Need your help. Need your help now.'

'Okay, calm down.' Annie was always calm. Very matter of fact, full of common sense. 'What's the problem?'

'Bones under my house. Boris took the floor up and there are bones.'

'Human bones?' Oh, yes, *now* she's interested. She loves crime novels.

'I don't know. I haven't seen them, I'm in Artarmon. But I don't want the police involved unless they really *are* human. So I thought—' I outlined the plan to her.

She was silent for a minute, thinking. 'I'd have to send Julieanne.'

'Noooo!' I wailed. 'Not Psycho Woman.'

'She's the only one here, apart from that contractor she's sleeping with. The good-looking one.'

'How does she *do* that?' I asked, momentarily distracted.

'I guess they're too busy looking at her tits to notice the madness in her eyes,' Annie said.

I debated with myself. Julieanne versus the police. Julieanne and I had a history, and not a pleasant one. It was a close call, and if I hadn't promised Jennifer Jay a shoot, I'd have gone for the police as the lesser of two evils.

'Oh, send her,' I said. 'I'm putting the camera crew in, too, so we'll get some footage for the show out of it.'

'And our agreement is in place?' Annie asked, suddenly businesslike. 'We get to use the footage as we choose in our exhibitions?'

'All signed and agreed to. What time could Julieanne meet me?'

'You know her. A bone to chew on? She'll get straight on her broomstick and fly.'

So I collected the camera crew—Terry, Dave and the production assistant Mirha—and followed their huge Ford V8 back over the Harbour Bridge (most of the ABC's cars are old). Sydney Harbour looked fabulous as always, even on this grey day, giving a sense of space and air and light to the middle of the city. Outside of peak hour, just five minutes off the bridge and you're turning into Johnston St, the main road that cuts right through Annandale. Seven minutes and you're pulling up at my place. I love how close it is to the city.

Annandale was built in the second half of the nineteenth century for the new professional and merchant classes that had arisen in Australia after the gold rush. It was a mix of large two-storey houses with lots of wrought-iron lacework on the balconies, beautiful plasterwork and fireplaces and lovely staircases, and tiny plain workers' cottages in narrow laneways where the labour force had lived. Guess which kind I could afford?

There's a long and complicated story attached to how I could even *think* about buying a house in Annandale, one of the nice inner-city suburbs. It involves my grandparents dying, my parents moving into *their* house in Annandale, then redeveloping their own big block in Western Sydney and putting townhouses on it, and then giving a townhouse each to me and my siblings. I sold mine. With that money, and the sale of the little flat I had, I had *just* enough money to buy the most run-down, tiny house in the worst street in the suburb.

But it was worth every penny. I loved to walk down the wide streets shaded by old, old trees to the park by Blackwattle Bay on the harbour, across from the boatyard where the mega-rich moored their white ultra yachts and craftsmen restored old wooden boats, plank by careful plank. At sunset the air was full of fruit bats heading home to the Moreton Bay figs in the park, and watching them fly across the city skyline under the moon was enough to make me fall in love with Sydney all over again.

Then again, I've always loved Sydney. Even in the rain, which was still coming down steadily.

Boris was sitting on a milk crate inside the open front door, drinking a coffee from the shop around the corner. He couldn't possibly have visited the shop without telling Gracie, the owner, all about the 'skellington'. I was sure the story was already spreading through the city. We'd have media all over us before we knew it. Well, I thought smugly, the ABC's got the exclusive.

We trooped in, leaving our umbrellas outside. The middle of my floor had been pulled up, the chipboard sections leaning against my pristine new walls.

'Boris!' I said reproachfully, pulling them away and inspecting the damage. 'Keep them off the new plaster.'

'Sorry, miss, I just chucked 'em down when I saw—' He pointed towards the bare ground under the floor.

'Oh. Yes. Okay.' I peered in, jostling for position with Terry and Dave. All I could see was a white bit of something sticking up from the hard-packed earth. There were some other disturbances in the earth around it, but they looked more like the edges of broken crockery.

'Mate, can't see shit down there,' Terry said. 'I'll bring in the lights.'

I hoped my ancient electrical circuits would take the load.

Boris, cheered by having other men there, pulled up more sections of chipboard and hauled them out to the skip on the road.

Terry and Dave carried in the lights while Mirha began to write up the shooting list and get the releases ready for the talent. A release is a document that says you allow us to film you and use the footage in our show. Anyone who appears on camera has to sign one, and it includes permission to use stills or photos in social media as well. Mirha is twenty-one (all PAs are in their early twenties, for some reason). As always, her hijab, loose top and trousers in various shades of turquoise were the height of style; her perfect grooming always made me feel like a slob. She smiled nicely at Boris and asked him to sign a release.

Boris was a good ten years older than Mirha, but he didn't seem to be thinking much about the girl back home in Croatia right now. He had some impressive muscles, thanks to his work, and he was flexing all of them at the same time. It made it quite hard for him to sign the paper. I don't think he even read what it said. He grinned, showing off the gold tooth, and Mirha giggled.

The main room of my house makes an L shape. As you walk in the door, the room stretches the width of the house. About ten feet in front of you is a corridor that leads to the kitchen out the back. Originally there had been a bedroom on the other side of the corridor, but the wall between that room and the parlour had been pulled down to make a bigger living space. It would have been nice to have pulled the corridor wall down, but it supported the floor above, so it had to stay. My plan was to have a dining alcove where the bedroom had been.

Terry set up lights in that area and one on the staircase that led to the bedrooms. 'Mate, just get down in the hole, will you, and don't look at the camera? Just want to set up the shot.'

Boris got in the hole, resting on his crowbar and trying not to look at the camera, as instructed, but having trouble because Mirha was standing right behind it, as PAs do, and he kept checking that she was still watching him. Terry's lights were warming up the small space nicely. They might even help my plaster dry out faster. He set up the camera and adjusted the lights while Dave fiddled with his recorder, getting some atmosphere down before shooting started. A sound technician always lays down an atmosphere track. It's an empty soundscape which can be used to provide a sense of continuity to a montage of shots, or which can fill in the gaps between edited conversations. It's the mortar of sound editing, and ideally it has no identifiable components.

I took a few shots for the program's Facebook page. We'd use them when the episode went to air, but I tweeted a couple out straight away—we had a lot of teachers who followed the show's Twitter account and we liked to give them a heads-up on a new episode so that they could plan lessons around it.

Archaeology for little ones—Australian history under your floorboards!

Then Julieanne came through the open door and all three men immediately straightened up, sucked in their stomachs and smoothed back their hair, like they'd rehearsed it. Terry and Dave began handling their tech equipment with what they clearly hoped was masculine vigour. Terry even did that thing with his fingers where you make a rectangle and look through it, pretending he was setting up a shot of Julieanne. Dave extended the boom microphone in a frankly Freudian gesture.

'Hi,' she said, smiling sweetly at Terry and Dave and ignoring me. I don't think she even noticed Mirha. Then she turned the smile on Boris, who blushed. 'Isn't this exciting?' It really was a terrific impersonation of a nice person.

That sounds bitchy. Look, there are many people in the world who like Julieanne Weaver. There are many people in the world who like me. However, Julieanne and I do not like each other. We never had. It was one of those instant antagonism things—on her part at first, and then on mine. I still don't really understand it.

Julieanne was one of those tall, blonde, blue-eyed women who look like they are channelling Barbie—Executive Barbie, in this case, thanks to the raw silk navy trouser suit and navy stilettos. I wondered just how gorgeous this new contractor she was sleeping with was. She didn't usually dress quite this well for work.

I didn't have to wonder long, because someone tall, dark and, okay, not quite handsome, but definitely attractive came through the door. Pale skin, good bones, maybe a bit lanky. I instinctively stood up, sucked my stomach in and smoothed my hair back, then realised what I was doing and laughed at myself. He smiled at me and I was suddenly conscious of my old jeans and cotton top, my standard work clothes. My part of the ABC is dag city. If I wore a suit to work everyone would think I had a job interview. Besides, my work takes me into factory floors, farms, fish markets … I have to be ready for anything a location can throw at me. I keep gumboots and overalls in the back of my car, and a respectable skirt and blouse in case I have to interview someone who might care how I look.

Julieanne's guy didn't seem to notice the clothes. Like Julieanne, he was peering into the hole. Terry looked at me and I twirled my finger to indicate he should start shooting. He signalled Dave and they both began doing their thing, while Mirha took notes. The cameras are almost soundless, so neither Julieanne or—what *was* his name?—noticed.

'I'm Poppy McGowan,' I said to the other archaeologist, since Julieanne clearly wasn't going to introduce us.

'Bartholomew Lang. Call me Tol.' He glanced around briefly but I'm not sure he actually saw me. He couldn't wait to look back to the hole.

'I'll have to change,' Julieanne announced and looked at me for the first time. I pointed up the stairs to the bedrooms—those rooms were in pretty good shape as they'd only been added to the house about twenty years ago. They had chipboard floors, too, but those were solid and dry.

Julieanne disappeared upstairs, carefully skirting the hole in the floor and the light on the steps, but Tol jumped right into the hole. Terry followed the movement.

'Wait for me!' Julieanne said, moving faster.

'Mmm,' Tol replied, bending over and inspecting the bone. 'I think you've got an animal here. At least, I hope you have.'

'Why?' I asked, peering down, but keeping out of camera range.

'Because these'—he pointed to something invisible on the surface of the bone—'are butchering marks. Whatever this was, it was chopped up and probably eaten. So let's hope it isn't human, eh?'

He smiled up at me wryly, and I couldn't help but smile back. God, he was attractive. Hazel eyes, a long, thoughtful face and wonderful hands. I'm a sucker for hands. I had to remind myself sharply that I had a boyfriend and Tol had a girlfriend and this was business. And I had to get them out of here quickly so Boris could finish pulling up the floor and the electricians could come in on Thursday.

Tol poked at the bone a bit more with those long-fingered, sensitive hands. I told myself to stop drooling. Looking away from his hands made me realise that, unlike Julieanne, he was in ratty old jeans and a faded polo shirt. Then he pulled a tarnished, pointed trowel from his back pocket and began to scrape the dirt away. The lights glinted off the trowel and out of the corner of my eye I saw Terry nod with satisfaction. I took a shot for social media. It was a very Indiana Jones moment.

'Where's the hat and leather jacket?' I blurted out like an idiot.

Tol looked resigned, as though lots of people had made that joke in the past, but he was still a little amused. 'In the car, actually,' he said. 'But no whip. The trowel is my weapon of choice.' He brandished it briefly at me and I laughed. Couldn't help it. Really. There was just something about the gleam in his eyes.

Then Julieanne ran down the stairs in, God help me, khakis, like she was going on a dig in the desert. But that would look good on screen. She handed Tol a trowel and brush and jumped brightly into the hole, then took them back again. The other men craned forward to get a better view as she bent over the bone.

'What do you think?' she asked Tol.

Wow, she must really like this one. I'd never heard her ask someone else's opinion before.

'Sheep,' he said. He scratched a little more at a different spot and pursed his lips. 'It's got a tail.'

'A tail?' she said, standing up straight, trowel in hand. Her blue eyes sparkled with anticipation. I felt my stomach drop. Anything that excited Julieanne about my floor was bad news for me.

'Pretty sure,' he said. He turned politely to me. 'I've done a fair bit of digging in the Middle East and you get a lot of animal bones there.'

'We have records from the early colony which mention fat-tailed sheep being brought out by the First Fleet, but we've never had any proof they were farmed successfully!' Julieanne said. 'This could be a significant find about the early colonial food supply.'

I groaned, quietly. The cameras were still rolling.

'Let's wait for the carbon-14 dating,' Tol said, 'before we get too excited. It might be from much later. It might not even *be* a fat-tailed sheep. Some other breeds don't get docked.'

'Tomorrow,' Julieanne said, ignoring him, 'we'll start digging and document all this properly.' She regarded the bones in the dirt with great satisfaction, her mouth curving into a perfect toothpaste-ad smile. 'I love a real dig!'

She exchanged a collegial smile with Tol, who was also looking forward, it seemed, to a real dig. He waggled his trowel at her like Groucho Marx with a cigar, and she laughed.

My house, an archaeological site. I was doomed to spend my entire life at my parents'.

CHAPTER THREE

'How interesting!' Mum said enthusiastically. 'A real archae-ological dig in your own backyard.'

'If it was in the backyard I wouldn't mind,' I said gloom-ily, stabbing at my grilled pork chop with my fork.

'Stop playing with your food,' Dad said, as if I were five again. 'Eat it up, it'll do you good.'

I'd lost five kilos since I'd moved in three months ago. Partly it was because I was driven out of the house on long walks to get some peace and quiet. And partly it was because my parents believed in 'good, plain food', which meant no takeaway—the source of my extra kilos in the first place.

'Well, it doesn't matter if you have to stay here a little longer,' Mum said. 'We don't mind.'

They beamed at me, and I had to repress a rude word.

Don't misunderstand me. I love my parents. And my two brothers and my three sisters and my nieces and nephews and aunts and uncles and cousins ... you get the idea. I'd been grateful when Mum and Dad had offered to let me move home until the house was renovated. Otherwise I'd have had to rent somewhere, and that would have meant no new tiles in the bathroom, cypress pine instead of recycled Huon pine floorboards ... lots of little things I couldn't have afforded without their support. They only lived two blocks from the new house, so it was convenient. Dad was terrific about going over to let tradesmen in and closing up again afterwards. It was nice having dinner ready on the table when I came home. Even my laundry was done if I left it in the dirty clothes basket.

But.

I'd lived away from home since I was twenty, and I was used to being independent. Not isolated, mind. My mother had called me every day of my life since I'd moved out, except for the two years I'd spent in London working for the BBC, and you know what? I'd got to the point where it didn't drive me crazy any more. But talking on the phone once a day and living together ... big difference.

Mum and Dad had snapped right back to me being fifteen and them having a right to know everything about my life. Which was a problem, because they are very strict Catholics who think that having sex before marriage means you'll go to Hell. And not in any metaphorical sense—the fire and brimstone way. So they'd like to think I'm still a virgin, even in my late twenties, and unless they ask me out-right I'm not going to tell them any differently. Which makes sneaking time in with my boyfriend Stuart a bit tricky.

I rang Stuart after seven-thirty, because he likes to watch the news. Watching the ABC news is one of his rituals. Old-fashioned, I know. I've suggested he could vary the routine, but he says it helps him unwind. I don't want to give the wrong impression of Stuart. He's a great guy. He's clever, good-looking, very sweet—but he does have … habits. He's an accountant; a very high-powered one with an international firm, high finance, top end of town, all that stuff—and I guess he likes things to be well-ordered. Once the ritual is out of the way he's very flexible and he came straight over.

My parents like Stuart. They think he's suitable husband material, just the right kind of guy to settle me down and stop me being so 'arty'. He's not a practising Catholic, which is a black mark, but he was raised Catholic, and they assume he'll revert to the old ways once he has children. I can't actu-ally see that happening, but if it keeps them happy …

So you would think that when this highly desirable beau turned up at their door that they would tactfully excuse themselves to give us time alone, right?

'Come through to the kitchen, Stuart,' Mum said. 'We're just having a cup of tea.' You could visit my family at any time of the day or night and they'd be 'just having a cup of tea'. I once counted fifteen separate pots made in a single day.

So we sat around the kitchen table and my parents told Stuart a highly coloured and inaccurate version of what had happened that day while I tried to explain the reality.

'They're going to turn the house into a museum,' Mum said. 'Early convict life, real exhibits, maybe even some live sheep.'

'I could have a look at the bones,' Dad offered. 'See if they've been butchered by an expert or not.'

He could, too. Dad was a butcher and then became a meat inspector for the Department of Agriculture. He was one of the people who make sure our meat is fit for human consumption. I'd suggested doing a show on meat inspectors to Jennifer Jay but she'd gently suggested that perhaps seeing the sweet little lambs slaughtered and gutted would upset the children. I'd been really interested when Dad took me to the abattoir when I was six, so I didn't quite buy that argument, though the idea that the teachers wouldn't like it carried more weight.

'So they're digging up your floor?' Stuart asked me. 'No, thanks, Mrs McGowan, no more tea. I'll have some more cake, though.'

Since Stuart came on the scene five weeks ago, my mother had started baking a lot of fruitcake, because he liked it. She was shameless. When he came for dinner she made him his favourite meals. She'd offered to go over to his place during the day so the washing machine repairman could get in.

The only way I'd found to cope with this was to acknowledge the obvious: 'She wants me to get married and have babies,' I'd said to him after the third time he visited and was given fruitcake.

He had smiled understandingly. I hadn't told Mum, but Stuart had made it quite clear on our second date that he wasn't interested in marriage. That he liked living alone. And that the thought of having children made his flesh crawl. I, in turn, had made it clear that this was okay with me. I was looking forward to at least some time living alone in my beautiful little house. Maybe not the rest of my life, but a while. And, well, did I mention Stuart's a hunk? He looks like a champion surfer, all blond hair and tanned skin—one of his other rituals is running through the Royal Botanic Gardens every lunchtime. Living alone would be great, but living alone and having a gorgeous boyfriend would be better.

'What's that going to do to your schedule?' Stuart asked. He had helped me draw up the renovation schedule, complete with Gantt chart and checklists for each tradie.

'Buggers it completely,' I said.

Dad frowned. He didn't like any of us using bad language, even my brothers. Ours was really a very feminist family, if feminism means both boys and girls being raised by the same standards. The boys were expected to be virgins until they got married, too.

'Come around and have a look,' I said. 'It's sort of interesting.'

My parents made encouraging noises. It wouldn't occur to them to have sex on the bare floorboards of an unrenovated house, so they never suspected that Stuart and I might. Had, in fact, with the help of a yoga mat.

Stuart and I walked the two blocks to my house, sharing my father's golf umbrella. It could have been romantic, but Stuart was intent on sorting out the conflicting stories my parents had told him.

'They're using your house to shoot footage for the show?'

I nodded. 'The one on archaeology I set up with Annie.'

'So you'll be getting location fees,' he said with satisfaction. Location fees were paid to people whose houses or businesses were used to film in. Not to public places like museums or the zoo that had a publicity reason to help us, but to private citizens, to compensate them for the upheaval in their lives. And believe me, nothing upheaves like a film crew.

'Nope. ABC policy. No location fees for employees.'

He frowned. 'What about the electricity for the lights? Do you get reimbursed?'

I had never asked about that, but I bet not. Something like that was too open to abuse. 'Doubt it.'

'It should be tax deductible,' Stuart mused. 'You should take a meter reading every day before they start and again after they finish and calculate the charges, then you can include it in your return.'

Stuart would actually do that, even if it were only a few dollars in question. He was very good at keeping track of things.

'Mmm,' I said, as we turned the corner to my street. I was more worried by the phrase 'every day'. How many more days would my house be off-limits? It was private property, so they couldn't force me to agree to a dig, but a) Jennifer

Jay would think this was a great story, particularly as she wouldn't have to pay location fees and b) Annie would insist and c) my own historical conscience would stop me chucking the lot of them out in time for the electricians.

But maybe it would only take them a few hours to establish that the bones were not old enough to be from the early colony. And then my house could get back on schedule.

I had given Julieanne a key so that she could get in the next day, because it was Dad's golf day and I had to be at Luna Park early. We were shooting the 'before the gates open' material with another camera crew, and that started at six-thirty. But I wasn't pleased to arrive at my gate and find my door still open and Terry's lights blazing.

'Check the meter straight away,' Stuart said, but I charged into my living room, ready to shout at Julieanne about invasion of privacy and breach of trust and a few other things.

'What are you still doing here? Oh—hi,' I said.

Tol was the only one there, hunkered down, carefully scraping dirt from around one of the crockery bits. He looked up and smiled.

'I thought, if we could get a date on one of these sherds, we could settle the whole argument about whether this is really a historically significant site. We'll carbon-date the bones, but it takes time. Hi,' he added to Stuart.

I introduced them and they nodded at each other.

'I suppose you didn't consider the expense of the lights to Poppy?' Stuart said, rather belligerently.

Tol blinked. 'No, I didn't. I thought it was more important for Poppy to get the dig over with before the electricians came in.'

At least someone had been listening!

'And?' I said eagerly. 'Can you date it?'

'Help me get it out,' he said. He handed me his trowel and handed me into the pit.

Tol picked up a medium-sized paintbrush and crouched down, gesturing for me to do the same. Hunched over, we seemed even closer, and I was having trouble concentrating.

'Just clean around that sherd,' he said.

I took firm hold of the trowel by the blade, to keep it steady.

'What do you think the handle's there for?' he asked, amusement in his voice. He put his hand over mine and eased my fingers back until I was holding the handle. I was conscious of the warmth of his skin and of Stuart glaring at us.

'Now try.'

I aimed the point of the trowel at the pottery, but Tol grabbed my hand again.

'You'll scratch the sample,' he said. 'Just scrape it gently away sideways, like this.' He guided my hand as he spoke, so that I was pushing dirt away from the pottery rather than stabbing at it.

'Are you two going to be long?' Stuart asked, a definite note of complaint in his voice.

'Now that Poppy's helping, it shouldn't take long at all,' Tol said cheerfully.

'Take some photos for Insta, will you?' I asked, handing Stuart my phone.

Stuart scowled, but complied. It didn't take long. Ten minutes later, after photographing the pieces 'in situ', as Tol said, I climbed out of the pit.

Tol eased the small piece of brown pottery I had uncovered from the ground. 'I've already mapped its position,' he said, as though we were about to criticise him. He lifted it up to the light and brushed some dirt from the broken edge.

'I'll have to wash it—' he was saying when Julieanne walked in, dressed for dinner in a slinky blue jersey dress that made Stuart's eyes pop out.

'Tol! Are you ready?' Then she saw the pottery in his hand. 'What are you doing?' she asked. Her tone was not pleasant.

'I've already photographed it,' he assured her, but that wasn't the problem.

'How could you work on my site without my permission?'

Tol went very still. 'Your site?'

'Of course it's mine!' she said, low and hard. I winced. It would have been better if she'd yelled. 'I'm the official museum archaeologist. I'll be lead author on the papers.'

Tol relaxed. 'Oh, I don't care about that,' he said. 'I just thought Poppy would like to get a firm date as soon as possible so she can get on with her renovations.'

'She won't be doing any renovations any time soon,' Julieanne said. 'This is a major site. An important discovery. It has to be fully excavated. Right out to the walls.' She looked around as though she'd like to knock the whole house down immediately.

I must have looked stricken, because Tol climbed out of the pit and patted me kindly on the shoulder. 'Excavating right out to a wall isn't such a good idea,' he said, trying to make a joke of it. 'They have a tendency to fall down on top of you if you do that.' He smiled at me. 'I know about walls. Don't worry. Yours are safe with me.'

How could I not like this man, even if he was Julieanne's current squeeze? And he had a beautiful voice, warm and smooth and reassuring, like hot chocolate.

'If the other material in the strata is of late date—'

'That won't prove anything!' Julieanne said. 'There's been building, earthquakes—'

'Earthquakes?' I protested. 'When?'

'The Newcastle quake from the seventies was felt here,' Julieanne said, then ploughed on. 'There's no way to tell about dates for the bones until we get the carbon-14 results. That could be days. Weeks, the way they're backed up at the lab. In the meantime, I intend to get right down to bedrock.'

'We're on clay,' I said. 'Bedrock is six feet down! Maybe twelve! You are not digging a twelve-foot hole in my living room!'

We glared at each other.

'I vote we just put the floorboards back over it and pretend it never happened,' I said, knowing that would infuriate her. But even I wasn't prepared for the full Psycho Woman treatment.

'You're a Philistine!' she shouted. 'You don't care about history! You were always trying to sabotage the real historians when you worked at the museum, and you haven't changed!'

I knew what she was talking about, of course: one of the worst afternoons in my life, when I had to listen to Julieanne nominate a stump-jump plough as the central piece of an exhibition, even though it didn't fit in the display case we had to work with. She nominated it sixteen times, even though the curator in charge of the exhibition explained fifteen times that it was too big and she'd have to find another, smaller object instead. He was very patient. I, on the other hand, went from being exasperated to being bored to being downright scared of someone who was incapable of accepting that the world wasn't the way she wanted it to be, to being really, really cross, so the sixteenth time Julieanne said, 'But it would be much better if we could have the plough', I exploded.

'You can't have the plough because the fucking plough doesn't FIT THE CASE! Deal with it. Move on. Because we're sick of hearing about the plough, Julieanne.'

'How dare you!' Julieanne had gasped, and rushed out of the room.

If I hadn't sworn at her, which I don't normally do, I might have got away with it. As it was, I had to apologise the next day and the powers that be suggested it might be better if another audio-visual person worked on the exhibition, which was fine with me.

But I didn't work with her any more, and no one was going to make me apologise for defending my own house, even if she was more upset than I'd expected. It wasn't like her to lose it.

'I'm sick of hearing about the plough, Julieanne,' I said, sweetly.

She raised her hand as though she wanted to slap me across the face, then stiffened.

'Really?' I said. 'That would be assault before witnesses.'

Stuart and Tol had frozen. Julieanne breathed through her nostrils, her teeth clenched, hand still raised. I'd never seen her this angry, and I wondered why she was so stressed. It couldn't be just me—she didn't think I was that important.

'I'll get a historical protection order from the council,' she said. 'Then you won't have a choice! Come on, Tol.'

She swept out. Tol stayed a moment longer to put the sherd of pottery in a plastic bag and tuck it into his pocket. He was carefully not meeting my gaze. What was he doing hanging around with Julieanne? Was he a masochist? Then it occurred to me that maybe this was the first time he had seen Julieanne being Psycho Woman.

He turned towards the door, which brought him face to face with me.

'She feels very strongly about things,' he said apologetically.

'TOL!' Julieanne shouted.

'Have a nice evening,' I said, and moved aside. He quirked his mouth to one side and left.

I turned to Stuart wanting hugs and reassurance.

'What plough?' he asked.

CHAPTER FOUR

We turned off the lights and locked up. With a possible early start the next day if the weather was good, dallying with Stuart didn't have as much appeal as usual. Besides, Julieanne had a key. I'd be looking over my shoulder the whole time.

I found that I was, surprisingly, worried about Julieanne. All right, we'd had our differences in the past, but threatening to slap me—that wasn't like her. She had to be seriously stressed about something to let me get under her skin like that. Well. Not my problem. My house was my problem.

The rain had stopped and an easterly was shredding the clouds away from a crescent moon. The smell of the sea was surprisingly strong, and I breathed it in deeply, trying to feel calmer about my poor little house. We saw Julieanne

and Tol standing by a beaten-up silver Lancer as we skirted
the skip. Julieanne had put on a matching jacket that trans-
formed the dress into something surprisingly respectable.
Elegant, even. Tol looked dirty and comfortable. We were
going to have to walk past them, but I didn't want to talk to
Julieanne again, so we moved slowly down the path, hoping
they'd go before we got there.

'You can't come to the preselection meeting looking like
that,' Julieanne said loudly. 'You *know* how important this is
to me—why couldn't you have made an effort?'

Stuart winced. I made a mental note never to use that
approach with him. Not that I would. A combination of
whining and accusation doesn't work with anyone, as far as
I know.

'My place is only five minutes away,' Tol said placatingly.
'I'll meet you there.'

Julieanne sniffed disapprovingly—no, really, she did, just
like in Victorian novels. 'I suppose it's too much to expect
a suit?'

'Yes,' Tol said, quite pleasantly, but very firmly. 'Suits
are for weddings and funerals. And even then I don't wear
a tie.'

I approved. Very close to my attitude to stilettos, though
I had been known to make an exception for dinner with a
very attractive man. But it was not the right answer to give
to Julieanne.

'Nothing I do matters to you!' she snapped. 'Can't you see
that tonight is *vital*?'

Tol shifted his feet. 'Look, Julieanne, we've only been see-ing each other a couple of weeks, and you've always known I'm going back to Jordan … I'm not that comfortable being paraded around as though I'm a permanent fixture in your life.'

'Oh, just help me out! I can lock in the Christian vote if I turn up with a man—they suspect me of being lesbian as it is, because you never come to the meetings!'

I couldn't help it, I laughed.

She whipped around like a viper ready to strike. 'Shut your mouth, Poppy!'

'Sorry,' I said. 'It's just the thought of you as a lesbian is—ridiculous.' So was the idea of her in Parliament. I'd heard rumours she was trying for preselection for the Australian Family Party, a splinter group of right-wing hard-liners, mostly funded by the Pentecostal churches. Maybe that's what she was stressed about. I hadn't believed the sto-ries, but even more, I had trouble believing they'd preselect a single, childless young woman whose morals more closely resembled Mary Magdalene's than the Virgin Mary's. But clearly, Julieanne was sculpting her image, and Tol was part of the package.

Looked like he was only now finding that out, and not liking the idea.

'Just don't introduce me as your fiancé,' he said.

'I'd never do anything like that,' Julieanne said, looking hurt and vulnerable. She moved closer to him and began whispering, stroking his chest, laying on the sugar with a trowel. His face softened. She really did look fabulous. I guess I could understand how a man could get blinded by that. For a while, at least.

We walked past them at a brisk pace and were almost to the corner when her voice rose in a shriek.

'You're ruining my life, you selfish bastard!'

Stuart and I looked around involuntarily. Julieanne pushed Tol with both hands so that he staggered, only prevented from falling by a rather sharp picket fence. Then she turned her back on him and walked fast in the other direction, her heels clicking on the footpath.

Tol just watched her go. Then he went to the car, pressed the key fob, and tried to open the door. It took him a couple of tries and I realised his hand was shaking. Was it with distress, or anger? I would absolutely have understood if Tol had wanted to whack Julieanne. But I was glad he hadn't. Very glad, for some reason.

Then Tol was in his car and pulling out from the kerb. He'd be all right.

'Come on,' Stuart said, his voice thick with distaste. 'I could do with a cup of tea.'

I laughed, and tucked my hand through his arm. 'Well, I happen to know where you can get one.'

CHAPTER FIVE

Tuesday

As I ate breakfast, the rain started pounding on the roof, and I groaned. No excuse to put off the dig. Luna Park would have to wait. I sent the appropriate emails.

At least I didn't have to rush out the door. I spent some time on my own social media (which tends to get neglected in favour of the program's). My last post complaining about my renovations being delayed had received lots of sad face emojis and sympathy, with my friend Alex offering to come over and evict the archaeologists in person. Which I'd have paid to see, because although he's a big guy, butch he is not.

It would take too long to describe Alex properly, but I'm a bit like his big sister—he's been one of my best friends since he was sixteen and I was eighteen. He runs a musical instrument shop. Did I mention he was gay? After offering to evict the archaeologists, he had made a crack about fat-tailed sheep, which started a hilarious if very rude thread, complete with Freddie Mercury GIFs. It was very funny. It did make me notice, though, that my friends were far more successful in cheering me up than my boyfriend had been the night before.

While I was online, I checked out the Australian Family Party's website. It still looked a very bad fit for Julieanne to me. Highly religious and very, very conservative. What on Earth was she doing in that company?

Annie called me while I was having my second cup of tea.

'Julieanne's already put in a complaint about you,' Annie said. I could hear the laugh in her voice. All right for her. 'I just opened the email.'

'Did she tell you she almost slapped me across the face in front of witnesses? I could've had her charged with assault.'

'Oh, shit. I'm glad she didn't—I need her for the fund-raiser. She's very good at schmoozing money out of rich old men. And you want the footage for your show.'

'She's going to ask for an historical preservation order from the council!'

'It'll sort itself out,' Annie said soothingly. 'Are we booked in for the Shakespeare?'

Annie and I were theatregoers. Had been ever since uni. This time, it was a production of *Much Ado About Nothing*, which was one of our favourites.

'Yep. Two weeks from today. All set.'

We discussed where to go for an early dinner before-hand, her children's latest crises at school ('Ruby keeps contradicting the teacher! And worse, she's always right!'), her cat's objections to dry food, and a few other mat-ters pertaining to some friends who were getting mar-ried. A proper natter, in other words. It was very calming. A return to normality.

So there I was, letting in Boris, and Terry and Dave and Mirha and Julieanne and Tol and three students and the PR girl from the museum who doubled as the staff photog-rapher. Did I mention my house is only twelve feet wide? It was crowded in there.

As on all shoots, the crew liked tea before starting, and archaeologists are apparently the same. Fortunately, although my kitchen is small, my family is not, and I'd set up tea-making facilities with a host of old mugs donated by various aunties. I'd even remembered to bring milk. I dis-pensed tea to everyone except Boris.

I pulled him out the front door into the scant shelter of the little porch.

'You don't have to hang around today, Boris. If they fin-ish early I'll call you. But I doubt we can get back in there before tomorrow at the earliest.' Boris was always working on two or three jobs at once, so I didn't have to worry about him being out of pocket if he didn't stay.

He looked disappointed. 'I can help,' he offered.

We stared through the doorway. Mugs in hands, Terry and the crew had taken possession of the small dining area to set up their gear. The lights were still in place from yesterday and they flared on, bright and hot, sending sharp shadows onto the corners and ceiling. The PR girl had squeezed in next to Mirha, who was trying to get the students to sign release forms, but there wasn't room enough for them to wield a pen. I thought it was typical that Julieanne should mentor only male students. The first two were a buff Indigenous guy from out west—a Barkindji man, I think Annie said—and a very young one who looked like he had Indian heritage. They both had the physiques of bodybuilders, but I thought her standards had slipped with the third one, who was pale and skinny and covered with acne. As we watched, Mirha waved them through to the kitchen and slipped out the door between the dining area and the corridor to follow them. Terry started filming.

Julieanne and Tol were down in the hole, happily levering up chipboard and chucking it up towards the doorway.

'Watch my walls!' I said.

'See, miss, you need me,' Boris said, and leapt in to gather up the chipboard and bring it out to the skip. As each board went, another section of bearer and joist was revealed.

They took out most of the lounge floor, leaving only the boards in the dining alcove, as well as a section running to the stairs and another to the corridor. Julieanne got the students in from the backyard, and instructed them on how to set up a three-dimensional grid with string lines stretched from wall to wall, and make a computer copy of it to scale, so they could mark the location of any finds exactly. It would have been interesting if this had been the first time I'd seen it done, but three years at the museum made it old hat to me. Terry filmed it all, though.

'When do they start digging?' Mirha asked me quietly.

I shrugged. 'Once they've set up the grid, they photograph everything, then they start with the trowels and brushes.'

She sighed.

'It's like filming,' I said. 'Everyone thinks it's exciting but mostly it's waiting for the clouds to pass or the aeroplane to go away.'

She nodded. Filming outside, in particular, is subject to interminable delays.

While Julieanne, Tol and the students had been setting up, the PR girl had found the folding chairs I had in the back shed and set them up under the sun umbrella I'd put up in the backyard. There was just enough room for three people to huddle there out of the rain.

The yard was one of the reasons I'd bought the house. Unlike most of the houses around here, it had grass and bushes instead of paving, and it was cool and restful and quiet. As they could only fit one student in the pit with Julieanne and Tol at any one time, the other two and the PR girl were soon established out there, chatting and texting and watching their phones.

If it had been any other shoot, I would have slipped away to the office to do some real work, but this was my place, and I was waiting to get Tol alone. I needed to get the skinny on how long they'd be.

Eventually they took a coffee break, with Mirha doing the honours in my tiny kitchen. Tol looked at the mug of instant that she offered him and visibly recoiled.

'No, thanks,' he said.

This was my chance. 'There's a good coffee shop around the corner,' I said. 'I was going to get myself one. Want to come?'

He stuck the trowel in his back pocket and headed for the door without even looking at Julieanne, picking up Terry's umbrella to cover us both.

Gracie, the owner of Bar Napoli, is actually Graciella, and she hand roasts and grinds her beans because she thinks machines suck the soul out of them. As Tol and I came in and he closed the umbrella, she beamed at me and scowled at Tol. She didn't like Stuart, either. She's never liked any man I've brought into the place. I don't know why, but I suspect that forty years with her husband Roberto has soured her on men altogether, and I don't blame her. Roberto is— well, that's not relevant.

Tol, sniffing with true appreciation, said, 'Malaga Mountain Blue.'

Gracie peered at him suspiciously. 'Si,' she said. 'What you want?'

'Cappuccino, grazie, bella signora,' he said, and smiled.

And before my eyes, Gracie actually blushed and sashayed over to the coffee machine. She knew I always took a latte.

'You are such a schmoozer,' I said.

'Guilty,' Tol admitted, smiling down at me in much the same way he'd smiled at Gracie. Hah! I was made of sterner stuff.

'What about my floor?' I asked. 'Could you date the pottery?'

He grimaced. 'Not exactly. We've got a range, but that kind of domestic ware was made and imported into the colony for about sixty years, starting in 1802, so it's not much help in excluding the possibility of an early fat-tailed farm.'

'Bugger,' I said gloomily.

'The carbon-14 will be back in a few days. That will settle the date. We ought to be able to get an accurate estimate, within fifty years.'

I knew about carbon-14 from my museum days. All organic material—that is, anything that has once been alive, animal or plant—has a certain proportion of the atom carbon-14, which decays into carbon-12. Comparing the proportions of carbon-14 with carbon-12 determines how old the organic material is.

I pulled out my phone. 'I have to call the electricians. You're not going to be finished in two days, are you?'

He shook his head sympathetically.

'When?' I demanded. 'Maybe I can get them to reschedule.'

'Look …' he hesitated. 'I'd be happy to do a quick and dirty, get the dates from the bones and be out by the week-end. We can probably get most of what's there to find out by then. We might miss a couple of small sherds, but nothing major. It's not like the site is going to turn into a tourist attraction, so we don't have to preserve the strata or anything. But—'

'But Julieanne won't do it that way.'

He was saved from answering by Gracie coming back with the coffees. He thanked her, paid for them—waving away my money—and we silently went back out into the rain.

As we walked under the umbrella, I was conscious of his shoulder rubbing mine—his arm, actually, because he was quite a lot taller. He had a loose, relaxed way of walking. Very different from Stuart, who was tense and contained almost all the time. Tol seemed so ... sane. What was he doing with Julieanne? I had to know.

'How long have you two been together?' I asked, trying for nonchalance and sounding like an airhead as a result.

'A few weeks. We met at a conference, and Julieanne told me about this consultancy. I'm between digs, so it seemed like a good idea ...'

From his tone, it didn't seem like such a good idea any more. Or was I just being hopeful? I looked up at him. The umbrella created an oddly intimate little island for the two of us. He looked at me, his eyes warm, looking more grey than hazel this time.

'And now?' I just couldn't resist probing a little deeper, but it was a mistake. His face closed down.

'Oh, I'm not really a colonial archaeologist. I'm more at home in Jordan than Annandale. I won't be sticking around here for that long.'

Well, that was a warning if ever I heard one, and I paid attention. My theory goes that, unless he's an absolute lying bastard, somewhere in the first couple of meetings a man will lay his position on the line. He'll say something like 'I'm not really looking for a permanent relationship', or 'I've never been that interested in kids', or 'I like living alone'. The mistake a lot of women make is that they don't listen. Or worse, they think: *But he'll change when he gets to know me.* Nuh. Maybe once in a thousand cases.

Usually, what happens is the woman spends a couple of years in happy almost-domesticity (sometimes complete with living together) and then when her biological clock starts ticking and she makes noises about marriage or children, the man will turn to her and say, 'But I told you I wasn't interested in that.' He feels justifiably annoyed when she melts down, because as far as he's concerned he's been honest the whole time. She's bereft because although he insists he loves her, it's not the kind of love she thought it was.

I admit it, I was disappointed when Tol said he'd be leaving soon. In fact, I was surprised by *how* disappointed I was. But better a little disappointment now than a lot of heartache later. Besides, we were both already involved with other people. I gave myself a mental shake and firmly took Tol off the 'potentially beddable if I break up with Stuart' list that lurks far in the back of my mind. The whole thing had only taken a split second.

I smiled at him. 'That sounds interesting.' It also explained his reference to Jordan last night, when he was warning Julieanne not to turn him into her fiancé.

'It is.' He told me about the job he was going to in Jordan the rest of the way to the house, and I could feel him relaxing as he described the desert and the digs. 'In fact,' he said as he replaced the collapsed umbrella on the porch and opened the door for me, 'the only thing I missed in Jordan was the conversation of women.' He smiled exactly the way he had smiled at Graciella, but I was armoured against it now.

'Schmoozer,' I said.

We walked in, both laughing, and collected dagger looks from Julieanne and Dave, because they were filming a segment where Julieanne was examining a fragment of pottery and describing it to one of the students.

Terry wasn't happy with the shot. 'Poppy, you get in and we'll do it with her explaining to you,' he said. 'He's too tall to get them both in a mid shot.'

I glared at him. I didn't like being on screen, and Terry knew it. Technically, I'm in charge when we're on a shoot, but try telling that to an experienced camera operator with fifteen years on you.

So I put on some lipstick, fixed my hair (curlier than ever because of the rain) and climbed into the pit.

Julieanne looked pissed off, but she wasn't fool enough to make an enemy of Terry. She cooperated, and she did know her stuff. She gave a concise, interesting description of the pottery, which showed the influence Chinese ware had had on English ceramics.

I reminded her this show was for six-year-olds, and she sighed in a long-suffering manner. But anyone who works at the museum has had to deal with school groups, so she gave a neat little word-picture of the kind of household this might have come from, complete with examples of how the kids in that household would have lived. I tried to look intelligent and interested, and asked a couple of questions I hoped we could cut out later.

'Right,' said Terry when the take was over, which was what he said when he was satisfied. 'Let me reset the lights for some close-ups of the ground.'

'Good one, Julieanne,' I said, trying hard to be fair. 'The kids will be really interested in that.'

She rolled her eyes, climbed out and went over to Tol, who was still standing by the door, sipping coffee with the expression of a man in love. With Graciella, no doubt. Julieanne slipped her hand into his trouser pocket and brought a phone out. She checked for messages and frowned, then dialled a number.

'Eliza, hello, this is Julieanne. May I speak to Matthew, please?'

She waited, her face tense.

'Well, when *will* he be available?' Whatever the other woman said strained Julieanne's patience and her good manners, but she managed to control herself by hitting the wall with her fist even while her voice was as sweet as honey. 'Yes, I'd really appreciate that, thanks, Eliza. Bye.'

She ended the call with a vicious tap and glared at Tol. 'Stupid cow. Surely they have a result by now? If I didn't make it, the least they could do is *tell* me.'

Tol murmured something soothing and she snorted.

'No, it would be *just* like Eliza bloody Carter to not pass the message along. She thinks all women should be barefoot and pregnant. I've got to go.'

I was astonished that Julieanne would pass up the opportunity for more showing off on film, but Tol didn't seem surprised, so I guessed he knew where she was skiving off to. Carter, I remembered, was the name of the head of the Australian Family Party. So perhaps Julieanne hadn't got preselection?

The day went on as before, mostly boring, interrupted by briefly exciting bits where Tol or one of the students located a piece of archaeology and alerted Terry so he could film them 'finding' it. Then they had to get the PR girl—I really ought to find out her name, I thought each time—to photograph the find in situ. Then the diggers would mark it on their 3D grid, and uncover it slowly with trowel, brush and fingers.

Most of it, unfortunately, was the same kind of domestic ware we'd already documented, or more bones. Mid-afternoon, I called the electrician and told them the story. They were interested but said they couldn't fit me in for another three weeks if I didn't make the Thursday slot. Reluctantly, I cancelled. No way would this lot be out of here by the day after tomorrow.

Boris got bored and went away to work on another job. I noticed he got Mirha's phone number first. So much for the girl in Croatia.

Terry is a fan of *Home and Away*. Don't ask me why. But it means that, unless there's a very good reason for overtime, he works an eight-hour day: six- to seven-hour shooting day, so he can get back to Artarmon, upload the footage and lock up the gear, and be home by seven. He says it's not the same when he has to stream it. So he and Dave packed up just after four, and we all went home.

The moment the lights go out on a set is a strange one. My house seemed smaller, suddenly, and drabber, and colder. I didn't like it. Yet at the same time, it was as though an intruder had climbed back out the window and left me in peace.

I followed Tol through the door with a deep reluctance, and looked up at the late afternoon sky. The clouds were clearing.

'I probably won't be here tomorrow,' I said to Terry as he loaded the Ford. 'If it's clear, Ben and Molly and I will be at Luna Park.'

'Better you than me,' he said. 'Anything special you want?'

'Just keep them from destroying my house.'

He winked at me and I felt comforted.

Before Tol climbed into his battered old Lancer, I gave him my phone number. Just in case anything came up the next day. Really.

He waved at me as he drove off, and I waved back. I was glad I didn't have to say goodbye to Julieanne. I'd had just about enough of Dr Julieanne Weaver.

Which was too bad for me, because when I got home Mum and Dad were watching a current affairs show about the rise of the Australian Family Party, featuring an inter-view with the two of the four candidates for preselection for a marginal seat in Sydney's west. Julieanne was one. This interview was clearly where she'd skived off to. She came across as sober, intelligent, reasonable, public spirited, conservative, even kind and compassionate. Maybe she *was* conservative—we'd never discussed politics. And she was undoubtedly intelligent. But the rest was PR bullshit, and I had to admit she was good at it. Even her clothes were perfect—a suit in mid-blue, softened by a feminine blouse in pearl grey, with discreet pearl earrings. In one long shot, I could see she had on classic navy court shoes, the sort flight attendants wear, except more expensive. I'd never seen her in anything except flats or follow-me-home stilettos. Somehow, those shoes made me realise how serious she was about becoming an MP.

The other candidate was more obviously hardline right— a middle-aged lawyer, family man, father of three, deacon at the Radiant Joy church—although that only came out via a surprise question from the reporter. The party was clearly downplaying its relationship to the church, trying to allay the fears of non-religious conservative voters. All in all, this guy represented everything I disliked about the right: bombastic, too sure of himself, didn't care how his policies would affect the poor, happy to marginalise gay people, black people, anyone not like himself. In comparison, Julieanne shone like a lighthouse. If I were a conservative voter, I might think I'd found a winner. I might vote this nice, good-looking cardboard figure into Parliament and let her run riot through our laws and traditions.

With any luck, she wouldn't get preselection, and the voters would recoil from the hardliner. Cross fingers.

CHAPTER SIX

Wednesday

Luna Park is one of my favourite bits of Sydney. It's small by amusement park standards, but its location right on Sydney Harbour, next to the bridge, makes an outing there a real treat. I had Ben (camera), Molly (sound) and Jade (PA) with me, as Terry, Dave and Mirha were locked in to the archaeology shoot.

The day was intermittently cloudy, which made for a long shoot, waiting for the light to be right so that the shots of each ride would match.

It was great fun, though. Did you know that after the mechanics test each ride, they have to run it three or four times just to make sure it's safe and to get the oil moving around each part smoothly? On the last try, they let me go on by myself. It was like I had my own private amusement park. Could there be anything cooler than riding the Spider all by yourself out over the waters of *Sydney Harbour* on a warm spring morning? Well, maybe if someone compatible had been sitting next to me it would have been better, but it was still one of the best days I'd had in the job. I uploaded some photos to the show's Instagram and Twitter feeds, and a couple to my own accounts as well.

Sydney Harbour in the early morning reminds me of what it must have been like in the old days, when everything travelled by boat because the roads were so bad. Yachts, tug boats, tall ships under sail getting ready for their first tourist jaunt of the day. Little dinghies full of men going home to put their dawn catch in the fridge before they got ready for work, rowing eights, single sea kayakers threading their way along the shoreline. And the ferries, of course, zig-zagging from wharf to wharf, collecting and decanting passengers just like in the 1800s. It's a working harbour, not just a tourist playground, and in the post-dawn hours you can see that clearly.

At Luna Park the last ride to be tested is always the little roller coaster, which I love, so I was very annoyed when my phone went off just before I stepped into the coaster car with the mechanics—just me and the boys, riding our own coaster. So cool!

'Yes?' I snarled into my phone.

'Terry says they can't get into your house. I thought that woman from the museum was supposed to meet them?' Jennifer Jay never introduced herself to her team. We were expected to know her voice.

'She was,' I said, and made 'wait for me' motions to the mechanics. They tapped their watches, so I got into the car still talking. The U-shaped safety bar came down over my shoulders and pressed me into the seat.

'Well, the man's there, but he doesn't have a key.'

'Get them to go round and get the spare from Mum,' I said, as the ride winched slowly up the long, long hill at the start.

'Okay.'

Jennifer Jay hung up and I tried to put the phone in my pocket, but I couldn't reach past the bar. We were at the top of the hill, looking west over the busy harbour. No time to squirm—I tucked my phone into my bra and grabbed the bar, and laughed and laughed as we went over and soared down.

The last laugh I had for some time.

Five minutes after I got off the roller coaster, feeling that curious combination of dizziness and cleanliness that they always give me, my phone rang again. I checked my watch. It was still only nine-thirty, although it felt much later.

'There's a body in your living room,' Jennifer Jay said.

'No, it's only sheep. I told you,' I said absently, checking my shooting schedule to make sure that we'd got all the shots we'd planned. The camera crew would stay on for the rest of the day to get 'colour'—people riding, playing games, eating—but I needed to head back to the office to confirm tomorrow's shoot at the warehouse where they kept all the stuffed toys for the games.

'That woman's dead.'

'What?' I put the clipboard on a bench and sat myself next to it. 'What woman?' I had an unpleasant feeling I knew the answer.

'That woman from the museum. They got the key from your mother and there she was. Dead.'

I'm glad to say that my first thought was not *This is going to stuff up my renovations*. First, I thought of Tol. He had been there, Jennifer Jay had said before. Had he found her? Poor thing. Secondly, I thought of Julieanne, and that was when I felt very cold. All right, I hadn't liked her, but it was hard to imagine anyone more intensely alive. Julieanne dead. Impossible. She *can't* be dead, part of my brain was saying. I only saw her yesterday.

I felt disconnected from my body. The noise of the park retreated and the bench under me felt a long way away.

'Did she fall into the hole or something?' I asked. Broken neck. Cracked spine. I hoped it had been fast, that she hadn't lain there for hours hoping for someone to come … I started to shiver.

'No idea. The police are there now. They're trying to stop the boys from filming. You'd better get over there.'

That wasn't as callous as it sounded. Really. Terry's instincts would all be about the story. I was more concerned about—well, yes, about my house, but also about Tol and Julieanne and … I guess she had other friends? I knew very little about her, really.

I explained to the camera crew—who said, 'Wow!' and 'How awful for you!' with equal sincerity—and left just as the giant mouth at the gate began gulping in the first of the crowds.

The trip home seemed longer than usual, and too short. I didn't want to face what was waiting for me at home.

It was worse than I thought.

The narrow street was blocked by two police cars and an ambulance and the house was taped off as a crime scene, with two young constables, one male and one female, standing outside my gate to move rubberneckers along. There weren't any—my house is in a side street and not too many people pass by. So they seemed quite pleased when I approached and gave them a chance to be official.

'Nothing to see, ma'am,' one said to me.

'I live here—I mean, I own the house,' I said.

The two of them exchanged glances and then the young woman went inside the house and came out a moment later to beckon me to the door. She stopped me going inside but I could see into the room.

The filming lights were still on but Terry's camera and Dave's sound equipment were missing. I wondered where they'd gone—I couldn't imagine them leaving the site of a story.

A story. My gut clenched hard. This wasn't a story. It was Julieanne, dead. Actually dead. I felt disconnected again, and put out my hand onto the new plasterwork. The smooth coolness helped, but I still felt helpless as I looked in.

My little living room was even more crowded than the day before—people in white overalls in the pit, two men watching, another man videotaping, and a woman in a straight brown skirt and cream blouse who looked strangely at home, leaning against my dining alcove windowsill and talking on a mobile. Everyone had those disposable booties on.

I caught a glimpse of feet behind the crouched bodies of the two—what? Scene of crime technicians, I guessed they were. The feet were wearing the same shoes Julieanne had worn on TV the night before, and they were stained with the dark brown clay of the pit.

They seemed pathetic. Seeing them should have made me compassionate towards her, aware of the vulnerability of human life. God knows I did feel that. But the only clear thought I had was that Julieanne would never have got down into that pit in those shoes.

'She was pushed,' I said involuntarily.

While I had stared at Julieanne's feet, the woman detective had finished her phone conversation and come across to me, balancing neatly on the bearers to walk across the pit.

'What makes you say that?' she asked.

'She'd never have worn those shoes in the pit,' I said. We sized each other up. She was slightly taller, so just above average, and sort of ... middling. White, with mid-brown hair that wasn't quite mousy, mid-blue eyes, a not-stunning but not-plain thin face, a slim but not remarkable body. Ordinary, except for the intelligence in those eyes.

'Detective Sergeant Chloe Prudhomme,' she said.

We shook hands. One of the other detectives, a young bloke with short blond hair, very pale eyebrows and an earring, turned to listen, but didn't introduce himself.

'Poppy McGowan,' I said. 'It's my house.'

She nodded, and flicked open one of those little note-books that TV cops always use. 'You work at the ABC? And that's why there's a film crew here?' Her tone indicated that she didn't much like the film crew.

I nodded. 'We were planning a documentary for the education section about archaeology, so when we found bones under the newel post, we thought it would be a good opportunity to get footage for the show.'

I looked over at the pit, where the scene of crime officers were climbing out.

One of them had blood on his white gloves. He picked a long hair off one finger and slid it into a bag another officer held ready. I felt sick. Julieanne's hair. Julieanne's blood. I wanted to turn away but I felt, obscurely, that I owed it to Julieanne to face what had been done to her. Yesterday she had been energetic, ambitious, *alive*. Now she was lying so still she no longer looked real—just a prop in a CSI show.

The detective consulted her notebook again, moving slightly to block my view. It was a relief to look at her instead.

'Did you report the bones to the police?' She sounded like she knew the answer already and didn't approve.

To my annoyance, I felt an urgent desire to explain myself. To win her approval. Was this just a response to being asked questions by a police officer, or was there something about this detective? I suspected it was her.

'No,' I said. 'I didn't want to bother anyone until we were sure they were human, so I called the museum, who are collaborating on this show with us, and they sent out a couple of experts to assess the finds. The bones were sheep.' I tried not to sound too conciliatory, but also not too smug at having been right. I'm not sure I succeeded with either.

'Hmm,' she said. I couldn't think of her as Detective Sergeant Prudhomme. It was too much of a mouthful. In my thoughts, at least, she'd have to be Detective Chloe. 'And Ms Weaver was one of the experts?'

'Dr Weaver,' I corrected automatically. It made me sound like a prig, though Chloe just nodded and made another note. The experts at the museum were fanatical about keeping up the distinctions between them and the students, and had drilled us all about using their proper titles. My mobile rang and Detective Chloe frowned, so I just reached into my bag and turned it off.

'And Dr Lang,' I added. I arched my eyebrows. 'Where is …?'

'Dr Lang, the students and your film crew are in the backyard,' Chloe said, still looking at the notebook. 'You worked with Dr Weaver?'

'I used to work at the museum a couple of years ago, before I went to the ABC.'

'Did you get on with her?'

I froze. Now, suddenly, I understood all those stupid people in crime shows who lie to the police even though they know they are innocent. I think it goes back to childhood: never admit doing something wrong—you'll get punished for it, even if it isn't what the adult is asking about. I overcame the eight-year-old in me who wanted to say, 'Yes, miss, I'm a good girl', and shook my head. Surely it would be less suspicious to admit to not liking her than to have them find it out later?

'No, actually, I didn't like her at all, and she didn't like me.'

Detective Chloe seemed surprised at the admission, and the corner of her mouth quirked. I suddenly thought that I might get to like her. The blond guy wasn't so impressed. He made a satisfied noise and wrote something in his notebook. Chloe ignored him.

'Fair enough. Thanks. We'll need to speak to you again when we have a time of death confirmed, but could you just explain where you were last night after seven and this morning until nine?'

I gave her all the details: my parents' address, phone and so on; Luna Park from six-thirty; contacts there; the film crew's names and contact numbers. But my mind was racing.

'If you're asking about my whereabouts ... does that mean it wasn't an accident?'

She cast a quick glance behind her, where the police camera operator was leaning over the pit. I tried not to think about what he was filming. The blond cop cleared his throat in what he probably thought was a menacing manner. Or maybe he was just reminding Chloe to be careful, because she shot him an amused glance.

'We're treating it as a suspicious death,' she said, her voice conscientiously formal. 'I'm not at liberty to say anything else at this time.'

A scene of crime person, a young woman with pink hair peeking from under her overall hoodie, came up to me. 'We'll need your fingerprints,' she said, holding out a scanner like security systems use. I went through the process, not just with one finger like you do for security, but with all ten.

'Got that? Good,' Chloe said to the techie. She turned to me. 'We'll need the prints of everyone who's been in the house lately.'

I gaped at her. 'Are you kidding? I'm *renovating*. This place has had tradies in and out for weeks.'

She looked annoyed. 'You must have records.'

'Sure. But—my family's been here, my boyfriend ...'

'We'll need their details,' she said firmly.

Detective Chloe followed me as I went to get the renovations file folder from the small upstairs bedroom I would eventually use as my office, carefully not looking down as I climbed the stairs. Julieanne deserved some privacy, I felt. These other people had the right to be inspecting her, but I didn't. I could accord her that dignity, at least.

All the bedroom had in it at the moment was a small card table and a plastic stool. I handed the folder over with some reluctance. It was my bible—all my quotes, all my notes on internal hardware, plaster roses, plumbing fixtures, colour schemes.

'*Please* don't lose that,' I said.

Detective Chloe nodded without speaking, flicking through the pages as we went down the stairs and looking less and less happy when she saw how many quotes I'd had.

'Names and addresses of other people who've been in the house?'

'Um, the film crew and the museum people—' I started.

'Done,' she said.

'My boyfriend.'

'Details.'

I gave her Stuart's contact details.

'Most of my family haven't been here for a while,' I said. 'Since before the plastering was done. Except Mum and Dad.' Something occurred to me that I really had to clear up now. 'By the way,' I said. 'Should I change my locks?'

'Pardon?'

'Julieanne had my spare key. Was it with her? Or should I get the locks changed?'

Impatience, annoyance—they passed over her face in a flash and vanished. 'Martin?'

He consulted a list. 'Yep, there was a key in her purse which fitted this lock.'

That was a relief.

One of the constables came up behind me and signalled to her. We both turned. A man in a council uniform was standing just inside the gate.

'What's this?' Chloe asked.

The council guy waved his clipboard. 'I have to inspect this site and deliver a historical preservation order.'

Oh, shit. Julieanne really had gone to the council. When had she had *time*?

Chloe noticed my expression and jumped to a conclusion. 'Who applied for the order?' she demanded.

The man read his notes. 'A Dr Julieanne Weaver.'

'Did you know about this?' Chloe asked me.

'Julieanne talked about it, but I didn't think she'd actually do it. I mean, I *was* letting them dig. She didn't really need an order.' I knew I sounded defensive, but that was how I felt.

Chloe had taken the clipboard from the council man and read it over. 'This could stop your renovations completely,' she said slowly. 'At least for some time …' She let the implication hang in the air: I had a motive to get rid of Julieanne before she applied to the council. 'What happens now?' she asked the council man.

'After I inspect the site—'

'You can't inspect this site,' the blond cop butted in. 'It's a crime scene.'

'Confidentially—and I *do* mean confidentially—Dr Weaver is dead,' Chloe said. 'How will that affect your order?'

The council man looked confused. 'I don't know, to tell you the truth. I'll have to check with the planning department.' He reached for the clipboard, but Chloe held it back.

'What's your name?'

'Marco Fozina.'

'I need a copy of this,' she said. She handed over a card. 'Get it couriered to this address care of me.'

Fozina nodded, then peered into the open doorway, clearly fascinated. 'Is that where …?'

Blond cop moved across to block his view. 'We'll be in touch, Mr Fozina.'

Reluctantly, the man left, casting glances behind him.

Chloe turned and looked at me.

'*I* didn't kill her,' I said. 'I'm not that much of an idiot. Even if she got the order, all it would mean was more time. It isn't like they can take my house away from me.'

'Are you sure?'

I hesitated. I couldn't remember the exact wording of the Heritage Act, but I was pretty sure that no politician would have voted for a bill that would enable the government to take away voters' houses over a few bits of bone and pottery. New bypasses, that was different.

'Pretty sure,' I said. 'And I would have checked before I killed anyone over it.'

'If you were calm. But if you were angry with her?'

'Hah!' I said. 'I've been angry with her lots of times, and I've never laid a hand on her. Why would I start now?'

Blond cop laughed bitterly, trying to show his cynicism and world-weariness. 'People snap sometimes,' he said.

Oh, for heaven's sake! 'What is your name, anyway?' I asked him.

He looked startled. 'Detective Constable Martin.'

'Steven Martin,' Chloe said, her tone slightly rebuking. I guessed it was police procedure to give full names to civilians, but I understood why this guy didn't. He must be very sick of the jokes. I immediately thought of two I could make, but I resisted. I *am* capable of controlling myself.

'What about Tol and the guys?' I asked.

I saw her note my use of Tol's name.

'They'll be allowed out as soon as the deceased has gone to the mortuary.'

'Oh, come on,' I protested. 'That's not fair. At least let Terry get some shots of the body being carried out. The other networks will be here by then, and *they'll* be filming.'

She stared at me. 'Are all you television people this callous?'

I flushed. 'Terry used to be a news cameraman. And well, frankly, if Julieanne Weaver has died in my front room, I think the ABC should get an exclusive. It's my job to think like that, detective sergeant.'

It was a tense moment, and Chloe opened her mouth to say no, I'm pretty sure. But then two TV news wagons from the commercial stations roared up the street before being stopped by the barriers. Their cameramen jumped out, cameras on shoulders. I looked pointedly at them and then back at Chloe.

'Oh, all right,' she said. 'But no filming until they're outside the front door.'

She sent Detective Constable Martin out to the yard and he came back leading the film crew. I saw that, although Terry was holding the camera across his chest rather than on his shoulder, the lens was pointed towards the pit, and the red record light was on. If mister blond cop was too stupid to see that, it wasn't my job to tell him.

Chloe stood back and let them out. She took a good look at the camera as Terry went past, but he'd turned it off by then and there was nothing suspicious to see. He winked at me and swung the camera up to his shoulder as soon as he was clear of the doorway, motioning for Dave to get the sound going. I realised this was my cue. Damn. I'd never wanted to be a news reporter, but I could imagine what the NewsCaff director would say if he found out I'd had a chance to do a doorstop interview and bailed out.

'Detective Sergeant Prudhomme,' I said, 'can you tell us about your investigation?'

She wasn't happy, but she bit back what she wanted to say and trotted out the officialese. 'The body of a woman has been found at this address and we are treating it as a suspicious death.'

I wanted to call it quits there, but the other camera operators were crowding the gate, trying to get the story, and Terry nudged me firmly in the back to keep going.

'Is it true that the body is that of Dr Julieanne Weaver, from the Museum of New South Wales?'

'We won't be releasing the identity of the deceased until family have been notified, and we would appreciate the media cooperating with us on that.'

One of the things I did know about Julieanne was that she had no family—only child, dead parents who'd migrated from England, so no aunts or uncles or cousins. I didn't have to worry about a relative finding out about Julieanne's death on the news. I blanked on what to say next. What other questions would a news reporter ask? Then I had a brainwave.

'Dr Weaver was seeking preselection for the seat of North Hughes for the Australian Family Party. Could there be a political aspect to her death?'

But I'd pushed too far.

'As I said, we are investigating this death as suspicious but that's all the information I have at this point.'

She turned and went back in, closing the front door firmly behind her. I resisted the impulse to use my key to follow her in for more questions. Apart from anything else, she'd just take the key away.

I knocked on the door instead, and DC Martin whipped it open with a nasty look on his face.

'I just wanted to tell you, she doesn't have any family in Australia. Only a couple of cousins in London.'

He scowled and shut the door in my face.

Terry stopped recording and took the camera off his shoulder. 'I don't have an outside broadcast van here, so I've got to get this back to NewsCaff now.'

I nodded.

'Good job,' he added, and slapped me on the back.

As he and Dave pushed out the gate, I realised that they'd given me the perfect cover. If I followed them, the waiting news ghouls wouldn't know it was my house—they'd just think I was a strangely dressed reporter. I put my head down and crowded up behind Dave as he made his way through the rapidly growing crowd. Annandale residents may ignore a couple of cop cars, but they emerge pretty fast when the news crews show up.

Terry was chortling when I caught up with him.

'We are going to scoop the lot with this one! We've got footage of the house, of the pit, of her in the pit, of her talking to Poppy in the pit—it's bloody gold, mate! Bloody Walkley Award stuff.'

Now I wasn't defending Terry to Chloe, I felt all her distaste for turning Julieanne's death into a story. But it was his job, and mine, and I've always felt that anyone who watches the news regularly has to accept the process that gets those stories on air. It was just that right now I didn't want to be a part of it.

Terry and Dave packed the stuff in the car and looked around for Mirha, only then realising that she wasn't with them.

'I'm not going back in there,' I said, but the door opened again and Mirha and Tol came out, both looking rather shocked at the pack of reporters straining forward over the fence. Tol simply ignored them and made for the gate, his face closed down, shouldering his way through the reporters and cameramen.

'Come on,' he said to Mirha, implying she should shelter behind him. Mirha waited just a moment too long, and the mob closed behind Tol with her still on the doormat. Mirha looked around and her face lit with relief when she saw us.

'Go get her, Dave,' Terry said.

Dave humphed a bit, but he went back and pulled some reporters away from the gate. The two constables looked a bit harassed and much too young to cope with all this hassle.

'Get away, you lot, she's just our PA,' Dave shouted, and they fell back, which gave Tol a chance to walk quickly off towards the corner. I hesitated for a moment—should I go back to work or talk to Tol? Then I thought of my parents seeing this on the news and decided I'd better go and see them first. Which solved my other problem.

'I'm going to tell Mum and Dad,' I said to Terry, and took off down the street while the reporters were regrouping around the gate.

Tol had turned the corner, which suited me because I didn't want Terry to get any idea about me interviewing him.

'Tol!' I called, rather breathlessly, as I ran up behind him.

He turned, scowling, but his face cleared when he saw it was me, and he waited. I didn't know what to do. My impulse was to give him a hug, but I hardly knew the man. I compromised with a hand on his arm.

'Are you all right?'

His mouth twisted in a not-smile, but his eyes were bleak.

'Poor Poppy. You're never going to get that rewiring done.'

I hit him on the arm. 'Trust you to think of that. Come on, come and have a cup of tea at our place.'

He hesitated.

'It's just around the corner,' I offered. I didn't think he would be tempted by fruitcake, but—'My dad makes great coffee.'

'God, I could use a coffee,' he muttered, and fell into step beside me.

We didn't talk. I suspected he'd been talking to the police too long and was glad of the silence.

When we let ourselves into the entrance hall, Mum was on the phone to one of my many aunties. She sounded both worried and annoyed.

'No, I don't know any more than you do, Maree, all I know is what I saw on the TV. A body, they said, but it can't be Poppy because she wasn't at the house today. She's not answering her mobile—'

Oops. My phone was still off.

'Sorry, sorry,' I called, 'but I'm fine.'

Mum can move fast for an old girl. She whipped around, dropped the phone, took two steps towards me, grabbed my shoulders and shook me while inspecting me from top to toe, then went back to the phone. 'She's just come in, she's fine, I'll call you back. Will you tell the others? Thanks.' Then she turned to face me. 'Well?'

I became aware that Tol was laughing silently beside me, and I cast an irritated glance towards him, then smiled at Mum.

'Sorry, Mum. I had to turn off my phone. But I came back as soon as the police let me go.'

Immediately my foolishness was forgotten. Mum shepherded us through to the kitchen and shouted for my father.

'Bill! Bill! She's here! And she's brought someone!' She put the kettle on, moving on automatic, while I gestured to Tol to sit down.

'This is Dr Bartholomew Lang, Mum, from the museum. He was Julieanne's colleague.'

'Call me Tol.' He smiled at Mum as her face filled with concern.

'Julieanne? It was Julieanne who died?'

We nodded in unison, like marionettes. Mum made the sign of the cross, her face grave. My mum and dad had met

Julieanne while I was working at the museum. She'd been particularly nice to them, sweetness personified, and Mum had decided that all my ranting about her was just 'Poppy being difficult, as usual'.

'Was it an accident?' Dad asked, coming in from the garage, wiping his hands free of something. Dad always had a project going—usually some kind of woodwork for one of the family, although sometimes it was mechanical repairs. Restoring furniture was his favourite, and most of our houses were graced by beautiful cedar chests of drawers or bookcases which he'd picked up cheap at auction and brought back to life.

Tol got to his feet as Dad walked in—an automatic gesture of good manners that wasn't lost on my parents. He and Dad sized each other up as they shook hands.

'Tol Lang.'

'Bill McGowan.'

'Poppy tells me you make great coffee.'

Dad's face lit up. He'd got one of those benchtop cappuccino machines for Christmas but most of us preferred tea, so he was always glad to have someone to show off for.

'Won't take a minute. Cappuccino?'

'Yes, please,' Tol said with heartfelt emphasis.

'*Was* it an accident?' Mum asked, bringing us back to business.

'We don't know,' I said. I helped as she got the mugs down and brought out the inevitable fruitcake, then sat down. 'The police say they're treating it as a suspicious death, but they're asking people where they were last night and this morning, so I think they think it's *very* suspicious. They want to fingerprint everyone who's been in the house, including you two.'

Mum paused, kettle in one hand, teapot in the other. 'Murder?'

It's a strange word. We use it all the time: 'I'm going to murder that kid if he leaves his bike in the driveway again', 'I could murder a beer', 'The traffic was murder tonight'. But when it's real, when it's someone you know, that word echoes around a room and around your head. Perhaps it was because I was sitting down quietly and thinking for the first moment since I'd arrived at my house, but suddenly I felt shaky.

'She was wearing the clothes she had on last night,' Tol said softly. 'I don't understand why she would have gone to the dig dressed like that.'

'To meet someone?' I wondered.

'She was supposed to meet me at my place,' Tol said. 'I waited until midnight before I went to bed.'

The coffee machine starting hissing and spitting, cutting off conversation, and Dad looked at Tol shrewdly. He reached into the bottom cupboard and brought out his treasured single malt scotch and poured one. He handed it over silently, and Tol took it just as silently with a nod of thanks and sipped it. I saw his shoulders relax a little as its warmth hit him.

Mum poured tea for the two of us, and I thought hard.

'So you don't have an alibi?' I asked delicately.

He shook his head. 'What about you?'

I shrugged. 'I was here,' I said. 'But I suppose I could have slipped out after everyone was asleep.'

In fact, this would have been impossible, as my siblings had discovered long ago (one of the advantages of being the youngest is that your older sibs get to make all the mistakes). Mum sleeps poorly and has the ears of a cat. No child of hers had ever succeeded in making it out of the house after hours. But I couldn't expect the police to believe that.

Dad handed Tol his coffee and made one for himself.

'But why would anyone have wanted to kill that lovely woman?' Mum asked. 'Perhaps it was political! Terrorists, maybe.'

My imagination baulked at terrorists targeting someone who hadn't even been preselected. Knowing Julieanne, it was far more likely to have been personal.

'She probably smacked someone across the face and they hit back,' I said gloomily.

'Poppy! As if she would. You've never been fair to that woman and now she's dead—'

'She threatened to hit me right across the face the day before yesterday,' I protested. I turned to Tol for support. 'Didn't she?'

'She did,' he said.

My mother's eyes narrowed. 'What did you say to her to make her do that?' she demanded. You can't win. Really.

'I told her I didn't want her digging a twelve-foot hole in my living room,' I said.

There was a silence. But my mother knew me too well. 'Is that all?'

'I may have said it more—metaphorically.'

That was enough. Mum was off. 'You can't go around swearing at people—'

'Um, Mrs McGowan,' Tol interrupted. 'It really wasn't Poppy's fault. Julieanne was being quite unreasonable.'

Hardly anyone had ever stood up for me. I felt a surge of warmth and gratitude, especially considering it was his dead girlfriend he was talking about.

'Oh.' Mum wasn't satisfied, but of course she would believe a total stranger before she would believe me. That's what being a mother does to you.

'So this girl had a bit of a temper?' Dad asked, putting his finger on the nub, as usual.

Tol nodded, reluctantly. 'I'm afraid so.' He took a big swig of coffee.

'I'll say a novena for her soul,' my mother said. She's really very kind. My eyes filled with tears and I grabbed her hand.

'Say one for us as well,' I said. 'We're going to be prime suspects.'

Tol didn't want to go to back for his car in case he was ambushed by the media, and neither did I, so I borrowed Mum's and drove him to the museum. The networks were there, too, but I went around to the staff entrance.

The museum is a big old sandstone building which has been dragged into the twenty-first century by adding a glass and steel exhibition hall. It looks out over the botanic gardens and down to the Opera House, which was shining white in the sun as we drove around the back to the service road and pulled into the loading dock.

'I'll fill Annie in,' Tol said, looking tired.

'No, I'll do that,' I said, and immediately felt stupid. He was a grown man, he didn't need me to nursemaid him.

He didn't seem to mind. 'Thanks, but there's no point wasting your time. I'll just have to tell the story a dozen times and work out what we're going to do about the dig.'

'The dig?' I was surprised. I'd assumed that the dig was over, even with the historical preservation order. Without Julieanne to push it through, the council probably wouldn't have been that interested in a couple of sheep bones. It wasn't as though I was trying to tear down a lovely old house—just the opposite, in fact. And I'd been fairly confident I could talk my way out of the order.

'I know Julieanne was the most interested, but if your site is connected with pastoralism in the early colony, we really should investigate. The police got me to give them the photos of the site from before—before Julieanne died. So they didn't have to take the bones as evidence, I suppose. That means the dig can still go on.'

'Oh, bugger,' I said.

He smiled sympathetically at me. 'We'll get the carbon-14 results back soon, and then we'll know what we're dealing with.'

I was reluctant to end the conversation. I knew that when he stepped out of my car, I'd be cold and vulnerable. With him there, I felt safe. But that was ridiculous. For the first time, I seriously considered the idea that Tol might have killed Julieanne. Surely that wasn't possible. Was it? How could I be sure? I *was* sure, deep in my gut, that it was impossible for him to do it deliberately—but it could have been an accident. In which case, I argued to myself, I was perfectly safe with him.

I'd been silent too long, and I saw Tol brace himself.

'Poppy?' he said hesitantly, his voice going up as though he were unsure of himself. 'Are you upset about the dig?'

'I'm not happy,' I admitted, 'but I think we have more to worry about than the dig.'

'I saw her, but I still find it hard to believe she's dead. She just looked—unconscious.' Tol stared blindly out the windscreen. I gently touched his arm and he covered my hand with his own. His was cold, but that wasn't why I shivered.

He turned to me and stared into my eyes. 'I—'

And then my bloody phone rang.

'I'll let you get that,' Tol said briskly, and jumped out of the car as though the devil himself were after him.

I snarled 'Yes?' into the phone as I watched him go across to the entrance. He paused in the doorway, then turned and waved at me before he disappeared inside.

'Yes?' I said again, more politely, feeling ridiculously happy that Tol had waved.

'Are you all right?' Stuart's voice was high and disapproving. Bugger, I should have called him. 'I just heard some story on the news about a woman's body being found at an archaeological dig in Annandale.'

'Julieanne,' I said automatically.

'Why didn't you call me?' he said. 'I thought it might have been you!'

'Sorry, sorry,' I said. 'You're right, but the police have been questioning me.' It wasn't a lie. Not really.

'Oh,' he said, placated slightly. 'What about?'

Sometimes I wonder about Stuart. I know he's intelligent. He got the university medal for accountancy. He's considered brilliant in his field. But sometimes he seems to have no grasp of reality.

'Uh—because they found a dead body in my house?'

'But surely it was an accident?'

'Maybe not.'

'You're joking!'

I really didn't want to have this conversation. 'Stuart, look, I have to get back to work. I'll see you tonight and fill you in then.'

I hung up. I didn't want to sit in the car and stew—Tol would have had enough time to see Annie by now. I needed to decompress, and there was no one better than Annie to do it with.

But before I got to the back door of the museum, she came out at a clip, clearly looking for me. Bless her.

How to describe Annie? She's my age (six days younger, actually), incredibly competent, chic in a way I'll never be, organised, whip-smart, and does not suffer fools. At all, let alone gladly.

We met on the first day of uni and have been friends ever since. I rely on Annie for a regular dose of common sense and endless kindness. She's the most generous person I know. She also manages to be a great mother to three kids and has a very lovely husband. There are times I feel quite incompetent in comparison—but she just laughs at that.

She gave me a hug and then held me at arm's length to inspect me. 'Are you all right? You look like death warmed up. Come on, come and have a coffee.'

We went across the road to the little café in the park opposite. I wasn't sure I could deal with yet another cup of tea, but an ice-cold ginger beer seemed like a good idea. I needed the sugar hit.

'Tol told me what happened. Give me your version,' Annie said, so I did.

She listened with that particular focus that has allowed her to climb to the top of her profession so young, and then drew in a long breath and let it out again. It was hard to read her expression, but she patted my hand as she might have patted her cat, Mycroft, and I felt marginally better.

'Murder.'

'I think so,' I said.

'You poor sausage,' she said.

'Poor Julieanne.'

Shaking her head, Annie downed the last of her latte. 'Yes. Poor Julieanne, which is something I never thought I'd say. I can't quite believe she's dead. This is going to be a dog's breakfast. I'd better get back and get the Minister's office up to speed.'

I walked out with her and waved as she went back into the museum. But before I could get back in the car, my phone rang.

'Meet me in the lobby at Ultimo. I'm leaving now.' Jennifer Jay's voice was crisp.

Although I was very tired, I was oddly glad to have something to do, and someone to tell me to do it. It would take me much less time to get there, so I read some of the texts on my phone. I answered Alex first, of course. He was delirious with curiosity.

Tell me everything!!!!!!!

I told him everything and left it to him to spread the news to the fifteen friends who'd sent me the same message, then drove to the ABC.

Jennifer Jay arrived with her normal haste and I joined her to go through security.

'What's up?' I asked as we swiped our staff cards.

'NewsCaff have decided that you should be involved in the planning on this story. Maybe do some of the reporting.'

NewsCaff is short for News and Current Affairs.

'I'm not a reporter!' My voice rose in a squeak.

Jennifer Jay cast me an amused glance. 'You did all right this afternoon. NewsCaff was very pleased with the police doorstep.'

I swallowed and tried to get my voice under control. 'Let me rephrase: I don't *want* to be a reporter.'

'Tell that to Tyler.'

I did, when we reached NewsCaff, which looks a lot more upmarket than our production office, but no tidier. The NewsCaff boss, Tyler Haddin, sat me down and congratulated me on the interview I'd done with Chloe. Tyler was mid-fifties, balding (and shaved to conceal it), pink-skinned as though he had regular facials, and dressed in the behind-the-scenes TV uniform of jeans and polo shirt. He had sharp little eyes that missed nothing and a mouth like a trap, but he was smiling at me.

'I don't want to be a reporter,' I said. 'I'm quite happy as a researcher.'

His smile disappeared. I guess he has a lot of people beating on his doors, wanting to be reporters, and it took him by surprise that I wasn't one of them. He changed tack.

'We need you.'

'Why? It's not like I can get into the house or anything. The police are still there. And when they go, I can let your crew and one of the regular reporters in.'

'It's a scoop, sweetheart,' he said, immediately putting me offside. I don't like being called sweetheart by people I've only just met. Patronising bastard. 'Having the inside straight only happens once in a lifetime. And having an insider in a murder investigation—that's fabulous! We're planning a series of stories—not just the news segments, but stories on *The Daily Report*, the *Australian Story* people are interested, maybe an hour-long documentary … we *need* you.'

'Why?'

'Because everyone's going to talk to you. What about the boyfriend, this Lang guy?'

'Tol,' I said automatically.

'Tol, okay. Will he agree to an interview?'

'I'm not going to interview Tol.' My tone that time must have got through to him. He raised his eyebrows. I clarified: 'I'm not going to interview anyone I know.'

'But maybe you can set it up for one of our other reporters?'

I felt very reluctant to involve Tol in any media scrum, but then I realised that if we had an exclusive, the others would leave him alone.

'Maybe,' I said.

'And we have exclusive interviews with you—we'll get you down to wardrobe and make-up soon, so Toby can talk to you for tonight's program—and access to the house—'

'Hold on!' I objected. 'I didn't say I'd do an interview with Toby.'

Both Jennifer Jay and Tyler looked at me in complete astonishment.

'Jennifer Jay, talk some sense into her.'

But she didn't have to. This was TV, and TV news at that. Forget sentiment, forget reticence, forget shyness. Even at the ABC, ratings mattered, and an interview with me would be good for ratings. As an ABC employee, I was expected to be loyal unto death. That's only barely an exaggeration— ABC people are fanatical about the organisation.

'Okay,' I said. 'But—'

'Great!' Tyler said, clapping his hands. 'And then maybe we can get you to cover the Australian Family side of things. You don't know them, do you?'

I shook my head. I didn't mind that—I was much more interested in finding out about the political stuff.

'I could start with Eliza and Matthew Carter. They were her main contacts there, I think.'

'Great!' Tyler said, and clapped his hands again. That could really get on my nerves. 'I've got someone getting their contact details. We'll do your interview with Toby and then you can go right out with a crew. We've got to move quickly on something like this. If they make an arrest the whole thing's sub judice and we won't be able to say anything.'

I might not have been a news reporter but I knew that once someone was arrested, the media had to stop reporting on the crime until it came to trial.

I hoped Chloe would make an arrest soon.

'What do we know about a Detective Sergeant Chloe Prudhomme?' I asked.

Tyler whistled. 'Is she in charge? She's on the fast track. Some insiders are saying she's heading straight for commissioner in a few years. Honors degree in politics and criminology, very connected family. Her mother is a Highmark: they have half-a-dozen QCs, two judges, three MPs, you name it. Apparently the family took it badly when she decided to be a cop, but she went for it anyway. You be careful of her, sweetheart. She's a very smart cookie.'

'Yeah,' I said. 'That much I could tell.'

They hustled me off to wardrobe and make-up and I was tarted up to look respectable. I sent Jennifer Jay out to the car to get my good shoes, but they wouldn't let me wear the nice skirt and blouse I kept in the boot. Instead they gave me a newsreader's power suit from the wardrobe stock.

'Sweetheart, you're representing us now, not the kiddies,' Tyler said, although he made sure first that Jennifer Jay couldn't hear him. He really was a patronising sod.

While I was in make-up, a press release came through from the cops to say the coroner had declared Julieanne's death officially suspicious. That hit me with a thump. I'd been hoping they'd decide it was an accident. I felt unclean, and for the first time I understood Lady Macbeth's exclamation, 'What, in our house?' Of course, she was covering up murder, but she'd known what emotion to counterfeit—bloody Shakespeare always knew what the real feelings were. I had a sense of my sanctuary being defiled, and it made me angry. Someone had killed Julieanne on *my* turf. That made it personal. I wanted them caught.

I said as much to Toby, who was chatty and charming right up to the point the cameras rolled, and then morphed into a hard-hitting interviewer determined to get to the truth.

'What's it like, being a murder suspect?' was his first question.

'Uh—I hadn't really thought about that,' I said stalling for time. I couldn't let him get me on the back foot. 'I've been thinking more about Julieanne and how sad her death is.'

Chew on that, hardliner. I'd seen and done enough interviews to know how to turn the conversation. I wasn't going to let him control it all. Perhaps that sounds cold, but anyone who's been involved with the media develops a thick skin and a calculating mind in situations like this, and I was thankful for it. I'd seen interviewees who didn't really understand that the host's job was to get shocking revelations and tearful confessions, and who'd ended up sobbing, feeling ambushed and betrayed.

'You knew her well?'

'I worked with her at the Museum of New South Wales,' I explained, and went into the story of how she came to be digging in my living room. I skated over any conflict between us, and clearly Toby's researchers hadn't talked enough to Terry and Dave, because he didn't bring it up.

'And now your home is a crime scene,' he prompted.

My eyes filled with tears at the thought of my poor little house invaded by police and cut off from me. But I knew better than to actually say so. I had to excuse the tears in some other way.

'It's terrible to think of Julieanne just lying there ...'

'Losing a friend must be very hard.' Toby was all sympathy, building the moment for the audience.

'I wouldn't say we were close friends,' I said, walking a fine line between truth and appearances. 'More colleagues. But it's a terrible thing to have anyone you know cut down by violence.'

He nodded, encouraging me to say more, but I shut up while I was ahead.

'The police are investigating anyone who might have had contact with Dr Weaver in the last few days,' he prompted.

'So I understand.' Out of the corner of my eye I could see the floor manager giving Toby the wind-up sign, saying we were out of time, so I thought I'd give them a nice emotional grab to finish on. 'I just hope the police can arrest the monster who did this and let Julieanne rest in peace.'

'Thank you very much for talking to us,' Toby concluded, and the floor manager yelled, 'Cut!'

'Great ending, Poppy, thanks,' Toby said, detaching his lapel mike and getting up.

I joined Jennifer Jay where she was waiting with a manila folder. She handed it to me.

'Details on Australian Family,' she said. 'Some interesting stuff in there. I'll see you later. Good luck.'

Tyler sent the work experience girl to the canteen to grab lunch for us while we looked through the folder in one of the screening booths.

The Australian Family Party had been started ten years ago by an evangelical preacher, Amos Winchester, who had come out from America twelve years before that to set up a mission of the Radiant Joy Church in Sydney. The church itself was doing fine—growing fast, like a lot of the Pentecostal churches, pulling in young people and donations with lively services and good singing and an absolute certainty about right and wrong. The Radiant Joy Church believed that homosexuality was evil, women should be subservient to men, and only Christians would be let into Heaven— pretty standard stuff that reminded me of the Catholicism of my parents' youth.

A few years ago, Winchester had teamed up with an unexpected mover and shaker: Samuel Stephenson, a businessman who had parlayed a family bakery into a multi-million dollar franchise operation, before selling it all to concentrate on church and party. He was a true believer, obviously.

The party had fielded a few candidates in local elections in the suburbs of the major cities, but they'd only had one elected: Matthew Carter, who'd taken over as leader of the party when Winchester retired from everything except church work. Carter was MP for Cumberland, a new seat in Sydney's north-west created when an existing electorate had been split in two to allow for the huge population growth in that area. He had benefited from the long-term sitting member choosing to stand for the other half of the seat, and by a domestic violence scandal involving the Liberal candidate. The incident gave Carter the perfect soapbox to espouse family values. It had worked. He didn't have a land-slide, but he got a clear majority.

Now a by-election was coming up because a state govern-ment MP had dropped dead in a brothel—a fact known to most journalists but firmly denied by everyone else involved. The government had only had a majority of one, so if Carter could get an Australian Family candidate elected, they'd have the balance of power. No wonder Julieanne had wanted to be preselected.

Tyler showed me some archival footage of Carter in full electioneering mode. I could see why the voters had fallen for him: he was good-looking and charming: about forty (not too old, not too young), energetic, a perfect toothpaste advertisement smile, wavy brown hair, strong jaw—lord, you could sell just about anything with this guy as your rep. He was clever too, I had to give him that. He spoke reasonably, rather than preaching, and he used phrases like 'moral common sense', to avoid actually saying the word 'God' out loud, in case he scared off the non-Christian voters.

'Yeah, they're trying to distance themselves from the church,' Tyler confirmed. 'That's still where they're getting most of their money, but Carter's realised he won't get the votes if the electorate know he's a God-botherer.'

I already disliked Matthew Carter. Was that fair? I believed in God, after all. I'd even been going to church again since

I moved back in with my parents. ('If you live in our house, you live by our rules,' they said, which I thought was fair enough when you realised that they honestly thought I'd go to Hell if I didn't attend Mass.) Why should I think the worst of Carter because he was evangelical? On the other hand, our archbishop was the same kind of hardliner, who lumped every gay person, everyone who'd had pre-marital sex and everyone who used contraception into the same pit of Hell, and I didn't like him either. It made me feel better to think that I was even-handed in my prejudice, rather than sectarian.

'Who's that?' I asked, pausing the tape to point at a woman standing behind Carter as he made his victory speech on election night.

'Keep it going,' Tyler said, so I pressed play.

Carter beamed at the adoring audience of supporters and said, 'And of course, the person on this earth I most have to thank—' (oh, very smooth, implying God's help without claiming it) '—is my wonderful wife, Eliza.'

She came forward for the obligatory kiss and smile. She looked like a blonde, slightly more conservative, Jackie Kennedy in the White House days: little pastel suit, pearls, perfect make-up. And she was good-looking. Not Julieanne's brand of sex appeal, but the smooth, controlled prettiness that's a combination of good bones, perfect grooming and rigorous self-discipline when the dessert cart goes past.

Their children joined them on the platform: twin boys, eight or ten, short-haired like their father, in navy jackets complete with ties, and a blonde teenage girl who looked so wholesome she could be in an ad for milk. How did they get a fifteen-year-old to wear a Laura Ashley dress like that? Bribery or threats of eternal damnation?

I shrugged. The kids all looked proud of their dad, although I noticed the girl stepped behind the others so she'd be out of the spotlight. Shy? Embarrassed? Everything's embarrassing at that age.

Someone knocked at the door of the screening booth and I stopped the tape. Terry and Dave.

'We've been seconded for the interim.' Terry looked happy, an old warhorse back in armour.

'I'll meet you outside,' I said, and they waved and left. I turned to Tyler. 'Because you're not sure if you'll be able to use any of the material I get?'

He didn't even have the grace to look embarrassed. 'It's a risk,' he admitted. 'Don't want to tie up one of our crews if we're not going to get anything. Besides, Terry's good. He just slowed down a bit too much for us. But getting interviews—none better. He'll show you the ropes.'

I sniffed and put on my borrowed respectable blue jacket. I felt like one of those poor little boys, stuffed into uncomfortable clothes just so the grown-ups could have a nice show.

'What if they won't talk to me?'

'Then we're no worse off than we were.' He patted me on the shoulder. 'Go put the boot in, sweetheart.'

CHAPTER EIGHT

Carter's electoral office was a fifty-minute drive away, out in the suburbs, at the retail end of a business park located across a highway from a huge sprawling suburban development full of McMansions. Perfect for him: sponsors and voters both within spitting distance. The church, discreetly, was more than a kilometre away, but still within easy reach.

We pulled up in the car park and considered our options. Carter had one of the shops that faced out but the door had a CLOSED sign that was visible from where we sat. There were several other news crews camped out on the footpath. Carter either hadn't arrived or hadn't left yet, but clearly he was planning to give no more than doorstep grabs.

Should I take the crew in or go in by myself first?

Terry was sure. 'You head in, they'll talk to you because it was your house. Then you establish yourself as sympathetic, and mention you were coming past with a camera crew on your way back from a shoot and dropped in. See if you can get them to suggest an interview.'

I drew in a deep breath, feeling like an undercover cop about to go into a gang stronghold. Which was ridiculous. I was a professional, doing my job, and these were politicians—they loved media. In fact, I was doing them a favour by giving them air time.

I got out of the car and walked across to the office, trying hard to look competent but not a journo. When I got to the door, one of the reporters—a Channel 10 junior reporter, one I'd seen on kids' TV—said, 'They're not giving interviews. They say he'll be out when he's finished his electoral business and we can get a grab then.'

I nodded thanks, but knocked on the door anyway.

A middle-aged Anglo woman peered out suspiciously and glared around, but seeing that I wasn't followed by a camera crew, she reluctantly opened the door a crack.

'Yes?' she rapped out.

'My name is Poppy McGowan,' I said quietly. I bent closer and cast a look back at the reporters and camera crews, implying the need for secrecy, and lowered my voice almost to a whisper. 'It was my house that Julieanne Weaver was found in.'

I would have kept my voice down even without the need to impress her. The last thing I wanted was for the other crews to figure out who I was and ambush me instead.

The woman's eyes lit with interest—everyone loves a murder—and opened the door. She took my arm and pulled me inside, then slammed the door shut and locked it firmly.

'Vultures!' she said.

The room seemed very crowded. Half the space had been partitioned off into a private office, and the rest was full of desks and people—a dozen or so, some working the phones, some on computers, and half just there because they could be. I saw Carter's daughter, looking more believable in jeans and a hoodie, but neither Carter nor his wife were visible.

'I hoped to talk to Mr Carter?' I asked.

The door guardian nodded. 'Just a minute.' She went back to the office and disappeared inside, leaving me with all those pairs of eyes staring at me.

What the hell. In for a penny ...

'Hi,' I said. I repeated what I'd told the door guardian, and there was a rustle of interest, but no one said anything, although several people nodded. One guy in the corner immediately got on the phone. I tried to listen, but all I heard was him asking for 'Mr Stephenson'. Interesting that Samuel Stephenson kept a spy in Matthew Carter's office.

I smiled, casually walked over to the desk where the daughter was standing and leant against it, as though pre-paring myself for a long wait.

'You knew Julieanne?' the daughter asked. Her name was Patience, I remembered from the file I'd gone over again on the drive out.

I gave that half-smile/half-grimace which is good man-ners when claiming acquaintance with the recently dead, and nodded. 'I used to work with her,' I said.

'She was seeking preselection,' Patience noted, her voice flat, eyes on the phone in her hand. Her earbuds were in, but I couldn't hear any music and there was no video playing. I was used to my nieces, whose faces showed every fleeting emotion, but Patience's face gave nothing away. I couldn't tell if she had liked Julieanne, but I suspected not. This girl didn't seem like a fool to me.

'So I heard,' I said, putting just a little disapproval in my tone.

Her eyes flicked up to mine and her mouth curled very slightly at the corners, as though she were satisfied that I shared her own opinion of Julieanne.

The door guardian came out of the office and beckoned me over. 'Mr Carter will see you now.'

It reminded me of taking one of my aunties to an appointment at a specialist's office. They always seem to have those older receptionists whose main job is making sure you appreciate the Great One's condescension in agreeing to see you at all.

Matthew Carter got up as I came in and walked around his desk to shake my hand. Although he gave me the two-handed politician's shake, his face was befittingly sombre. As phony as a designer knockoff. His wife was sitting in a guest chair facing the desk, and she swivelled around to look at me, her face calm and politely interested.

'Miss McGowan,' Carter said. 'How can we help you?'

I returned the pressure of his hand and finally he let me go, stepping back around the desk but not sitting down, as though ready to usher me out at any moment. I sat in the remaining guest chair and saw Eliza's eyes flicker, but made sure my face showed nothing but mild concern. Carter sat down slowly.

'You know it was my house that Julieanne was found in?' I asked.

'Yes, terrible,' Carter said automatically.

'Um, I'm not a member of the party, but my family are very supportive of your ideals,' I said hesitantly. Which was true. My parents think the Australian Family Party makes a lot of sense. Thank God the sitting independent member in our electorate is a Catholic, or they might even be voting for this lot. 'I guess I just wanted to talk to you because we've both sort of been dragged into this … It would be a shame if Julieanne's death hurt anyone else in the party.'

Carter warmed slightly, and Eliza smiled.

'I work for the ABC,' I said (hiding nothing, so they couldn't accuse me of setting them up later), 'and the word around the newsroom is this may have a political link.' I'm not a liar by nature, and I wasn't going to tell any lies, but this wasn't how I usually got interviews. Trickery was what it felt like.

'No!' Eliza said vehemently. 'This has nothing to do with the Party!' You could hear the capital letter. She sounded vaguely Marxist, which was funny, really.

'The news director can't see why her museum work would have led to this. And her personal life seems … stable.'

'That woman's personal life was as disgusting as a sewer,' Eliza said, her voice thick with contempt.

Carter made a sound of protest, and Eliza's whole manner changed immediately.

Casting her eyes down, she murmured, sweet as pie, 'But I shouldn't judge.' She looked up at him through her lashes and I saw that he was smiling down at her. The smile had something odd at the centre of it—it wasn't simple affection; there was a dark edge to it, as though he liked seeing her back down completely at the merest hint from him. Power. He liked power. No surprise there. And she adored him. What do the Americans say? She thought he hung the moon.

'I'm absolutely sure that Dr Weaver's political ambitions had nothing to do with her death,' Carter said. 'Dr Weaver', not 'Julieanne'—he was distancing himself as fast as he could. 'It wasn't as though she had been preselected. In fact …' He leant closer and dropped his voice. 'I can tell you in confidence that the party had reached a decision *not* to preselect her.'

Yeah, right.

'It's a shame you can't make your position clear to the electorate,' I said.

Carter cast a glance at the door. 'A media scrum isn't the right place to make a considered statement,' he said ruefully. 'They'd try to derail me, put me on the defensive.' He laughed a little and spread his hands. 'Sorry to insult your profession, Miss McGowan, but in my business you learn to treat the media with caution!'

'Oh, I know. I work in the education department myself. News is a bit too cutthroat for me.' *So* true.

They relaxed even further. Education is such a *nice* department. So worthy.

I hesitated, then said, 'Um … I just dropped in on my way from a shoot … my camera crew is outside in the car … If you wanted to do a proper interview, I could get it to news …'

Carter and Eliza exchanged glances and I saw her nod fractionally.

'That might be very helpful,' he said.

So I went out through the office, told the door dragon I'd be back in a minute, returned to the car and leant in through the open window.

'Would you like to do an interview with the delightful Mr Carter?' I said.

'Good job, love,' Terry said.

As we went past the media contingent outside the door, the Channel 10 reporter asked querulously, 'What's going on?'

'ABC exclusive,' Dave said smugly, eliciting an interesting range of swear words from the waiting journos.

While Terry and Dave set up the lights, I stood in a corner of the office and wondered why neither Eliza nor Carter had asked me a single question—about the house, about Julieanne's death, about my involvement, not even about why I was there. Could they be that self-centred? Or did they already know the answers?

Patience came to stand beside me.

'Are you a reporter?' she asked accusingly.

'I'm a researcher for ABC Kids,' I said. 'But I had a camera crew with me, and your father thought it might be helpful to do a more controlled interview than he'd get from that lot out there.' I nodded towards the windows. Even through the blinds, you could tell that there was a crowd outside. More were arriving every minute.

'Oh,' she said.

'Did you know Julieanne well?'

'I hated her,' Patience hissed. Her face contorted. She really had hated Julieanne. Then her expression melted into confused sorrow. 'But hate's a sin. And now she's dead and I can't make amends.'

She brought out all my auntly instincts.

'Well, I wouldn't worry about it,' I said bracingly. 'When you're as much a bitch as Julieanne was, hatred happens. Just shows you've got good taste.'

This was an approach to sin that Patience had clearly never encountered before. 'But I should repent my sin,' she said. 'For the good of my own soul.'

I shrugged. 'Okay. If it makes you feel better. But if God is just, He's not going to blame anyone who hated Julieanne Weaver. At least, I hope not, or I'm in real trouble!'

Patience laughed, and then covered her mouth with her hands, glancing around to see if her parents had seen. 'Are you a believer?' she asked. Which meant: *Should I be talking to this heathen?*

I tried to imagine one of my nieces—who all go to Mass every Sunday—asking a total stranger if they believed in God. Not only would they not do it, it wouldn't even *occur* to them that it might matter. Maybe I should introduce Patience to them.

'In God? You bet,' I said.

She relaxed and leant her shoulders against the wall. 'There are so many people who aren't,' she said, as if that were both inconceivable and frightening.

'Like Julieanne?'

'Her! She *pretended*. She'd pray with us at home before meals, and she'd even started coming to church on Sundays, but it was just *politics*.'

My imagination boggled at that. Julieanne in church? Then something else clicked.

'So Julieanne visited you at home?'

Patience nodded. 'The last few months, she was there all the time. In meetings with Father, and with the other elders.' So much for Carter pretending he hardly knew her.

Carter ushered his daughter out and closed the door behind her, then took his seat behind the desk. I was surprised that Eliza wasn't there to watch.

Terry signalled he was ready and I took my position, remembering watching senior journos do hard-hitting interviews. With government ministers, they usually went for the jugular straight away, but with other people, they often started out nicely and then put the knife in. Hmm.

'Rolling,' Terry said.

'Mr Carter, Julieanne Weaver was found dead this morning and the police are treating it as a suspicious death. Do you have any comment?' There, a nice straight question to let him get his prepared statement off his chest. I couldn't believe it had only been this morning, though. It felt like a year, at least.

'Dr Weaver's death is a tragedy, and our thoughts and prayers are with her family at this tragic time.' Oh, he was good. Once you can fake sincerity, you've got it made.

'Dr Weaver was seeking preselection for the seat of North Hughes. Do you believe that her political ambitions may have led to her death?'

'Absolutely not!' Carter leant forward. 'There can be no possible link. I'm sure the police will find that Dr Weaver was killed by an intruder.'

Nice theory, except for the fact that the house was locked up tight.

'Would Dr Weaver have gained preselection?'

He hesitated. It was nicely calculated, and it looked convincing. 'I haven't received permission from the party to announce the candidate yet, but I can tell you that it would not have been Dr Weaver.'

'Why not?'

He blinked. He wasn't expecting that one. 'While Dr Weaver was an intelligent, energetic person, we felt that she was not quite the right person to represent the party.'

'Was that because she was a woman?'

He blinked again, and ran a hand through that carefully cut blond hair. 'No, certainly not! Women have a great deal to offer as MPs.'

'Because she wasn't married, then?'

He hesitated. 'We are a party which represents the family. It's difficult to understand the needs of families if you don't have one of your own.'

Really? My single-woman hackles rose and I started to enjoy grilling him.

'So if she'd been a married woman with children, she would have been preselected?'

'Not necessarily. It would have depended on the qualities of the other candidates.' He smiled. 'And I'm glad to say that the quality of the other candidates is very high indeed.'

'But she would have had a better chance if she'd been a mum?'

He shrugged a little. 'As I said, it's important that our MPs fully understand the needs of families.'

'But doesn't Australian Family believe that a mother should be at home, looking after her children?'

He hadn't seen that coming and he'd walked right into it, but he was quick. 'Whenever possible, we believe that children should be raised by the people who love them the most, yes. But someone also has to look after the needs of children in the wider arena, and that's what Australian Family is dedicated to.'

He'd be ready for any other challenges on that subject, so I changed tack. 'Dr Weaver has spent a great deal of time with your family over the last few months. Is this a personal tragedy for you?'

I could see him restrain himself from glaring at me.

'Dr Weaver, as a candidate for preselection, clearly needed to meet with party officials. My house was often the venue for those meetings, but they were purely business, as was my relationship with Dr Weaver.'

'Did you like Dr Weaver?'

'Yes! Everyone at Australian Family liked her.'

I smiled confidingly. 'Now, you know that's not true, Matthew. Her opponents for preselection didn't like her.'

It was a guess, but it was close to a certainty. I followed up while he was choosing his words.

'Isn't it true that there were sections of the party who felt that Dr Weaver's personal life didn't match the standards required by Australian Family? That her commitment to God, for example, was suspect?'

Carter licked his lips. Hah! I had him on the run.

'A commitment to God isn't a prerequisite for joining our party. Only a commitment to the needs of the family.'

'But it is a prerequisite for preselection, isn't it? Aren't the members of your preselection committee overwhelmingly members of the Radiant Joy Church? And didn't some of them question Dr Weaver's true beliefs?' I would have, if I'd been them.

'All the candidates' backgrounds are carefully checked before we select them,' Carter said, dropping into safe explanation mode. 'Dr Weaver was no exception.'

'Checked by a committee made up of church elders?'

'By a private investigator, actually,' Carter said disingenuously.

'And the committee?'

'Many of our committee are, indeed, members of local churches. But not only the Radiant Joy Church. Many Christians understand what we are trying to defend, and they support us.'

Back on message. Very good, Mr Carter. He was getting impatient and angry. I probably only had one more question. Let's make it a doozy, I thought. I made my voice as earnest as I could.

'Mr Carter, do you believe that Julieanne Weaver is in Heaven?'

He looked like I'd poleaxed him, and didn't reply for quite a few seconds, which would stretch out meaningfully on screen. Surprisingly, I caught a glimpse of tears in his eyes.

'I'd like to think so,' he said slowly. 'But no one can judge anyone but themselves.'

'Matthew Carter, thank you very much.'

'Thank you, Poppy,' he said automatically.

Terry said, 'Cut!' and then turned the lights off and started to move the camera to the other side of the desk. 'Right, let's get the noddies and the questions from you, Poppy.'

Carter glared at me and stood up, and I thought I'd better pre-empt his explosion.

'You were so good, Mr Carter! I knew you would be.' I dropped my voice and gestured him aside as Terry brought the camera around his side of the desk so he could get the reverse shots of me. Carter was crowded out and stepped across to me automatically.

'I thought I'd better ask you some difficult questions so the news director wouldn't think it was a whitewash. I knew you'd be able to answer. You were great,' I simpered. Could he really believe that? But his ego was big enough to believe any amount of female adoration, and he calmed down.

'I see. That's a dangerous game, Poppy.'

'But you were terrific! Wasn't he, Terry?'

Terry shrugged. 'Sounded okay to me.' He gestured for me to sit back down. 'Let's get the questions.'

'I'll leave you to it.' Carter turned at the door and looked at me. 'I'm not sure whether to thank you or not, Poppy.' There was a little humour in his eyes. It was the first time I'd come close to liking him, and I realised that when he was relaxed he did have a real charm. I wondered if Julieanne had fallen for it. I smiled back at him and pretended to misunderstand.

'I don't need thanks, Matthew,' I said. 'I was glad to help.'

He went out looking slightly chagrined and closed the door behind him.

Terry and Dave filmed me asking the same questions over again, and then a series of 'noddies'—me appearing to listen to Carter's answers and nodding in comprehension or encouragement. The two bits of vision would be cut together so it looked like it had all been shot at the same time: my question, his answer, my nod, and so on. A little piece of television illusion that happens every day.

As Terry and Dave were packing up the lights, Carter came back.

'So,' he said, rubbing his hands together. 'All finished?'

I nodded. 'There's just one thing …'

'Yes?'

'If I go back with that interview, the news director is going to ask for the name of the private investigator.'

Carter frowned. 'Oh, I don't think I can reveal that.'

'Why not?'

It stopped him. He didn't seem to be used to direct questions. 'Uh, because it's confidential.'

'Why?'

'Because any details of Dr Weaver's personal life are confidential.'

'Of course,' I agreed. 'He won't be able to reveal anything to us.'

'So why do you want the name?'

'*I* don't,' I said, with convincing earnestness. I really didn't. 'But the news director will, and I'll get in trouble if I don't have it … it's not like the investigator will say anything, but it would be great if I could give news the information.' I smiled sadly. 'They think education is a bit naff, you know.'

He thawed a little. 'I suppose it wouldn't do any harm. His name is Garry Monahan.'

'*Thanks!*' I gushed.

Carter went out and Terry and Dave shouldered the equipment. I picked up one of the cases.

Before we went out the door, Terry said, 'You're good at that poor little girl stuff.' His tone was faintly accusing.

'Hey, when you're dealing with a patriarchal arsehole like Carter, you've got to play the gender card as hard as you can,' I said, laughing.

We went through the door and found Patience just on the other side of it, glaring murderously at me. Whoops! She'd heard.

I shrugged. 'So shoot me. I don't like your father.'

Her face went curiously blank. 'Everybody likes Father,' she said, in much the same way as she might say, 'The sun gives off light.'

'Not me,' I said.

She turned on her heel and went to the kitchenette behind Carter's office, disappearing as though she were hiding. That was interesting.

Carter and Eliza were nowhere to be seen, and the dragon let us out the door without comment.

We drove back to the city in silence except for ABC 702 on the radio, and I wondered if Carter's tears had been based on religion, or on something more personal. What had been his real relationship with Julieanne?

CHAPTER NINE

I have to admit, it was a sweet moment when Tyler turned to me after viewing the tape and said, 'Not bad. I don't suppose you got the name of the private investigator?' and I said, 'Garry Monahan.'

After that, I gave my borrowed finery back to wardrobe and thankfully went home. I was exhausted, even though it was only five o'clock. Luna Park seemed a lifetime ago. As I pulled into a parking spot near my parents' house I tried to remember what I was supposed to be doing tomorrow. The warehouse with fluffy toys. That was it. At least that didn't start until nine.

My parents were quite excited about the scene of crime tech who had come to take their fingerprints. She liked fruit-cake too, it turned out. I yawned my way through dinner and slumped in a lounge chair with a cup of tea afterwards, waiting for the interview to show up.

There was a short piece on the news about Julieanne's death, complete with a quick grab of Julieanne explaining the significance of the pottery and footage Terry had shot of the pit and the living room. The strap at the bottom said *Exclusive to the ABC*. Reference was made to Julieanne's bid for preselection. The anchor told viewers there would be an interview with Matthew Carter on *The Daily Report*. My parents were hyped about me showing up on the news, and even more excited about me being on *The Daily Report*. Just like a real reporter! Mum rang everyone in the family and got them to record it.

'I can get copies from work,' I said.

They didn't listen.

I smiled as I heard Mum on the phone. She'd never say so to my face, but she kept making comments like, 'Well, of course, she's very good at her job' and 'They're very pleased with her, you know'.

I got up to put my cup in the dishwasher and gave her a hug as I went past.

She patted me absently on the back and to my aunty in Brisbane said, 'Well, it's an ill wind.' I guess she meant that at least Julieanne's death was helping my career.

I'm sure Julieanne would have been delighted.

My Aunty Mary arrived in time to watch *The Daily Report* with us, complete with her special apricot rum balls and yet more fruitcake. She settled down comfortably on the lounge and announced happily, 'I'm dying, you know.'

'Shh,' my mother said. 'It's starting.'

I logged in to Twitter—there were always people live tweeting #dailyreport and I wanted to see the reaction.

The show did a background piece on Julieanne and the Australian Family Party before they showed the interview. They'd managed to get a grab from Annie, bemoaning the loss of a valuable employee. Annie's upset was genuine. Even though Julieanne was a bitch, she was a very capable and knowledgeable bitch, and she'd be hard to replace. Then they played the interview.

I winced as I watched it, of course. You always do. Because the mastoid bone carries your voice from your throat to your ear, as well as the sound coming through the air, we all think our voices are deeper than they are. Whenever I hear my voice on tape, I think I sound like a five-year-old. And no one else thinks it's odd, so that means I really do sound like that.

Twitter was having a ding-dong row between left-leaning cynics and members of the Radiant Joy Church. They were certainly up with the social media pile-on. I wondered how many of the people in Carter's electoral office were involved. Sure enough, I found the profile of the woman who had let me into the office; she was being vicious to anyone who criticised Carter.

Then—rather oddly, I thought—*The Daily Report* showed the interview with me. I would have done it the other way around, but I understood when they threw from the grab of me saying, 'I hope the police can catch this monster,' to a quick interview with Detective Sergeant Chloe Prudhomme, who was discreet and polite and didn't give anything away, apart from appealing to anyone who may have been in my street the night before to come forward to police.

'You were wonderful!' Dad said.

My mother nodded. 'You really came across as being very professional.'

I could have wished that they didn't sound surprised, but that's what happens when you're the youngest of six: everyone is always astonished that you can tie your own shoelaces. It makes me very defensive. Normally, I would have said something like 'I *am* a professional, Mum', but she'd been so nice about me on the phone that I just smiled and said, 'Thanks.'

Even Twitter didn't criticise me too much, and I got a few new follows. The woman from Carter's office had disappeared completely from the stream, along with quite a few others. Only interested in Carter's rep, obviously.

'Now, Mary,' Mum said. 'What are you dying of this time?'

'It's my blood pressure!' she said. 'I could drop dead at any moment. The doctor said so.' There was a world of satisfaction in her voice. I tried not to smile, but I heard Dad turn a derisive snort into a cough.

Now her husband was dead, Aunty Mary amused herself with hypochondria. But ever since she had sailed through getting COVID-19 like a twenty-year-old, the family was less inclined to take her seriously.

'That's terrible,' Mum said obediently (when someone says they're dying you have to be polite, even if you don't believe it), and then they were off on a long discussion of symptoms and medicines and the immorality of healthcare funds.

I left them to argue it out. Alex called before I got up the stairs to my bedroom.

'You were fabulous!' he said.

'I sound like a five-year-old.'

'A *clever* five-year-old, sweetie!'

I had to laugh.

There was a shout in the background at his end, and he went on, 'Rick says don't forget that Ruby's party is on Sunday and what should we get her?'

Ruby is Annie's daughter; she's turning eight. 'Books about dragons. She loves dragons.'

'Dragons *are* cool,' Alex said. 'How's the house thing going?'

I caught him up on the council debacle, then spent an hour answering all the worried messages from friends, and thankfully went to bed. I had weird, anxious dreams about fat-tailed sheep chasing Julieanne across a big church.

It didn't occur to me until morning that Stuart hadn't come over as he'd promised.

CHAPTER TEN

Thursday

The police showed up at the soft-toy warehouse the next day.

If you want surreal, I recommend you be interrogated about a murder in a big, big shed full of fluffiness: pink poodles and neon snakes and bears with red hearts appliquéd to their stomachs. And in the middle of all that stood Detective Sergeant Chloe Prudhomme, furious that I'd gone and interviewed Matthew Carter.

'I didn't tell him anything,' I protested. 'And you know what? He didn't ask me anything.'

That stopped her in her tracks. 'What do you mean?'

'I mean that I showed up there and *told* them it was my house that Julieanne had been found in and they asked me not one single, solitary question about it. All they cared about was getting the political message across.'

'Single-minded?'

'Or else they already knew all about it.'

Chloe mused over that. 'Two ways that could happen: they were involved, or they'd already got all the details from someone else.'

'Like who?' I was happy to encourage her to be suspicious of someone else.

'Lang?'

I screwed my face up. 'Don't see it, myself. He's not exactly political.'

Defending him was a mistake. It brought her back to her original line of questioning.

'So, how well do you know him?'

I shrugged. 'Only met him the other day.' I was having trouble sorting out the days—was it three, or four, since Boris had found the bones?

'The students say you were very chummy, going off for coffee together, walking home together after we let you go. Are you having a relationship?'

I wish. The thought came involuntarily and surprised me. *Stuart*, I thought next. And a small part of my mind whispered, *But not Julieanne. Not any more.* I shook my head to clear it, but Chloe took that as an answer.

'Do you want a relationship?'

'I have a boyfriend.' Even if he wasn't much in evidence lately.

'Not an answer.'

'Look, Tol's cute, but no man is cute enough to kill for.'

'Answer the question. Do you want a relationship with Dr Lang?'

I stared at her. The shrewd blue eyes bored into me. What the hell.

'Tell you the truth, I'm damned if I know,' I said.

She seemed to accept that. We turned and walked down an aisle full of purple aliens.

'What about him? Does he want one with you?'

'Hasn't mentioned it if he does. Hasn't called me to see how I am or anything.' I couldn't help the faint tone of bitterness in my voice, and I saw Chloe register it.

'If he killed Weaver over you, contacting you would be the stupidest thing he could do.'

And right on cue, like we were in a movie, my phone rang. It's him, I thought as I pulled it out of my pocket and excused myself to Chloe.

'Hello?'

'Would you like pasta or pan-fried chicken breast for tea?' Dad asked.

Sometimes you just have to laugh.

'Chicken, thanks, Dad.'

'Okay. Pick up some milk on your way home, will you?'

'Sure. Bye.'

My father doesn't say goodbye, he just hangs up. I grinned at my friendly detective sergeant, who was now standing in front of a fetching background of bright pink flamingos. There was a very Las Vegas feel to those flamingos.

'That was my dad,' I said.

'So I gathered.' She studied her notebook for a minute, letting the silence lengthen. 'Detective Constable Martin thinks you did it. It was your house, your alibi isn't that great, you didn't like her, you fancied her boyfriend, she'd threatened to slap you around in front of witnesses and to top it all off she was getting that preservation order served against you. He reckons you just lost it and pushed her.'

I ignored all that and fastened on the interesting bit.

'Is that how she died? She was pushed and hit her head or something?'

Chloe looked annoyed with herself. 'I can't release that information until the forensic pathologist makes a formal report. Is that all you've got to say?'

'What do you want me to say? "I'm innocent"? Of course I'm innocent! But all of that is true, so it's no good me standing here bleating, "But I didn't do it, officer", is it? What worries me is that if you concentrate on me, you're going to overlook the real murderer.'

'It might not have been murder.'

'Accident?'

'Manslaughter, say. Possibly even self-defence, Poppy.'

I realised that she was offering me a way out, good-cop style. Confess to me, she was implying, and we can make it okay. I know you're not really a murderer, Poppy. Just tell me the truth and I'll help you.

'Julieanne Weaver had a lot of enemies,' Chloe said. 'You don't, Poppy. That tells me something.'

'Yeah,' I said. 'It should tell you that one of them did it.'

She pressed her lips together and strode a few paces, then turned and regarded me sternly. The effect was spoiled a little by the fluffy devil figures brandishing pitchforks behind her. Perhaps I was getting a bit hysterical, but I couldn't help noticing that the black and red ones had smaller pitchforks than the white and pink ones. Was that a subtle reminder from the designers: beware devils who pretend to be angels? God, I was tired.

'There's only a limited amount of time that I can help you in, Poppy,' she said. 'If you refuse to cooperate.' I wondered if there was some kind of interrogation school that taught detectives to use the suspect's name a lot when they were being good cop.

'Cooperate in being railroaded?' I said. 'Didn't do it, Chloe. Wouldn't do it, Chloe. Am not going to say I did when I didn't, Chloe.'

Okay, maybe all the parroting of her name was a mistake, but wouldn't you have been peeved?

She wasn't happy. She collected Detective Constable Martin from the front door where he'd no doubt been waiting to give her a chance at good cop. Next time, I bet, he'd be unleashed in full bad-cop mode. Something to look forward to.

It seemed as though they seriously suspected me. I confess, I hadn't expected that, and it unsettled me. Or maybe they suspected Tol more.

I wished that I'd got his number when I'd given him mine. But that was an oversight that could be remedied. As soon as we'd finished at the warehouse, I left, refusing offers of free fluffiness (ABC policy again), and went to see Annie.

CHAPTER ELEVEN

When I got to her office, Annie was on the phone laying down the law to a subcontractor who had failed to deliver some display cases on time. With a final 'See that you do', she hung up and turned to me, getting up and coming around the desk to give me a hug.

'Poor possum,' she said. 'You've been in the wars, haven't you?'

I hugged her back and almost cried. She's tiny, really; her head only comes up to my ear, but right then I felt like I could lean on her as hard as I liked and she'd cope.

'A bit,' I said.

'It was a good interview, though,' she said judiciously. 'Tell me everything.'

So I filled her in, including the fact that I was apparently suspect number one.

'Oh, how stupid,' Annie snapped. 'I could point out at least four people right in this building who would have liked to kill her more than you.'

'Would you mind telling Detective Chloe about them?'

Annie looked thoughtful. 'I just might,' she said. 'For a start, there's Paul Baume.'

Paul was curator of domestic technology, which covers everything from spoons to dishwashers and, incidentally, had introduced me to Stuart at a museum event a few months ago. Paul and Julieanne had been a couple for almost eight months—which may have been a personal record for her. They'd broken up only a month or so ago; right before Tol appeared on the scene.

'What happened there, anyway?'

'Just between us?' Annie asked. I nodded. 'Well, I heard he asked her to marry him and she not only turned him down, she laughed at him. Said she had her eye on someone a lot better connected and a lot better off, and he'd just been a smokescreen.'

'Really? Sounds like something Detective Chloe really should know. "A smokescreen" could mean a married man.'

'Mmm. That's what I thought.'

'Paul was upset?'

Annie bit her lip. She quite liked Paul. But her sense of loyalty to me won out.

'He was ropable. More than that, really. I think he really had been in love with her. Finding out she'd played him the whole time was a very deep cut. He hasn't had many other relationships, you know.'

Most of the curators were sane, happily partnered, reasonable people. But the job did also attract the slightly unusual type. This type of curator is obsessive about their speciality, with poor social skills, few friends and no interest in being 'normal'. Paul was definitely one of them. He was also, when you got past the awkward front, witty, well read and very sweet. When he'd taken up with Julieanne the people who liked him had assumed that she'd been impressed by his physique and that he'd demonstrated some of his better qualities to her while they were working together on a project about early washing machines.

Annie hadn't been sure if Julieanne was a good thing in Paul's life or not. 'At least he's seeing someone,' she'd said when I'd told her to protect Paul by getting Julieanne transferred to another project.

I nobly refrained from saying 'I told you so' now.

'Ropable enough to push her in a pit?'

'Was she pushed?'

'I think so.'

Annie thought this over. 'Maybe.'

'I don't want Paul to be the killer. Who else?'

'What about Gerry?'

'Oh, I like that much better.'

Gerry Collonucci was supposedly Julieanne's boss, but she routinely ignored his directions and, worst of all, insisted on making press releases to the media instead of letting Gerry, as head of the department, get the glory. Annie hadn't intervened because Gerry hadn't complained and also because Julieanne was a much better front person for the museum than Gerry, who spoke with a distinct adenoidal twang of which he seemed to be unaware. Gerry was also renowned for using his power over student placements to get routine admin jobs done for nothing—and for taking credit for junior archaeologists' work. So no one had worried too much that Julieanne stole some of his thunder. Annie had kept him on because he was a surprisingly good historian, but I knew that she'd put him on notice to improve his management or he'd be out. Gerry, it would be fair to say, seriously disliked Julieanne—and as her boss, he had a legitimate reason to be on site.

'I know that look,' Annie said. 'What are you planning?'

'A chat with Gerry?'

'You be careful. You're not Miss Marple, you know. Let the police do their job.'

'Mmm,' I said. 'But what if they arrest me?'

She was silent, then said doubtfully, 'They've got no real evidence. The DPP would throw the case back at them.'

The Director of Public Prosecutions has to approve any major prosecution—that is, the police could arrest me but they couldn't take me to trial without DPP approval.

'Great—and meanwhile I'm in jail, stripsearched, mugshotted, locked in …' I shuddered. 'I'm going to talk to Gerry.'

'You know he's got a hell of a temper,' Annie cautioned, seeing me to the door. 'If he figures out you're trying to investigate …'

'Exactly why I'm calling in the heavy guns—NewsCaff.'

I rang Tyler and asked if he'd like an interview with Julieanne's boss. He jumped at it, so I went into Gerry's office armed with that greatest of all powers: an invitation to fame.

Curator's offices come in two types: neat and messy. Gerry's was the messy kind. Every surface was covered in objects, fragments of objects, papers, drawings, reference books and bricks. Yes, bricks. Gerry's particular speciality was the manufacture of bricks in Australia up until the end of World War Two. He could look at a brick and tell you not just where it was made, but when, and who the foreman was, and where they got the clay from. And he would—at length—if you showed the slightest interest.

Gerry was at his desk, meticulously checking a catalogue of finds. I could see the tiny drawings or photos and the descriptive text next to each, but I couldn't tell which dig it was from. One bit of early colonial pottery looks like every other bit to me. But not to Gerry. He was frowning, and he shook his head at me as I came in.

'I'm not at all happy about this classification,' he said, tapping his hairy forefinger on the page. 'Sandra's got it down as 1860s, but the glaze looks a little deep to me for that. I suspect it's no earlier than the eighties.'

'Eighteen-eighties isn't far off,' I said, sitting in the guest chair.

'*Nineteen*-eighties!' he snapped. 'The company reissued some of their classic designs then, and this was one of them. If it is, it compromises the entire stratification.' He threw the folder on the desk and glared at me, eyes hostile. He never did like me. 'And what do *you* want?'

'I came to see if you'd do an interview for *The Daily Report* about Julieanne's work and why she was interested in the bones in the pit.'

He thought about it, weighing his dislike for me against his desire to be on national TV. Ego won. 'All right,' he said, as though he were granting me a big favour. He relaxed slightly and pulled at his shirt, which stretched tightly over his belly. What is it with fat men? When women put on weight, they go and buy new clothes that fit. Men just keep squeezing themselves into the old ones. Do they think no one will notice?

What the hell, I thought. I could pussyfoot around and try to be subtle, but Gerry had no feelings to hurt, and we'd never been friends. 'I also want to know if you killed Julieanne.'

He went very still. 'Wh—why would I have done that?'

'Now that's interesting,' I said, getting more comfortable in my seat. 'Most people would say, "No, of course not!" But not you. I wonder why.'

'Because I know what you're like, McGowan,' he growled. 'Always poking your nose in. Always getting people to tell you things you shouldn't know.'

Ah, yes. I remembered. One of his students, in the course of telling me the story of her life, had let slip that Gerry had put the hard word on her, and asked me what she should do. Have sex with him to save her position on the team or stand up for herself and get the boot? I'd sorted that one out simply: 'Tape the next conversation and you'll have enough on him to make sure of your place on the team until you graduate.'

'I didn't even tell Annie about that,' I protested. Only because the girl had begged me not to. She hadn't wanted to get a reputation as a troublemaker, and I understood that, since I had that reputation myself and found it tiresome. 'I could have got you fired.'

'I suppose you could have,' he said grudgingly. 'Do you know what the cops have got on me?'

I shrugged. 'They're far too busy questioning me to tell me who else they're talking to. But I do know you resented Julieanne.'

'Hah! Everyone resented her. She invited it.'

'No argument from me.'

He mellowed a little more, and leant back in his seat. 'Anyway, I've got an alibi.'

'Really?'

'Yep. I was with Jake at the pub. I've told the cops.'

The tall, acned student who had been at the dig at my house. My imagination boggled at the idea of him and Gerry at the pub, drinking amicably.

'How convenient for both of you.'

He smirked. 'Isn't it?'

'Chloe Prudhomme isn't going to believe that.'

'Let her try to prove differently,' Gerry said, leaning forward with both hands on the desk. 'We'll swear it on a stack of Bibles.'

I wondered why Jake was prepared to do that. Had he disliked Julieanne too? Or was there some other advantage to him in it? Like guaranteed access to the best digs? Or being given lead authorship on one of the papers that would come out of the research? I suggested as much to Gerry, but he just kept on smirking.

'Try to prove it, McGowan,' he said, and chuckled.

I couldn't let him get away with that. 'Oh, I'm not going to prove it. I'll leave that to the cops.'

His smile disappeared.

'I'll get someone from News to ring you,' I said, and got up. I turned back at the door, just like Columbo. 'What about the next morning?'

'What?'

'What were you doing the next morning?'

He sat up straight and frowned, his fingers gripping the edge of the desk.

'The cops didn't ask me that.'

'Didn't they? Perhaps they already knew.'

I had seriously disturbed him.

'I thought she was killed the night before.'

'Why did you think that? She was due at the house to open up—why assume she'd gone back late at night?'

He sat there, his mouth open but no answers coming out.

I smiled at him. 'No alibi for the morning, Gerry? Shame. But never mind. There's still time to manufacture one.'

It was a good exit line, and I made use of it.

It seemed to me that Gerry had been relieved that the police were only interested in him because of a known dislike, as though there was something else they could have found out about. Worth considering. I called Tyler and gave him Gerry's contact details and told him that someone else should do the interview because Gerry couldn't stand me.

He laughed. 'Lots of people hate you, huh?'

'Lots more love me. Do you want an interview with her ex-boyfriend, or not?'

'Shit, yes,' he said, sobering. Of course he did. Ex-boyfriends were always the top suspect. Next to current boyfriends, which I didn't want to think about.

'I'll see what I can do.'

I hung up and stood in the corridor, considering. Chloe had already spoken to Gerry, apparently. Had she talked to Paul too? Probably. But Paul wasn't the easiest person in the world to converse with. I might get more out of him than she had.

Should I go and talk to Paul, or should I find Tol and see how he was? I sighed. If I wanted to steer the police away from me, I had to have something more than Gerry's undoubted sleaziness. Paul it was.

Paul's office was as neat as Gerry's was messy: tidy to the point of weirdness. If it weren't for the museum poster on the wall, it would have looked as though no one used it. Not a pen on the desk, not a paper in sight. The computer screen didn't even have a Post-it note stuck to the edge. The only personal thing was a photo of his parents' wedding, with his mother (who is Chinese) rocking a fabulous Audrey Hepburn look and his father (Anglo) seeming surprised he'd managed to catch someone so beautiful. I wondered if that was how Paul had felt about Julieanne.

Paul, at first sight, looks like a typical museum guy, with the slightly too long, untidy straight hair, the glasses, the vague expression in the eyes that suggested the brain behind them was otherwise engaged, the faint frown indicating confusion with the world ... then he stood up to greet me and it was like someone had transplanted his head onto GI Joe's body.

'Paul!' I said in astonishment. 'You've really been working out!'

He'd always been fit, but now he looked like Schwarzenegger. Or at least Chris Hemsworth as Thor—the in-shape Thor, not the fat one. A couple of months had made a huge difference. I wondered if he was taking steroids.

'Not much else to do these days,' he said, embarrassed.

'I didn't realise you were such a gym bunny.'

'Oh, I don't go to the gym,' he said, looking a little shocked. 'It's very unhygienic, you know. People *sweat* on those machines. I've set up a home gym.'

Of course. I'd forgotten Paul's thing about germs. I wondered how he'd brought himself to have actual sex with Julieanne. Assuming that they had.

'You know they found Julieanne at my house,' I said, plunging in.

His eyes filled with tears, but he blinked them back. 'Yes. I saw the news. In your living room ... I suppose you'll be selling, now?'

I was dismayed by his air of distaste. Selling hadn't occurred to me—it was still *my house*.

'I'm not going to let some bastard push me out just because he had a problem with Julieanne,' I said fiercely.

'But ... wouldn't you always ... remember?' he asked, astonished. It was clear he couldn't imagine living in a house where a dead body had lain, for however short a time.

'She was on the ground, not the floor. I'm putting new floors in,' I reassured him.

'I don't think I could ever visit you there, Poppy.'

I chose to misunderstand him. 'Of course, it would be too hard for *you*, Paul,' I said earnestly. 'You were so close to her, weren't you?'

He went very still. 'For a while,' he said softly. 'But it didn't last.'

'You called it off?'

'*She* called it off, two months ago. Didn't you know that?'

I shrugged. 'Doesn't sound like Julieanne to me. I've never known her to dump anyone until she had someone else lined up, and Tol didn't arrive on the scene until last month. So I assumed you'd thought better of it. I didn't blame you.'

He was very quiet. I don't think Paul had ever really thought about Julieanne's motives before. He'd just taken it as natural that someone like her would get tired of him.

'I never did understand what you two had in common,' I prompted.

'Sex,' he said simply.

'Really?' I tried not to let my incredulity show, but it was tough.

He nodded.

'Sex is necessary to the proper, healthy functioning of the human body, you know, Poppy,' he said. 'Absolutely necessary.'

I pushed away questions about what he usually did if it was so necessary, and focussed on Julieanne. 'And she ...?'

'She had a very good, wholesome attitude to sex. She liked it simple. Frequent. No—no frills, so to speak. It was very refreshing.'

I didn't want to do it. It was like jabbing a kitten. But I had to know what he really thought of her now.

'It wasn't enough for her, though, in the end?'

His face darkened. 'She used me while I was convenient, I suppose. But she said I wasn't presentable enough for her political ambitions. My *social skills* weren't good enough! She wanted me to—to schmooze people. Go to parties.' There was plenty of anger there, but then his voice dropped. 'From what she said that last night, I think she even wanted to get *married*.'

He was so appalled by the idea, I almost laughed. 'I heard it was you who wanted to get married.'

'Absolutely not.'

'So are you sure it was you she wanted to marry?'

He hesitated. 'Who else?'

'Someone she'd been seeing secretly, maybe?'

He turned positively puce. I wondered again about steroids and roid rage. I'd never known Paul to get angry before.

'She lied as easily as she breathed,' he said through gritted teeth. 'Who knows?'

I thought I could risk one more question before he got really aggro.

'Did you love her, Paul?'

His big, square hands splayed out over the desktop. I thought about how quickly he could have overpowered

Julieanne. She was a tall woman, and pretty fit herself, but there was no way she could have resisted him.

'It doesn't matter whether I did or I didn't,' he said quietly, looking at his hands. 'She didn't love me, and she's dead now.'

There was something in that tone, something flat and absolute, that made me want to run away. I didn't know why—was it a deep, deep grief, or something else?

I wasn't going to ask him for an interview, no matter what I'd promised Tyler. It would have felt too much like twisting the knife.

'Stay in touch,' I said gently and left, but I don't think he realised I was gone. I glanced back as I went to the door and he was still staring at his hands, his eyes wide and dry.

I wasn't watching as I moved into the corridor, and I bumped right into someone. They reached out to steady me.

Tol. Tol had been standing just outside the door. Listening? Waiting?

'What are you doing here?' I blurted out. His hands were still on the bare skin of my arms. Hot. Strong. *Get a grip, McGowan*, I told myself. But I couldn't make myself take a step back.

His eyes lit with amusement, and maybe something warmer. 'I work here, remember?'

'In the corridor?' I asked, finally edging back just a little, so that he could let go if he wanted to. He did, leaving my arms feeling cold, but he didn't move away. Instead, he leant against the wall, staring down at me intently.

'I was waiting for you,' he said. 'Are you all right?'

'Of course. Why wouldn't I be?'

He reached out and tucked a strand of hair behind my ear. It was a startlingly intimate thing to do, but he didn't seem aware of that. He kept studying my face.

'You look tired. Are the police bothering you?'

My lip trembled, which appalled me. But apart from Annie, he was the only person who seemed to be aware that this might be a difficult experience for me: everyone else either thought it was exciting or useful.

'They think I killed Julieanne.'

'Really? I got the impression they think *I* killed her.' He raised an eyebrow at me, just like Spock. I couldn't help it—I smiled. I love it when men do that. It looks so intelligent.

'Maybe they think we both did it.'

'Did you?'

The voice came from behind me. It was Chloe Prud-homme, looking grim. I realised that Tol and I must have looked like … conspirators, or even lovers, huddling in the corridor, our heads together. I blushed—furiously, which made me cross.

'*If* I had killed Julieanne Weaver,' I said, glowering, 'I wouldn't have done it in my house, and I would have had a much better alibi. And furthermore, you probably wouldn't even have known it was murder!'

Tol half-laughed. 'And if *I'd* killed her, I would have got Poppy to supervise, so ditto for me!'

I didn't know whether to be angry with him or laugh, too, and by the look on her face, neither did Chloe.

'Are you two lovers?' she asked bluntly.

Tol shook his head. 'No such luck,' he said with what sounded like genuine regret.

I felt the blush start again, but for a vastly different reason.

'But if you'd wanted to be, Julieanne was in the way,' Chloe suggested.

'We weren't *married*,' Tol said.

'Like she could have stopped us,' I said at the same time.

We paused for a beat, to see if the other had anything else to say, but Tol was silent, so I added, 'From where I stood, their relationship wasn't going to last long anyway. All I had to do was wait a few weeks.'

'Really?' Tol said. 'You thought of that?'

He sounded hopeful and I got panicky, wondering if I'd given too much away. Stuart, I reminded myself.

'Besides,' I said, 'I have a boyfriend.'

'Hmm.' Chloe didn't sound too impressed by Stuart's existence. 'Didn't look like that when I got here.'

She turned and walked away while we were still trying to come up with a response. I expected her to throw a line over her shoulder or come back for a final question, but she just kept walking down to Annie's office and went in, leaving Tol and me in a less-than-comfortable silence.

'Yep,' he said eventually. 'They think we both did it.'

We stood for a moment, not quite looking at each other, not sure what to do next.

'Well,' I said, 'I'd better get back to work.'

'Me too. Ms Prudhomme says we can get back to the dig next week.'

'Great,' I said glumly.

'Cheer up. I'll do my best to get you your house back as soon as I can.'

As I went back to my car I decided that my attraction to Tol wasn't just my hormones—he really was a lovely man. A lovely man who seemed to genuinely like me. Or a killer who was really good at schmoozing. Or just a man who wanted a fling before he went back to the rigours of archaeology in the Middle East.

After all, would a really nice man be smoothing back the hair of a woman two days after his girlfriend was killed? Oh, bugger. Reluctantly, I put away a charming image of Tol and me on Bondi Beach at sunset and concentrated on the increasing traffic as I crossed Anzac Bridge. At least he was going to be around my house for the next week or so … If the police found the killer soon, I could forget my suspicions and enjoy his company for a while. A fling didn't sound all that bad.

And Stuart? my conscience whispered. Stuart, I told it, had better pick up his game. He hadn't turned up last night, and he hadn't even called me today. A tower of strength he was not.

CHAPTER TWELVE

Maybe I'd been too hard on him. Stuart turned up after dinner (and the news) complete with flowers and lollies, suggesting we watch a movie. I wasn't going to let him get off scot-free, though.

'Where were you last night?' I asked, arms akimbo, blocking the door.

Surprised, he rubbed one hand over his hair as if for reassurance. 'It was Wednesday!'

Wednesday. Ah yes, Wednesday. Laundry night. Every Wednesday night Stuart did his laundry for the week. No matter what, apparently.

'Laundry.'

He smiled happily and kissed me on the cheek as though everything had been settled. What could I say? *Your laundry is more important to you than I am?* Any way you looked at it,

that was ridiculous, and saying it out loud would make me
ridiculous. I sighed.

'Come on in.'

And then we had a lovely night, watching a rom-com
and eating popcorn and imperial mandarins, which Stuart
produced like a conjuror, knowing they're my favourite. He
didn't even complain about having been fingerprinted.

I remembered, while kissing him goodnight, why I'd got
involved with him in the first place. He might not make
me shiver when he stood next to me, but he was kind and
warm and clever and didn't have any plans to disappear to
the Middle East, which was a big plus.

Even if he couldn't lift one eyebrow.

Friday

I had a day off in lieu of a day filming at the beach we'd
done two weekends before. That was the theory, anyway.
Around seven-thirty, when I was still sitting in the kitchen
in my pyjamas, I got a call from Tyler. Did that man live at
the ABC?

'Carter's agreed to another interview with *The Daily
Report*, but only if you do it,' he said.

'No way.'

'In depth,' Tyler said. 'Taking you over the whole operation. Preselection committee, party headquarters, the lot.'

'He's going to use it to announce the new candidate.'

'Sure he is. But he's going to announce it first on
the ABC.'

A silence. What could I say? *Let him take it to the commercial channels?* Never!

'Okay.'

'That's my girl.' Tyler actually sounded relieved, as though he hadn't been sure I'd agree. 'I've got the researcher to dummy up your questions—like she'd normally do for the interviewer,' he added in a hurry, as if he could sense me bridle even over the phone. I'd forgotten that the jour-nos often didn't do their own research for current affairs. No time, with their shooting schedule. It was different in kids' TV.

'Okay.'

'Camera car'll pick you up in half an hour.'

'Okay,' I said again.

'You'll be fine.' He obviously thought I was nervous. 'You delivered the other day. Did good, played hard.'

Football metaphors. Do I look like a front row forward?

'Thanks,' I said through gritted teeth.

'Half an hour,' Tyler said. 'Dress the part, sweetheart.' He hung up.

I really didn't like that guy.

At least he sent me Terry and Dave.

We drove to party headquarters, at the other end of the business park from Carter's office. As a start-up party, they didn't need huge premises, but they didn't seem to know that. They had two floors of a large office block: one of those ones with a lake and a waterfall in the courtyard and a food hall in the basement. The reception area had a glass wall so you could see through to the open-plan office beyond, where half-a-dozen people talked on phones and tapped at computers, just like in every other office in the country.

Inside, everything was blue: pale blue walls, baby-blue office dividers, grey-blue desks, tastefully matching blinds. The long reception feature wall was painted in what my Catholic sensibilities always thought of as Virgin Mary blue. It looked like an incomplete shrine waiting for a statue. And the receptionist was the acolyte, sitting tall and proud under a sign which announced: AUSTRALIAN FAMILY—PUTTING FAMILIES BEFORE POLITICS. Tall, slender, red-headed, stylishly suited and shod, she gave new meaning to the phrase 'well groomed'—the only odd note was the phone headset she wore like a tiara. She had an engagement ring the size of an almond glinting on her finger. I smiled to myself. The perfect female employee: not married, so not neglecting her husband or children for her career, but committed nonetheless to married life. As a subservient wife, no doubt.

'How may I help you?' she asked in hushed tones, as though she couldn't see the camera on Terry's shoulders.

'*The Daily Report.* We're here to see Mr Carter,' I said cheerfully and loudly.

The receptionist winced. 'Please take a seat,' she said, then pushed a button on the phone and murmured a few words into the headset. I was fascinated by her eyebrows, which were plucked into thin, perfect arches which reminded me irresistibly of Mickey Mouse ears. It was odd, when the fashion was for much thicker brows, and they gave her a perpetually surprised look. 'Mr Carter will be with you in a few moments,' she said in a congratulatory tone.

While we waited, Terry got some footage of her at work answering the phone, which seemed pretty busy considering it wasn't quite nine yet. She ignored him loftily, although she looked suspiciously at Dave when he started recording ambient sound, and when she spoke, her voice dropped even further, as though she thought he was spying.

I could have told her differently—Dave certainly didn't want to hear what she was saying, because that would constrain how he could use the atmos track. Besides, if he'd wanted to spy on her, he'd have used a different mike altogether.

After he finished, I wandered over to the desk.

'Have you worked here long ...'

'Samantha.' It was a condescension on her part, no doubt, to give me her name, but anything for the party.

'Samantha,' I said, smiling.

'I've only been in the party headquarters for a few months, but before that I worked for Mr Carter at his electoral office.'

She was a real acolyte, all right, in the religion of Matthew Carter—her eyes gleamed as she said his name. I wondered if there was a reason other than hero worship.

'He's very attractive,' I said casually, girl to girl.

But that was the wrong tack. She frowned and sat up even straighter. 'Mr Carter is an inspiration to us. It wouldn't matter if he were—were completely *ugly*! We'd still support him.'

'Oh, of course. Helps on television, though.'

That mollified her. 'It's all media these days,' she said disdainfully. Of course. All political parties hate the media. 'We're lucky that Mr Carter is so good at that side of the job.'

Yes, indeed. And right on cue, the door opened to let in Matthew Carter, followed not by Eliza but by the party treasurer, Samuel Stephenson.

Stephenson, the researcher's notes had said, was a longtime elder of the Radiant Joy Church. He'd been raised Anglican, had run wild as a young man, and had become born again at one of Amos Winchester's first Sydney missions. After studying accountancy at uni, he'd started his first bakery, Ruth's Kitchen. Now, having franchised that and sold the business, he functioned both as paid party accountant and volunteer treasurer—a dubious if not strictly illegal situation. With a background like that, I'd imagined he'd be a middle-aged man in a crumpled suit, probably a bit stout and red in the face.

Instead, he was as lean as a greyhound, dark-eyed, intense, his grey hair well cut. Not PR attractive in the way Carter was—the camera would make his nose look too big and his cheeks too hollow, turn the intensity into weirdness—but in person he was at least as impressive, maybe more. He had that trick that I'd seen in old police officers and experienced teachers, of looking at you very hard for a few seconds and then away, as though that was all the time he needed to assess and classify you. Arrogant. There was arrogance, too, in the way he wore his suit. He and Carter, both in tailor-made pinstripes, looked like models from a *GQ* article on the stylish older man.

I was suddenly fond of Terry and Dave, who slouched around in jeans and polo shirts and whose sole concession to personal grooming was wearing deodorant.

I smiled. 'Matthew, how nice to see you again!'

This was a useful trick. When I worked at the BBC, I discovered that in a hierarchical organisation, your status depended entirely upon whom you called by their first name. The person will start to treat you as an equal in order to justify *to themselves* letting you do it, because that's how humans are. With enough brazenness, you can improve your status startlingly.

I could see him think it through. Should he correct me and put me offside before the interview? He was tempted to, but Terry was already filming. So he turned to Stephenson and said jovially, 'Samuel, this is Poppy McGowan from *The Daily Report*.'

'How do you do, Poppy,' Stephenson intoned. I remembered from my notes that he was also a deacon at the church and no doubt used to public praying.

'How do you do, Samuel,' I echoed sunnily. We shook hands.

'Let's go through and we can show you around the office,' he said.

So we got the guided tour, which was about as riveting as any office tour ever is, except that, unlike every other office, almost everyone here was lily white (which I'd expected after seeing the staff at Carter's office). There wasn't a single nose stud or eyebrow ring or brightly coloured strand of hair on any employee, not one pair of jeans, not even a shirt without a tie. No skirt above the knee, no blouse opened to the cleavage. And every hair was in place. Almost. I felt sorry for one young man, who had clearly tried to wet his hair down into submission like his colleagues, but whose curls sprang defiantly upwards.

From what we overheard, the employees were either cold-calling potential supporters or fielding calls from the interested. I wondered where they got their list of potentials from.

As the camera rolled, Carter gave us an anodyne commentary and I made supportive, interested noises. Stephenson followed a pace behind Dave and Terry, a brooding presence.

Then we went into the conference room and there we found Amos Winchester, the founder of the Australian Family Party and still the pastor of the Radiant Joy Church.

I don't know what I'd expected. Either WC Fields or an eighty-two-year-old Colonel Sanders, I think. But Winchester was a small man, jockey sized, wrinkled and with arthritic hands, bright blue eyes and not much hair, who jumped up to welcome me with genuine enthusiasm. If he was as calculating as his two followers, it didn't show. He grabbed my hands and pumped them with energy, smiling, and I couldn't help but smile back. Out of the corner of my eye I saw Carter and Stephenson exchanging satisfied looks, and realised that they'd counted on my reaction. Everyone likes Amos, huh? How nice for you.

'I'm glad to have this opportunity to interview you, Reverend Winchester,' I said. The whole first-name thing has its place—but it doesn't work with old ministers or priests; they'll just put you in your place and smile while they're doing it.

'Call me pastor, child,' he said, the faintest trace of his southern American drawl still (deliberately?) there. I almost expected him to say shucks.

'We need lights in here,' Terry announced. I nodded and he disappeared with Dave to get them from the car.

'Are the rest of the preselection committee joining us?' I asked brightly.

'The only other member cannot, alas, make the time,' Stephenson said.

'That would be Wilfred Cooper?' I asked, checking my notes. Interesting. The only member of the committee not from Radiant Joy. I reckoned they wanted to make sure they kept control of the party image, and I wondered how much power Cooper really had, with these three so tight.

'Yes. Unfortunately, Wilf has other commitments.'

'Isn't he retired?'

'*Family* commitments,' Stephenson said admonishingly, as though no more had to be said.

I duly shut up. It wasn't worth pushing on—Tyler could always get Cooper's views later on.

'Disappointed you didn't get the full bench?' Winchester chuckled and I smiled back.

'It's always nice to cover all the bases,' I said. 'My news director can be a bit picky.'

'Nature of the business. It's a lot harder edged than it used to be.' He sighed. I waited for 'in my day' and sure enough, out it came. 'In my day there was a bit more respect paid to those who served their countries.'

I deliberately misunderstood.

'You served in the military?' I exclaimed. 'That's not in my notes …' I read through my briefing, as though looking for confirmation.

'No, no,' he said quickly, discomfited. 'No, I couldn't serve—bad lungs, bad lungs, you know. Tried for a chaplaincy but they wouldn't take me, so I had to serve my flock at home.'

He moved away to say something quietly to Carter, who glanced at me. They'd either think I was a bit dim or too sharp, I thought, so I smiled with as much air-headedness as I could summon on short notice. The more time I spent with these men, the less I liked them, and the more I wanted to skewer them publicly, for all to see.

I'd gone over the game plan with Terry. We were going for a long interview, long enough so that they would relax with me. I'd warned him I was going to ask a lot of Dorothy Dixers first, to let them get the party line off their chests. Then, with luck, they'd relax enough so that I could sneak in some more difficult questions.

But having Winchester there changed things.

'Is there any chance I could do an interview one on one with you, pastor?' I asked. 'Since you were the founder of the party …'

The great thing about sexism is that men who think women are stupider than they are truly believe it. So they are very, very reluctant to acknowledge that a woman may not be stupid. Thus far, I'd played to their expectations of a young woman who wasn't really a reporter, and their own mindset predisposed them to believe I wasn't a threat.

'I don't see why not, young lady,' Winchester said, like everyone's favourite uncle.

'That's wonderful,' I said.

Terry and Dave came back with the lights and began setting up.

Winchester came over to me and spoke confidentially. 'Now, just what questions did you have in mind to ask?'

Hah! As if.

'Well,' I said, vaguely, 'are there some you think I should ask?'

Enthusiastically, he started dictating a list—exactly what you might expect: why did you set up the party, what do you think of the present party leaders, are you happy with the direction the party's taking ... I dutifully wrote them down, and when Terry was ready I politely ushered Carter and Stephenson out the door and sat down opposite Winchester and asked each one of his questions as though they made up the hardest-hitting interview in media history. He beamed all the way through. When we got to the end of his questions he relaxed and leant back in his chair, as though the interview was over.

'Did you know Julieanne Weaver?' I asked, still smiling.

He went still, the way people who live in the public eye do when they're asked something difficult.

'Yes. Poor child. Yes, I met her a couple times.' His accent was suddenly more pronounced.

'More than a couple, surely, pastor? I believe that Dr Weaver met with the preselection committee for North Hughes quite a few times over the past months—and you are a member of the committee, aren't you?'

'We met a few times, maybe.'

'What did you think of her?'

He hesitated. 'Dr Weaver wasn't a member of my flock, you know, so I didn't get to know her well ... but she seemed like a very clever woman.'

'Clever? That's pretty faint praise for someone you were thinking of preselecting. She got through to the last round, didn't she?'

He shook his head. 'I'm not going to speak ill of the dead, child, and Matthew Carter is the person to ask about pre-selection. All I can say about Julieanne Weaver is that I'm praying for her soul and the soul of the poor misguided wretch who killed her.'

I couldn't ask the Heaven question again, he'd know I'd already asked Carter. I decided to play my trump.

'You know, it was my house that Dr Weaver was found in, and from some things the police have asked me, there may be a political angle to her death. Who hates Australian Family enough to attack one of your members?'

As I'd hoped, that brought him out fighting.

'Now wait just a minute, child! There's no suggestion that the girl was killed because she was a member of Australian Family. No suggestion at all.'

'Not even though she was trying hard for preselection?'

'That's got nothing to do with her death! God alone knows the truth of that, but I'll swear on my Bible that Australian Family had nothing to do with it!'

He realised just too late that the phrase 'had nothing to do with it' could be heard two ways; did he mean her death wasn't politically motivated or was he being defensive about someone in the party being guilty? I changed tack immediately.

'Are you worried about people like Julieanne—people who don't have a real commitment to God—taking over your party? Diluting its goals? Playing politics?'

'Matthew Carter's not going to let that happen,' he said stoutly.

'So Carter will protect the purity of the party?'

'He'll protect our ideals, ideals which the majority of people in this country share, let me tell you!' Yeah, right. Not according to the results of the same-sex marriage survey.

'How sure can your members be that another Julieanne Weaver won't get preselection? That whoever you choose will be worthy of their trust?'

'I'll tell you how! Because we've given the boot to all those image mongers, those PR advisers'—he made it sound like a curse—'who kept trying to make us like all the rest! We don't *want* to be *representative* and *progressive* if it means abandoning God's plan for us. We've shot that lot out the window and they won't be coming back!'

Before he could get launched into another election speech, I asked, 'Is God guiding the party, pastor?'

He smiled, suddenly relaxed. 'I truly believe He is, yes, ma'am, but even if He's not, the party is in good hands.'

The wily old fox! That was a good end line, I had to give it to him. I knew Tyler would be pleased with the stuff about the PR hacks, anyway.

After that, the interview with Stephenson and Carter was pretty bland. As expected, they announced the candidate for North Hughes, and she joined us for the last section of the interview. Carmen Broadhurst. Fifties, Anglo, greying hair cut smartly, pale blue Chanel-style suit, hazel eyes, contact lenses.

So, they'd thrown the other main candidate overboard, then. No loss. He'd been terrible in the interview he'd done with Julieanne.

They'd played it very smart. A woman, so they couldn't be accused of sexism, but a widow with grown children, so they couldn't be accused of encouraging a mother or wife to abandon her responsibilities. And she put on a good show. Intelligent but not too sharp, womanly without being too soft. She'd been in local government as an independent for a while, so she knew the ropes and she realised, by the gleam in her eye, that she was being handed a plum.

She didn't look like a killer to me. Then again, what did I know about killers?

'Are you relieved that the fight for preselection is over?' I asked her.

She shrugged, her time in local government coming in handy. 'I've avoided that kind of thing as an independent,' she said, 'but I understand how necessary it is in party politics.'

'What made you join Australian Family?' It was a Dorothy Dixer, but I was actually curious. She seemed too sane to really subscribe to some of their ideas.

'I think our politicians have ignored the needs of families for too long,' she said. 'They need a good sharp kick, if you ask me. And Australian Family is the only party willing to deliver it.'

Nice. Just a touch of the common people, but not enough to disturb the air of respectability.

'Are you a member of the Radiant Joy Church, Mrs Broadhurst?'

'No, no. I'm an Anglican.'

Oh, very good. Anglican sounds so respectable, although, in Sydney, it stood a good chance of meaning you were hardline.

'So you subscribe to Australian Family's attitudes to women?'

She smiled broadly. 'As far as I can see, Australian Family's attitude to women is that we play a crucial, undervalued role in this society and need to be supported more by government policy.'

'As long as that role is limited to wifehood and motherhood?'

'Those are the aspects of being a woman which are undervalued, wouldn't you agree?'

I just smiled and switched my approach. 'Did you know Julieanne Weaver, Mrs Broadhurst?'

Carter and Stephenson both opened their mouths, but she held up a hand to stop them. 'I'd met Dr Weaver at party functions, but I can't say that I actually knew her. I am, of course, shocked and saddened by her death.'

Oh, she was *good*. Just the right note of sincerity and sorrow. She wasn't going to put a foot wrong in this election. I thanked her for the interview and reluctantly decided that I liked Carmen Broadhurst.

Which was more than I could say for Samuel Stephenson.

He objected strenuously after the camera stopped filming.

'Those questions weren't in the agreement, young lady,' he said, staring down at me as if from the heights of Mt Sinai. Did he see himself as Moses? He did have a kind of Charlton Heston look about him, all jaw and cheekbones and blazing eyes.

I blinked ingenuously at him.

'Agreement, Samuel? Oh, I don't think my producer would have agreed to limit the scope of our interview. He didn't tell me anything about that.'

'But we understood—'

'We understood that you supported our aims, Miss McGowan,' Carter cut in.

'I can't let my personal feelings interfere with my professional responsibilities,' I said, then I dropped my voice confidentially. 'I think the real *Daily Report* people would have been a bit tougher, frankly.'

Carter and Stephenson exchanged glances and I could almost hear their thoughts. She's probably right, they signalled to each other.

'Thank you so much for your time.' I smiled brightly at Carter. 'Time to get this footage back, I think.'

Stephenson shepherded me out to the car.

'You've never thought about standing for preselection yourself, Mr Stephenson?' I asked while Dave and Terry loaded up the lights.

He snorted. 'I know my limits,' he said. 'I'm a good businessman, and that's where I can be of most use to the church. I mean, the party.'

'Not much difference, really, is there?'

He was silent, a slight flush of embarrassment on his cheekbones. I could prod just one more time, I reckoned, before he snapped at me. I signalled behind my back, hoping Terry could see me, that he would start filming.

'It's about the only political party that *does* put religious values first,' I said slowly.

'Damn right it is! We're the only ones prepared to state the truth, to stand up to the greenie leftie liberals who want us all to be gender neutral and have unnatural sex in front of innocent children!'

Well. That tapped a deep spring. Eyes blazing, he stared down at me with the fervour of the fanatic. I nodded. No good arguing back at someone like that.

Before I could figure out what to say, a woman parked her car next to us and hopped out. About Stephenson's age, small and quick like a sparrow, dressed all in brown, sensible shoes, stockings, dress and hat. The style reminded me of my grandmother, although this woman had to be a good forty years younger.

'Samuel!' she said, her voice high and breathless. 'You forgot your lunch.'

Must be his wife. She came around the car and handed him an insulated lunchbox. Navy blue. Very masculine.

Noticing me and the two men, she smiled hesitantly. 'Hello ... I'm Ruth Stephenson.' Aha! She must be the Ruth of Ruth's Kitchen. It was kind of nice that he'd named the business after her.

I held out my hand. 'Poppy McGowan.'

She shook my hand as though it were something she didn't do often.

'Thanks, Ruth,' Stephenson said. 'You didn't need to bring it up.'

'Oh, it was no trouble!' She smiled up at him sunnily, with clear devotion. 'I was just on my way to do the shopping for the youth disco tomorrow night. I must get on. Nice to meet you, Miss McGowan.'

'And you.'

'Yes, well,' Stephenson said. 'You'll let us know when it airs?'

'Don't worry, mate,' Dave said, 'you'll see the ads.'

That didn't seem to reassure Stephenson, but I hid my grin until he'd gone back inside the building.

'Tell me you got that explosion from him,' I said to Terry. He patted the side of his camera.

'Just camera sound, but I got it.'

I punched him on the arm in approval. 'Yay, you. Let's get it back.'

Tyler was reluctantly approving of the footage. He liked the Winchester interview. He was lukewarm about the kids. He acknowledged that Carmen Broadhurst was a seasoned performer and I'd got what I could. He loved the Stephenson outburst, but wished it had been Carter who'd said it.

'If we edit it right, we can put together a little montage of right wing outbursts,' I said.

He looked more cheerful. 'Mmm. All right. Job done. Thanks.'

News reporters usually worked with the editors on their own stories, but Tyler didn't trust me that much. I escaped with relief. News really wasn't the job for me. I didn't like conning people into telling me more than they wanted to.

CHAPTER THIRTEEN

I went back to work, so I could claim the day in lieu later, and changed thankfully back into my jeans.

But I found it hard to concentrate, and Jennifer Jay found me staring into my cold mug of tea.

'How's Luna Park coming along?' she asked, perching her hip on the corner of my desk.

'Fine,' I said, sitting up. 'Just tomorrow, getting interviews with some of the people who work there. Then we're ready to cut. Have you seen the rushes?'

She nodded. 'Not bad. I like the empty park and the rides going without anyone in them. Might be a bit spooky for the kids, though. We'll have to put happy music over the top.'

It always amazed me how you could change the whole meaning of a piece of film by using the right music. I had come to terms with it—it wasn't manipulative, I told myself, it was merely a different way of communicating. A much more effective way than words.

The Radiant Joy Church, I reflected, was famous for using modern music to draw in new members. I wondered if Tyler had covered that side of the story. I felt a suicidal urge to call him and ask if he wanted me to cover a service, but I pushed it down. I had to schedule the rest of the shooting for the archaeology program. We couldn't get into my house (yet), but we could shoot at the museum. I clearly needed to go there right now and do a recce. Monday was the first scheduled shooting day for that episode now Jennifer Jay had delayed the recycling episode, which I'd learnt from the big whiteboard that scheduled everyone's movements.

This program was all arse-about, as my grandfather used to say. Normally, I would do research, preliminary interviews, archival research, recces and so on, and then come back and write a script, and together Jennifer Jay and I would come up with a workable shooting schedule. Then I would go out with the crews, get the footage, bring it back to Jennifer Jay and she would do all the post-production, which is where images really become programs.

In other sections of the ABC, a director would be involved with the planning and go out with the crew and literally call the shots. But in education we were cash-strapped, so we only used a director for shows where we had actors. As long as I had an experienced camera operator, I could pull a documentary together as well as a director could—as long

as I had Jennifer Jay to supervise the editing, FX, music …
We made a good team.

The discovery of the sheep bones had caught me without a script ready for the archaeology program. I needed to
write that script and to do that, I needed to do the research
I would normally have done much earlier. The fact that I
already knew the museum inside and out was irrelevant.
And the fact that I might see Tol … coincidence, I assured
myself. Serendipity.

So I signed myself out on the whiteboard and headed
back over the bridge, feeling oddly lighthearted, enjoying
the bright skies and crisp wind off the harbour. A skywriter
was working over the Opera House. He'd got as far as
'Happy', which probably meant a birthday greeting, but I
was glad to settle for just the idea of happiness floating in
the sky.

I was parking in the museum's visitor's spot when my
phone rang. I hurriedly pulled on the parking brake and
dived for the phone.

'Hello?'

'Miss McGowan? It's Eliza Carter.'

This was interesting. Why would she be ringing me?

'Nice to hear from you,' I said. 'What can I do for you?'

She hesitated. 'I wondered … you're in contact with the
police, aren't you?'

'You might say that,' I said dryly.

'Do you know—have they said who they think …'

'Who they think killed Dr Weaver?' I supplied.

'Yes,' she said, her voice breathy as though she really cared.

'Sure they have,' I said, stringing her along. Then pity overcame me. 'They think I did it.' My heart thumped a little, as though saying it out loud made it more real.

'*You!* Why would they—how could they—why *you?*'

I bridled at the mixture of disbelief and barely concealed contempt. I might not like the police thinking I'd killed Julieanne, but being dismissed out of hand as a suspect was strangely insulting.

'I didn't like Julieanne, you know, Eliza. And she *was* found in my house.'

'I never thought of that ... Oh, that's—that's wonderful!' And she hung up. Just like that.

Wonderful? WTF?

Bugger that, I thought. I called Detective Chloe.

'Prudhomme,' she snapped after the first ring.

'This is Poppy McGowan,' I said. 'Eliza Carter just asked me who you suspected. When I said it was me, she said, and I quote: "That's wonderful!"'

There was silence for a long moment.

'She could be just relieved that her husband isn't a suspect.' But her voice was thoughtful.

'That's a lot of relief.'

'Yes,' Chloe said. 'Thanks.' She hung up. What, no one says goodbye any more?

My stomach growled, so I rang Stuart, who worked nearby.

'Lunch?' he said, sounding harassed. 'Sorry, I brought my lunch in from home today. If you'd given me notice ...'

Fine. If leftovers were more important than seeing me, then screw him.

I went into the museum, grabbed a sandwich at the café, and then spent a solid hour writing up a shooting schedule for Monday. I checked out the vaults, the displays, the public spaces, the offices. I decided to use Gerry's office for the interviews (all those bricks made great props), and organised with the curatorial assistants to have the right pieces from the collections available for filming in Annie's office, which had the best natural light. Annie was out at a conference all day, so I abandoned the idea of a nice soothing chat with her. Tol was nowhere to be found.

'Dr Lang?' the curatorial assistant said. 'He's at a meeting at Sydney Uni. Something about his Jordan dig.'

Of course. Jordan.

Time to go home and double-check the schedule.

I got back in the car and ten minutes later found myself, without thinking about it, on the expressway that led northwest. Right to Eliza Carter's door. I had her address from the initial briefing Tyler's researcher had done for me.

I'd been expecting a McMansion, one of the huge project homes which occupied swathes of land which in my childhood had been peach and dairy farms. But no, not a one-size-fits-most house for the Carters. They lived on the top of a hill in one of the original farmhouses. At least, I assumed it was original; it had been so tarted up and tidied and painted and landscaped that I doubted its first owners would have recognised it. There was a swing set on a very green side lawn, but that was the only sign that children occupied the place.

Patience answered the door. Maybe I'd been longer than I'd thought at the museum. I checked my watch. No, it was still school hours, just. She looked pale, but not sick enough to be at home.

'Hello!' she said, half-pleased and half-suspicious.

'Hi,' I said. 'Your mother called me. Is she in?'

'She's in the kitchen,' Patience said, leading the way through a *Vogue Living* formal room. No cute farmhouse décor here, this was serious money. Carter had gone for the Oriental-antique-meets-modern-Italian look, and if a professional designer hadn't been in charge, I'd be very surprised. I even saw a Brett Whiteley on the wall. He didn't get that kind of money from being a member of parliament, and I wondered what slice of the church's income came his way, and how he justified it to himself.

The kitchen, Eliza's domain, was another matter. Admittedly, it had every conceivable appliance in stainless steel, but it was rose pink and country styled. Corn dollies on the wall. Patchwork cushions on the window seat. Eliza Carter was at the bench, kneading dough. She had an apron on, but other than that she looked like she'd just walked out of the beauty salon. Not a smudge of flour, even. She looked less stressed than the last time I'd seen her—perhaps cooking was her hobby. Or perhaps the knowledge that I was the prime suspect was enough to bring that light to her eyes.

I didn't have to fake the annoyance in my voice when I said, '"That's wonderful"? Why is it wonderful that the police suspect me?'

Her hands gripped the bread dough convulsively and she stared at me. Her cheeks flushed. With shame, or anger? Anger would be more interesting. Would she abuse me for invading her home?

But she took a deep breath and let it out again. Then another. Determined to get control of herself before she said anything.

'Mum?' Patience asked. 'Are you all right?'

Eliza summoned a smile. 'Of course I am, darling. Miss McGowan just startled me.' She turned to me, smooth as milk. 'I was just pleased that the police had turned their attention away from the Party,' she said. She looked down at the dough and frowned before reshaping it and beginning to knead again. 'We're at a crucial stage. It's relatively easy to get one member in parliament. That's like standing as an independent.' She began to weave the dough into a complicated plaited loaf. 'But once you put two candidates up, the public is more suspicious.' She looked up and flushed again. 'At least, that's what my husband says.' Shame this time, definitely, about being caught theorising about men's business.

'So it's all right for the police to suspect an innocent person as long as the party's out of it?' I asked, a snap in my voice.

'The things the Party is trying to do are more important than any one person,' she parroted.

'Sounds like what the communists used to say,' I said. I was aware of Patience standing in the doorway, listening intently.

'How *dare* you!' That was genuine anger, twenty-four carat. Eliza's eyes flamed, her cheeks went bright red. She slammed the loaf down on the counter. 'How dare you even mention that word in this house! Godless, evil—' She was practically foaming at the mouth.

Patience moved forward soundlessly, as though preparing to intervene if it got physical.

'The Lord Himself guides my husband!' Eliza declared, getting control back.

Patience froze.

Eliza bowed her head. 'Lord, help this poor misguided girl to understand Your work. Help her to find her way to You and be set free by Your Holy Spirit. Amen.'

'Amen,' Patience whispered.

Being prayed over was strangely disquieting. I'd been prayed *for* lots of times: when I was sick, when I was studying for an exam, when I was involved with a boyfriend my parents didn't like. But that took place decently in private or, at worst, in silence in church. This public declaration was profoundly alien, and it unsettled me more than I would have expected.

'You should come to one of our services,' Eliza said, almost desperately. 'Then you'd see how important our work is.'

'All right,' I found myself saying. What was I thinking? The last thing I wanted to do—but the idea of seeing Matthew Carter in full flight was intriguing. Know your enemy,

I thought, and didn't stop to ask myself why the Carters were my enemy.

Patience was staring at me with astonishment. I shrugged. 'Research,' I said.

Eliza beamed at me. 'Call it what you like,' she said. 'The Lord is leading you.'

I so hoped that was true. But not in the way she meant.

As though my agreement to attend service had made us best friends, Eliza insisted on making me coffee and produced it, steaming, accompanied by homemade cake. She sat me down at the breakfast bar, apologising for the informality, and hummed as she finished the loaf and set it to rise.

Patience refused cake but her mother insisted on her having a large glass of milk.

'You're not well?' I asked.

She shrugged, uncomfortable.

Eliza shot me a conspiratorial look and dropped her voice. 'Her *friend* is visiting.'

It had been so long since I'd heard that particular euphemism that I actually looked around to see if Patience's friend was there. Then I realised. Her period.

'Ah,' I said. I was seized by a desire to call a spade a spade, but I suppressed it. 'You know, Eliza, there's something I still don't really understand.'

'Mmm?' she asked, eyes on the bench as she ruthlessly eliminated every speck of flour.

'I've known Julieanne Weaver for a few years now. And I don't really understand how she—er ... insinuated herself into Australian Family. She's—she was so *different* from the other party members I've met.'

Eliza's hands stilled. Every part of her stilled. Then she began to move again, sweeping the flour fragments into her hand and turning to dump them in the bin.

'She approached my husband at the electoral office,' she said, her voice very even. 'He thought … he thought that she might be suitable. An example that the party wasn't, um—'

'Misogynist?' I offered helpfully.

It did help, too. She pulled herself together.

'"Old fashioned" was the way my husband put it.' She turned back, face calm. Patience let a breath out. 'But I think he was misled,' Eliza said.

'She could be very convincing—to men,' I said. Something flickered across Eliza's face. Hatred? Scorn? Something strong, but gone too fast to identify.

'Men are not cursed, as we women are, with a natural understanding of evil,' she said. Straight-faced.

I looked at Patience. Is this what she was taught? That women were naturally evil? Well, it was an old idea. But in this modern, shining kitchen, with the sun beaming through the windows and the microwave cheerily displaying the time, it was frightening.

'The service starts at ten on Sunday,' Eliza said. She looked me over—the old jeans, the cotton top—and visibly refrained from asking me to smarten up for the occasion.

I took the last swallow of my coffee. It really was very good; Tol would like it. Eliza swooped almost before I'd put the cup back in the saucer and whisked them and the empty plate to the dishwasher. The interview was over.

'Patience will show you the way out.' She forced herself to smile. The MP's wife was back in force, every hair in place. 'I look forward to seeing you on Sunday.'

Patience took me silently to the door, which sprang open just before we got to it. Two little boys in school uniform—private school uniform, I noted—rushed in, calling, 'Mum, Mum, we're starving!'

It was the most normal thing that had happened since I'd walked in and I smiled involuntarily. Carter followed them in, and smiled back as though I'd aimed the look at him personally. Erk. I wondered how ready he'd been to be persuaded that Julieanne should join the party. And what kind of party had she joined?

'Poppy,' he said, with a question in his voice. 'How nice to see you.'

'Eliza has convinced me to join you on Sunday at the church,' I said.

There was no doubting the genuine enthusiasm that brought out. His whole face lit up and he grabbed my hand and shook it. 'That's wonderful. Wonderful. We'll see you then.'

The two boys rushed back and took hold of his arm, chattering about how getting a dog wouldn't really make any more work for anyone, and 'we'd look after it, Dad, really we would'. He grinned and shrugged, following them into the kitchen. Patience opened the door.

'Bye,' I said.

She waited until I was almost through before she said, 'I thought you didn't like my father.'

'I don't,' I said. 'And I feel sorry for your mother and you.' I looked at her, but she was staring at her feet, clad in sensible sneakers. 'Women aren't naturally any more evil than men, you know.'

She looked up sharply. 'That's evil enough,' she said, and closed the door in my face.

Fair comment.

Despite the cake, I was still hungry. I got drive-thru on my way back to lodge my shooting schedule with Jennifer Jay. It tasted even more delicious because I was sure that Eliza Carter would have disapproved.

CHAPTER FOURTEEN

'Do you think women are naturally evil, Mum?'

My mother snorted and handed me the teapot and the milk. 'Original sin's in all of us,' she said, and paused. 'But if you think about who causes the most misery in the world ...' She looked at the photo of her brother George on the wall. George had been killed in Vietnam. Mum shrugged, as though she didn't have to finish the sentence.

I considered it as we watched the news and drank our tea. Were men more likely to kill? Statistically, yes, no doubt about it. I'd written an episode on unlawful death for the Legal Studies program, and the statistics had been fascinating. The person most likely to die by violence in our society is a young drunk man. They get into fights, and they get killed. The interesting thing was that it didn't matter who started the fight. That doesn't have any correlation to who gets hurt.

For women, the statistics are more sobering. The most likely person to kill a woman is her partner, especially if she's about to leave or has just left. The most likely place is her own bedroom, closely followed by the rest of her house. Which made Tol and Paul the most likely suspects in Julieanne's death. But why couldn't she have been killed in her own house? I thought bitterly.

The thought stayed with me. Yes, why? And why hadn't I considered that before?

I went to bed wondering why Julieanne had been in my house late at night. In her dress-to-impress blue outfit, and her respectable expensive court shoes. She wouldn't have gone there to dig dressed like that, and the police hadn't mentioned other clothes being found there. Would they mention it? I decided to ask Detective Chloe. She might even tell me.

The most reasonable explanation was that she had gone there to meet someone. An empty house was a great place for an assignation. I really hoped nothing physical had happened before she was killed. Somehow I found the idea of Julieanne having illicit sex in my house more off-putting than the memory of her corpse. But surely the police wouldn't suspect me if there was evidence of Julieanne's sexual activity?

I would scrub the upstairs floors when the police let me back in, though. Just in case.

The next day I spent doing interviews with workers at Luna Park. It was Saturday, when Luna Park is at its best.

That's the way it works during the shooting season for a show. You do the work when you need to, and take time off later. It was a hectic, full-on day and I found it very restful. No one died. No one called me unexpectedly. No one questioned my motives or my innocence.

I came home cheerful and spent a few hours knocking together a rough script for the archaeology show from Mirha's production notes of what shots we had. Working a way around the footage with Julieanne in it was tricky, but fortunately Terry's one of those camera operators who believes in 'coverage'—that is, taking several shots of the same images from different angles and directions. So I had a reasonable amount to play with, and we could fill in with an interview with Tol back at the house. I pushed down an image of the two of us standing close together in the pit. Control yourself! I had Stuart, and Tol was going back to Jordan.

But I couldn't control my dreams.

At seven am on Sunday, I opened one eye and debated whether or not I really wanted to see Matthew Carter operating in his natural habitat, the conservative Christian church. I decided no, rolled over and went back to sleep.

At eight, my mother woke me up 'because you'll be late for church if you don't get a move on'.

Even though my mother had woken me every Sunday morning of my childhood with more or less the same words, this morning it sounded like a message from God, so I rolled out of bed and blearily made my way to the bathroom. A hot shower, a cup of tea and some cereal later, I felt human enough to explain to my parents that I was going to church elsewhere.

'Why?' my mother demanded.

'I've got to recce the Radiant Joy Church for the News-Caff people.'

She didn't look happy. Going to church didn't count unless it was Catholic.

'They might want to do another story on *The Daily Report*,' I added, only a little mendaciously. Tyler had been making noises about a follow-up.

Her face cleared a little. She'd enjoyed my brief doses of fame. I hadn't been able to bear watching the Australian Family interview, but she had, and so had the rest of the family. And if it was *work*—that excused a lot. People talk about the Protestant work ethic, but the Catholic one isn't too shabby either.

'I suppose you can go to Mass tonight,' she said.

Right. Twice in one day was too much for me. I'd figure out how to get out of that one later.

I doubted that skipping Mass was going to put me in Hell, as my parents believed. As for Heaven, I vacillate between the classic Christian image and reincarnation, which seems to me so much fairer than giving you just one shot at getting the whole being-human thing right. I like the idea of reincarnation; I find it soothing and reassuring. It makes me a heretic, of course, so it's best not to talk about it at home. And the only priest I raised it with backed away so fast he almost left skidmarks, so I've just filed it as one of those things I approve of that the Church doesn't, like contraception and gay relationships.

I drove west hoping it wouldn't be as bad as I expected.

The Radiant Joy Church looked a bit like a shopping mall from the outside. Not quite as big. Blank concrete walls, the lower floor all glass and automatic doors, a big lobby—actually, I thought, walking up the dark blue–carpeted stairs, it was more like a cinema than a mall. It had a lot of screens, just like a cinema, showing only the empty stage—sorry, altar: it featured a very simple wooden cross.

I passed a yellow-painted room with big glass doors labelled CHILDREN'S MINISTRY. It was filling fast with small, mostly blond, children who ran in happily and greeted what I presumed were the Sunday School supervisors (teenage girls) with enthusiasm. I'd checked out the very, very slick website—there was a Children's Ministry, a Youth Ministry, a Seniors' Ministry and something called a 'Happy Homes Ministry' which, on closer examination, turned out to be a school for brides-to-be to help them become submissive wives.

Lots of people smiled at me as I made my way into the huge horseshoe-shaped auditorium and slid into a seat at the back. Lots of white people—male, female, old, young—were smiling at me and nodding as though they recognised I was a newcomer. They all seemed to have very shiny teeth.

At ten o'clock sharp, the service started with a rousing rendition of 'Giving It All For Jesus', which everyone but me seemed to know and love.

One of the things I do like about the Catholics is that no one asks you what you're thinking. There's none of that standing up and witnessing business, no public confessions, no thought police. As long as you turn up to Mass, you're counted as one of the flock, and no one probes your private beliefs—which is how most Catholic women happily go to Communion and take the Pill as well, and live with the supposed dichotomy without the slightest qualm of conscience—even my sisters, who were virgins when they got married and would describe themselves as good Catholics.

The Catholics know where private thoughts belong—in the confessional.

That idea occurred to me very strongly at twenty minutes past ten, while I was listening to Pastor Amos Winchester invite his flock to 'come forward and witness to Jesus'. This means, apparently, coming to the state-of-the-art microphone and telling a story about how your life had been shit before you found religion and now it's fantastic, while your face is projected up onto a big screen, so we can all see the tears in your eyes. Then we'll sing a hymn praising Jesus.

I learnt far too much about total strangers. Ex-drug addicts, ex-prostitutes, ex-alcoholics. Even, to my astonishment, a supposed ex-schizophrenic whom Winchester had exorcised of the demons that had made him seem mentally ill. It was like Eliza Carter talking about the evil of women in her sunny kitchen—the combination of medieval thought and sleek, streamlined, modern setting made me very uneasy.

And the music! A full band, a percussion section bigger than the Sydney Symphony Orchestra, a choir (though not, to my disappointment, any gospel singing—it was all soft rock) and a sound system as sophisticated as the last Wiggles concert I took my nephews to.

The auditorium was almost as big as the Wiggles', and it was just as full, although the kids were older. These young people sang and clapped and listened attentively. They didn't lounge in their seats or look bored, they didn't surreptitiously check for text messages, they didn't roll their eyes when one of the witnesses choked up—and they sang loud and strong.

It was disgusting.

It was invigorating and inspiring.

It was profoundly disturbing.

I love to sing in church. I really enjoy singing hymns. I used to be in the choir, all that stuff. But although the songs at Radiant Joy were catchy and the words were all up there on the big screen so everyone could sing along, I just couldn't. I'd felt more at home in the Buddhist temple where we'd filmed a segment for a program on multiculturalism.

Then Winchester got up for his sermon. I relaxed a little. Winchester was familiar, at least. I felt like I'd been thrown a lifeline. But his American accent just crystallised why I was so uncomfortable. This approach to religion, it was an import, like American cop shows and McDonald's. There was something deeply alien—dare I use the word 'unAustralian'?—about all the ... the *sincerity*. I'd been to church in America—Baptist church, with my friend Raquel, in Washington, D.C.—and there the clapping and the raptness of the congregation had seemed just right. But not here.

It got worse. According to Winchester, God wanted His chosen people (that is, the Radiant Joy worshippers) to be prosperous—to have abundance. 'Pressed down and running over,' he kept repeating. My parish priest had always said that that part of the Gospel referred to spiritual wealth, but Pastor Amos took it more literally. He believed— strongly believed, by the look of him—that it referred to material wealth, and he assured his congregation so.

'God loves you!' he purred, his lapel microphone picking up every syllable as he strode from one side of the stage to the other. 'God loves you and He wants you to be happy. How do we know? Because He sent His only begotten Son to save you. Each and every one of you! You think He did that because He wants you to suffer? No! Suffering is a tool of the Devil! Accept Jesus into your life and suffering is at an end! Live as God wanted you to live, and you *will* prosper. Share your prosperity as God intended and it will grow tenfold!'

Sharing prosperity, it transpired soon afterwards, meant tithing to the church. Ten per cent, right off the top. I looked around at the hundreds of well-fed, well-dressed, apparently well-off people. If Amos Winchester got a tenth of everything they earned … shit, that was a *lot* of money. No wonder the church could afford to bankroll a political party.

The Carters, minus the little boys, were sitting right down the front, next to Samuel Stephenson and his wife, dressed all in brown again, who listened raptly to Pastor Amos. You could tell that Ruth was a leading example of the submissive wife. Occasionally she glanced up at Stephenson's craggy profile with adoration, and when he went to the podium to deliver a short address about the church financing a new ministry reaching out to 'troubled teens', she positively glowed with pride. He spoke well, I had to give him that, with authority and even a bit of charisma. But he didn't have Carter's charm. When Carter gave a speech of thanks to everyone who had been supporting Australian Family and invited them all to a fundraising barbecue, you could hear female hearts fluttering all over the auditorium.

Because of the horseshoe shape of the seating, I had a great view of Carter's group. I was more interested in Patience than the others. She sang and clapped and listened with the others, but when Winchester talked about prosperity and abundance, there was a slight frown on her face, an expression, not exactly of doubt, but of reserve. As though she'd like to be convinced, but wasn't.

She looked up as if she felt my eyes on her and smiled involuntarily as she saw me. My heart lifted and I smiled back. Patience blinked and looked away, but shot a couple of glances at me as the sermon went on. I tried to look respectful but I suspected that she saw through me, because when I sneaked a peek there was a tiny quirk to her mouth.

After the service I slipped out quickly and made my way to the end of the enormous parking lot where I had stashed

my car for a smooth getaway. If I lingered, I'd have to talk to
the Carters and Stephenson, and if they asked me what I'd
thought of the service I'd have told them, and then they'd
never have spoken to me again.

But as I was unlocking my car, Patience ran up, panting.
'What did you think?'

Maybe I could have schmoozed Stephenson if I'd really
tried, but I couldn't lie to Patience.

'I saw your face during the prosperity sermon,' I said. 'And
I have just one thing to say to you: Matthew 19:24.' The
Bible verse about it being easier for a camel to go through
the eye of a needle than for a rich man to enter the kingdom
of God.

Her face turned to stone. None of us like having our
worst fears laid bare.

'You said you believed in God,' she whispered.

'I do. But Amos Winchester isn't God.'

She turned and ran. Poor Patience. Being a teenager is
hard enough without having to cope with dodgy theol-
ogy. I remembered how intense I'd been about religion at
her age—full of desire to be good, full of anger about the
hypocrisy of adults. Not my parents. My parents are many,
many things, but hypocrites they're not. That's why I can
deal with their sometimes difficult attitudes. They live by
them, and try their very best to help everyone they meet.
But Patience … poor Patience.

CHAPTER FIFTEEN

Sunday afternoon was Annie's daughter Ruby's eighth birthday party. Jim, Annie's husband, is a ranger at Lane Cove National Park, so that's where the birthday party was. He's Indigenous—a Dharug man of the Eora nation—and runs courses in bush tucker and Indigenous Art at the park. I was born on Dharug land, in Parramatta hospital, and so was Jim, only two days earlier, which forms a weird kind of bond between us. Also, his twin sister Elsie and I had been friends since kinder—that's how he'd met Annie.

'Hey, cuz.' He greeted me with a hug.

'Hey.' I hugged him back. Jim was the hottest guy I'd ever met. Like one of those firefighters they get to do the calendars. But he was so lovely that, after a while, the hotness wore off and all you could feel for him was a vast affection.

Besides, he was a double brother to me, via both Elsie and Annie.

'Hi, Aunty Poppy!' Ruby and Miles and Peter, Annie and Jim's kids, ran up and hugged me. I gave Ruby her present—a stuffed purple dragon.

'Oh, she's so cool!' She sat on the ground to investigate it straight away.

Miles started to tell me about the party. 'Fairy bread! Party pies! Games!'

Peter is only four, and resents the fact that Miles is my godson, so he attached himself to my leg and started talking about dinosaurs. 'I like T-Rex best!' he announced.

'*Everyone* likes T-Rex best!' Miles said, scornful as only a big brother can be.

'I don't,' I said. 'I like parasaurolophus best.' True. The boys were silenced for a fabulous moment by my unexpected knowledge of dinosaurs (very experienced aunty, here) and their mother swooped in, dragged Ruby off the ground and sent them all off to greet the arriving guests.

'I need someone to set out the food,' she told me. Properly marshalled, I went to get the sausage rolls from the cook.

The party was at the café in the national park—a beautiful setting overlooking the Lane Cove River, surrounded by the tallest of gum trees. Only one drawback: the local birds are convinced that any food on any table is theirs. And when a raven or kookaburra decides it wants your fairy bread, it gets it.

So all the eating was done inside the café, but after the song was sung and the cake cut, the kids piled outside and were set to classic party games by Alex and his partner Rick, with help from me and Annie. Three-legged races, egg-and-spoon races, bobbing for apples ... Very appropriate for a historian's child. And fun.

Afterwards, Annie, Alex, Rick and I collapsed on chairs and had a cold drink while the small people ran around screaming, working off the sugar hit. Jim supervised down by the river to make sure no one drowned.

Alex and Rick are a study in contrasts. Alex is six foot three, with thick bright red hair and green eyes, and looks like an extra in *Outlander*—those Scottish highlander genes are strong. Rick is tall, too, but slender and dark, with big brown eyes and light brown skin; he says he has Persian and Italian ancestry as well as Anglo, but both so far back that it unfortunately doesn't count in terms of dual citizenship. They draped over each other in comfortable affection.

'Tell us a story, Poppy,' Rick said, as he always did when things were happening in my life.

I complied with a commentary on Radiant Joy Church. I had them in stitches parodying Winchester's sermon, trying to wash the bad taste he'd left in my mouth away with laughter. It didn't work. I felt off-kilter, out of sorts.

'He's the gay one, right?' Rick said.

Astonished, I sat up and stared at him. *'Amos Winchester?* Surely not.'

'We did a thing with them when their choir wanted to sing the *Messiah* last Easter.' Rick plays timpani for the Sydney Symphony. 'The symphony lent them a few people. I swear he was giving me the once-over.'

'Rick's gaydar is the best in the business,' Alex said, ruffling Rick's hair. 'And you know what those right-wing preachers are like. Always being caught with rent boys in seedy motels.'

Annie pursed her lips. 'Maybe *he* killed Julieanne. Her gaydar was pretty good too.'

But I just couldn't believe that. Winchester and rent boys? No, and no, and no. Not because he couldn't be gay. But because Amos Winchester was very, very smart, and very, very much in control. If he was having sex with a man, it would be with a man who had just as much to lose as he did. And, frankly, I suspected he was sincere in his beliefs. If he *was* gay, he was probably celibate.

But would he, or someone else in the church, kill to prevent an accusation? He didn't have a convenient wife to contradict it. Come to think of it, he'd never been married, which was odd for a man in his position.

'I doubt it,' I said. 'Whoever killed Julieanne really hated her, and Winchester wouldn't have given her the satisfaction of hating her.'

What a horrible sentence. A horrible thought. It made me feel unclean.

'What I don't understand,' Annie said, 'is why Julieanne was trying for preselection with Australian Family.' She shook her head. 'I can't imagine a party she'd fit into less.

Why not as an independent? Why not as a Green—they have a good chance, too, and she'd be right up their alley. She's done good work in rehabilitating dig sites back to native habitats.'

None of us could answer that, but it did make me think. Julieanne had approached Carter at his electoral office, but I didn't know when—was that part of a long-term plan? No one could have predicted that a sitting MP would have a heart-attack hump and create an opportunity via a by-election. Maybe she'd identified that Australian Family was missing members in her demographic? Or had it been pure short-term opportunism? None of it made sense.

After the birthday party was cleared up, I decided to go to six o'clock Mass and let the comfort of ritual, the ordered, calm process of the Eucharist, ease my mind. No one asked me for enthusiasm at St Brendan's, but I was expected to be reverent and that, I realised, was what I had missed most at Radiant Joy.

And when I went home and let myself in and my mother said, 'Have you been to church?' and I said, 'Yes, I went to six o'clock', as I might have done at Patience's age, I felt clean, and restored to some kind of balance.

My father said, 'Your dinner's in the oven', so I sat down and ate lamb chops and mashed potato and then I went to bed and slept better than my sister's baby.

CHAPTER SIXTEEN

Monday

The next morning, we started at nine at the museum and worked solidly through the schedule. I needed Tol for the interviews. Now that Julieanne was dead, he was the only archaeologist we had on film at the house dig. So at morning tea, after we'd shot all the pieces in the vault, I left Terry and Dave setting up the lights in Gerry's office and went in search of him.

Tol's office was one of those small, untidy spaces given to temporary staff—corners full of odd equipment there was nowhere else to put, old posters from long-past exhibitions fraying on the wall, dents in the filing cabinet drawers from frequent moving. Overlaid on the slightly grimy standard museum effects was essence of Tol: a trowel tossed onto a side table; his leather jacket hanging on his chair; a clutch of pottery sherds in the middle of the desk; three takeaway coffee cups in the bin; a fez perched on top of the hatstand. But no Tol. Then a step behind me and the slight scent of something male.

I turned, my heart beating as though I'd been caught in a burglary. 'Hi,' I said, trying for insouciance, 'ready for your interview?'

He smiled at me, but his brows twitched together at the last word. 'Interview?'

'Didn't Annie tell you? For the program we were shooting at the house.'

He didn't look pleased. 'I don't like doing interviews,' he said. It was a flat tone of voice with very little room for manoeuvre.

I wasn't going to beg him. 'Fine,' I said. 'Maybe we can hold a séance and interview Julieanne.'

He flinched and I immediately felt guilty. She had been his girlfriend, after all.

'Sorry,' I said. 'But—'

He sighed, a tad melodramatically, I thought. 'All right. Let's get it over with.'

He was grouchy all through the preparation, through the lighting set-up, the sound test, signing the release for Mirha the PA, acting like we were going to torture him. Then, as I sat down opposite him and gave Terry the sign to start film- ing, he smiled into my eyes and proceeded to give an imper- sonation of the loveliest, most charming, most interesting archaeologist in the world.

I wanted to slap him. Then he made me laugh with an outrageous joke about skeletons—the kind of joke that six-year-olds would love—and I wanted to kiss him. I flushed and frowned, but even Terry and Dave were grinning.

'What do you like best about archaeology?' I asked. The last question on my list.

Tol paused. All his other answers had been glib, rolling off his tongue with practised ease. This one he really thought about. I was expecting something profound, something philosophical, something inspiring.

'Walls,' he said. 'I really like finding walls.' He smiled at me with genuine warmth, offering me this insight into his soul, and God help me, I couldn't help but smile back.

'That's it,' I said.

Terry snapped the lights off with the usual effect of turning off the sun. We sat blinking for a moment while our eyes adjusted.

'Walls?' I asked.

Tol shrugged. 'That's why I don't much like colonial archaeology. Hardly any walls worth finding.'

But in Jordan there were lots of lovely old walls buried deep, just waiting to be uncovered.

'Some good news,' Tol offered. 'We can get back into the house tomorrow. And I went out to Sydney Uni the other day and recruited a bone expert who can identify the bones definitively for us. If they are fat-tailed sheep, we'll know tomorrow.'

'A bone expert?'

He shrugged. 'A mate of mine. It'll save you a lot of time.'

He *was* nice. Considerate. Funny. But there were no interesting walls in Sydney.

Terry and Dave left to set up in Annie's office. Mirha
followed them. Tol stood and I lingered, both of us unsure
what to say.

'Uh—see you tomorrow, I guess,' he said at last.

'Sure. Yeah. Tomorrow.' I sounded like a zombie in a bad
horror flick. Then he smiled at me again, but I thought,
Walls, walls, and kept a proper demeanour.

'Tomorrow,' I said with much more assurance. 'We'll be
there at eight-thirty.'

He grinned. 'I'll be there at nine. After I've had my coffee.'

In the doorway, Mirha cleared her throat and showed
me the shooting schedule for the afternoon. 'Terry says
how about lunch after we set up, and then knock this over
fast?'

'Good idea,' I said. Would Tol ask me to lunch?

'I've got a meeting with Annie,' he said, half-apologetically.
'See you tomorrow.'

I knew about that meeting. Annie had emailed me—she
wanted Tol to take over from Julieanne, at least temporar-
ily. I couldn't decide if I wanted him to agree or not. If he
was going back to Jordan eventually, better for my peace of
mind if he went soon.

I rang Stuart as soon as Tol was out of the room and
arranged to meet him at the Newtown cinema after work
for an arty French film he'd been wanting to see. And then,
while Terry was filming the bits and pieces of finds, I sat
down and googled Amos Winchester again. This time I
went through the information I found with an investigative
eye. Could he be gay?

He'd always been single.

He'd never been involved in any scandal involving a woman.

And, most shocking of all, he'd never been quoted, so far as I could find, saying that homosexuality was evil. He'd said a *lot* about marriage being between one man and one woman. Oh, yes. Quite a lot. But it was always couched as 'the foundation of society', 'the real kind of family' and so on. At no time did he ever say that gay people would burn in hell.

He said that about paedophiles. He said it about adulterers. He even said it about apostates. But not gay or lesbian people. Which was almost unbelievable.

His co-preachers, including Matthew Carter, had put themselves on the record as saying that only heterosexual sex was blessed by God. But not Winchester.

I read interview after interview. I watched several sermons from the church's website. Any time he was asked about LGBTQ+ matters, he turned the answer into a statement about family values. It looked as though he was answering, but he wasn't. Not once.

I was filled with a fresh and poignant admiration for him, as well as a deep and sickening disapproval. He'd clearly pulled off one of the great sleights of hand. His congregation believed, implicitly, that he *would* condemn homosexuality. Of course he would. They probably all believed that he had. But he hadn't. Never. Instead, he'd left the LGBTQ+ members of his community to hang in the wind, the target of everyone else in the church.

It was brilliantly done. It was disgusting. To collaborate with the bigots who would be happy to tar and feather gay people ... There was a degree of self-hatred there that was both awful and pathetic.

I had to ask him.

Face to face.

The movie didn't start until seven-thirty. I checked that the film crew didn't need me, and then I ran out to my car and rang the Radiant Joy offices and made a quick appointment with Winchester.

'He'll be at the church,' the receptionist told me. 'Supervising the installation of new lighting.'

The church parking lot was quiet, except for some tradies' utes and a couple of vans parked with reckless disregard across the disabled parking bays.

I went into the church and found my way to the—I realised I was thinking about it as the 'arena'. It didn't feel like a church to me, especially empty of everyone but Winchester, a couple of flunkies, and the men putting up the new lights.

He saw me come in and smiled benignly at me, motioning me to a seat in the front row and joining me there.

'Miss McGowan.'

I really wanted to say, 'It's *Ms* McGowan,' but I didn't. No need to antagonise him just yet. We sat. He was still smiling benignly. Could he possibly think I had come to him for spiritual guidance? Well, why not? I'd come to service, hadn't I? I'd told them my family supported their values. I could work with that.

'Pastor, service was very interesting.'

He nodded, still smiling.

'But I did want to ask you a couple of questions.' I took a deep breath. 'What is your position on homosexuality?'

He launched into the spiel I'd already heard or read several times about the man–woman family. I let him talk himself out.

'But that doesn't say anything about homosexuality, pastor. Just about what a family should be.'

His eyes sharpened, and his hands, loosely held in his lap, tightened. 'It's not my job to condemn people, Poppy.' Oh, smooth as honey.

'But you've condemned paedophiles. And adulterers. You've said they're going to Hell. What about gay people? Are they going to Hell?'

'That's up to the Lord.'

'But what do *you* think? Do you think that being gay is a sin?'

He looked over his shoulder at the lighting men, and pretended to see one waving at him. 'Oh, I think I'd better just go—'

'My friend Rick says you're gay,' I said baldly. 'He's met you. He's very gay, and his gaydar is excellent.'

I've never seen a living body go so still. It was kind of scary, although I didn't know if I were scared for myself, or for him.

'This isn't for the media, pastor,' I said quickly. 'I'm not going to out you on *The Daily Report*. This is off the record. But when I was reading your sermons and interviews, I couldn't help but notice that you never condemn homosexuality.'

He finally looked back at me. Buttoned down, in control. Mostly. There was just a tightness in his voice and his shoulders. 'I don't approve of homosexuality.' A pause. 'I do not practise homosexuality. I have *never* practised it. It is not Godly.'

I looked at him. He looked at me. I was pierced with pity for this old man who had grown up in a time when he could literally have been thrown into prison for who he was. Which didn't excuse his silence. Pity warred with anger that he had encouraged so much bigotry, of so many different kinds.

'Not Godly? Nor is letting gay members of your congregation believe that they are damned,' I said, softly. 'Do you know the statistics on suicide in LGBTQ youth?'

'That's why I don't condemn it,' he snapped.

Huh. Time for the big question. 'Did Julieanne Weaver realise your secret?'

'*I have no secrets!*' He stood up, standing over me, fists clenched. 'You go look, missy. Nothing in my life to find. *Nothing.* Julieanne Weaver realised nothing because there was nothing there. Never. Not once.' His voice quietened. 'Not once.'

I stood up, making him step back a pace. It put him off balance, and I steadied him with a hand on his arm.

'Not too late, pastor. You still have time to accept who you really are. Who God made you.'

He gaped at me. Was that a flicker of longing in his eyes?

No. It was hatred. He hated me for making him admit who he was.

Too bad. It made me sick to think of all the crap he spewed out every Sunday, and probably on every other day too. Prosperity gospel. Anti-everything. Give me your money or you won't go to Heaven. 'Family values' but God help you if you weren't heterosexual and married, no matter how much you loved your partner and children. And all the time hugging this secret to himself. I didn't care if he *was* gay and hiding it. It was no excuse.

As I drove back to Newtown to meet Stuart, I couldn't make up my mind. Should I tell Chloe? Amos had an alibi. There was no proof that Julieanne had ever twigged to his sexuality. No proof of what his sexuality was, really.

But what a motive for someone from the church!

Gossip wasn't proof. I decided I would sit on it, for now. I felt better about that; outing someone has always seemed to me to be a violent act. There'd been enough violence done.

Stuart's solid good sense was a nice antidote to the afternoon. Until we went into the cinema.

I liked arty French films, usually, but this one turned out to be about a beautiful blonde woman being murdered and her distraught boyfriend (tall, dark) descending into madness as it was gradually revealed that he had killed her in a fit of jealousy.

It's a sign, I told myself, sounding like my grandmother. I squeezed Stuart's arm in the dark and he patted my hand like I was a dog asking for a biscuit. I almost expected him to say, 'Good girl, shh, now.'

Afterwards, we walked down to a Thai place for dinner. It was a fine night and even though it was a Monday, most of the restaurants were open and full.

It was reassuring to be out among people who weren't worried about murder. I enjoyed watching the pierced, tattooed and brilliantly haired locals peacock down King St, mixed in with the nurses from the nearby hospital picking up takeaway on their way home. Stuart was funny and insightful about the movie, we drank a good Margaret River verdelho with our chilli beef, and I laughed for what felt like the first time in ages.

Stuart walked me back to my car.

'We'll be back in the house tomorrow,' I said.

He grinned. 'Thank god! We can have some time to ourselves.' His goodbye kiss was a lot warmer and his hands moved more freely. Normally I would have been just as enthusiastic, but I couldn't help remembering my suspicions about Julieanne. As soon as filming was over tomorrow I was scrubbing that floor. Maybe buying a temporary rug for it.

'Are you all right?'

I sighed. 'Just hoping the police will sort all this out quickly.'

Stuart patted my shoulder. 'I'm sure they will,' he said, but he sounded annoyed, as though he wished I hadn't spoiled the mood. Fair enough, but I didn't have the energy to make the situation better.

'Night,' I said.

CHAPTER SEVENTEEN

Tuesday

I put the key into my front door lock with mixed feelings.
I was desperately relieved to get the house back, but what
would I find inside?

At first glance, it all looked the same as we'd left it the day
Julieanne had been killed. The bare-earth floor, criss-crossed
by joists and bearers, the lines strung across the shallow
pit, the edging of chipboard around the walls and running
from the front door to the stairs. I felt vastly relieved. Then
I noticed details. Not all the string lines were there—some
had been pushed into the ground where Julieanne had fallen
onto them. The ground was mushed up by many, many
boot prints. There was black dust everywhere—fingerprint
powder, I figured. And worst of all, one bearer at the end

of the pit had a neat section taken out of it; the raw wood showed up bright against the aged outside. They hadn't sawn all the way through, just taken a section of the top of the bearer. One part of my brain planned to ask Boris to assess it for load-bearing safety. Another noted the dark stains on the side of the bearer just under the raw wood. Julieanne's blood.

I took a step forward so I could see the earth beneath the bearer. There was no terrible pool of blood—not even dried blood. So she hadn't bled to death. But that bearer had been the instrument of her demise.

My heart started thudding. I couldn't stand to look at those stains—and I couldn't imagine Tol working in that pit, staring at them, all day long. I rushed to the laundry and got the bucket and gloves I kept there and I perched on the joists and scrubbed and scrubbed until there was nothing on the bearer but water stains. I didn't look at the bucket. I knew the water would be a dark red-brown. I threw it out on the garden. The hydrangeas. Tried not to think about blood and bone being good fertiliser. Tried not to giggle with shock and horror.

I threw the gloves out, brought the vacuum cleaner down from the main bedroom and frantically hoovered all the fingerprint powder away. It was all I could do, but I knew it wouldn't be enough to erase Tol's memories. Lugging the vacuum cleaner up the stairs, I felt exhausted, and work hadn't even started.

When the doorbell sounded, I let the film crew into the house and waited while they set up the lights, seeming as normal as I could. They moved around the pit with circumspection at first, trying to show respect for the dead, but that wore off pretty quickly. It was just the same location that we'd been filming at the week before. I didn't know how I felt. The image of Julieanne's feet in the pit was vivid in my mind, but this was still *my* house, and I still loved it.

Terry got some shots of the pit and close ups of the bearer to give to Tyler for the evening news. Business as usual. But then, with a glance at me to make sure it was all right, he got down in the pit and stretched out the string lines, so it looked as pristine as it could. I smiled at him with gratitude. I'd wanted to do that but I just couldn't make myself get into the pit again.

Tol arrived at nine, complete with coffee from Graciella's and a tall burly man with a beard.

'Alain Parkes, Poppy McGowan,' Tol introduced us.

Alain looked far more like an archaeologist just off a dig than Tol. His boots had seen a lot of hard wear, he badly needed a haircut, his beard was bushy and his fingers were dry and callused as though he'd dug with his bare hands. He looked competent and experienced and very smart. But I noticed that his pale blue eyes blinked a little shyly behind his big glasses, so I smiled gently at him and thanked him for coming to help. He smiled back and relaxed a little.

'Fat-tailed sheep, eh?' he said.

'I hope not!'

He chuckled and we went inside, where he was introduced to the film crew and lost no time getting into the pit. Tol,

I noticed, hesitated a moment before he jumped down too.
I saw him glance at the cut bearer and go slightly pale, but
he kept working, so I didn't say anything. Alain, though,
spent a lot of time up that end of the pit, as though he were
deliberately shielding Tol from the view. A nice man.

I was glad we had more filming to do—it was acting like a
kind of antiseptic, clearing the room of Julieanne's memory,
overlaying the image of her body in the pit with images of
Tol and Alain earnestly squatting and discussing the ways
in which you could tell a fat-tailed sheep from a Cotswold,
North Devon or Teeswater, which had all apparently been
bred in the early colony.

'Can you explain to the camera what you're looking for?' I
asked Alain, but he couldn't. He froze as soon as he realised
that we were filming. I sighed and sat on the edge of the pit.
I'd dealt with reluctant interviewees before. 'Just talk to me,'
I said reassuringly. 'Tell me all about it.'

'If it's a fat-tailed, it'll be a Cape sheep,' Alain explained,
keeping his eyes on me. His shyness was evident at first but
began to melt away almost immediately as he got into his
subject. Experts are like that. 'The Second Fleet brought
some from Cape Town on their way out in 1790. But by the
early eighteen hundreds other breeds were being imported,
like the Teeswater, which is much bigger. They kept the tails
on, sometimes, but we should be able to tell from the size of
the femurs ...'

Tol, on cue, proffered a leg bone and Alain inspected it.

'Too big,' he said. 'Probably Teeswater, though it could be
a Lincoln, even, if it's a bit later.'

Tol handed over another bone.

'Tail,' Alain said succinctly. 'Mmm. Odd. Neither fat-tailed nor Teeswater. This is a Bengal tail. Seen a lot of them. Stringy-looking things.' He bent down and examined some of the other bones poking up through the dirt. 'Looks like there're several breeds here. Not as early as Julieanne thought, though. Eighteen hundreds, definitely, but probably later than 1820.' He peered more closely at one particular bone, which looked like all the others to me. 'And that's a cow rib, too.'

He and Tol exchanged glances and looked down at the pit as if seeing it in a new light.

'Butchery,' Tol said.

It took me a minute to realise what he meant.

'A—a slaughterhouse?' I asked, incredulous. 'My house was an *abattoir*?'

'Well, not your actual house,' Alain said reassuringly. 'That's much later. But the site ... yes, I'd say that whatever farm was here did its butchering in this area.'

He and Tol were watching me anxiously, clearly worried that I would find the idea disgusting. Little did they know.

The laugh started in my belly and worked its way up, leaving me helplessly giggling on the floor. 'Dad's going to love this!' I gasped.

Maybe I seemed a bit hysterical. Terry actually stopped filming and came over to see if I was all right, so I pulled myself together a bit and managed to say, 'My dad was a butcher. A meat inspector. Worked in abattoirs all his life! My grandfather too!'

The men exchanged glances and then smiled, half-amused, half-relieved that they didn't have to deal with a crazy woman.

'So …' Alain wasn't quite sure what to do next.

I took a deep breath and motioned to Terry to get back behind the camera. When he signalled that he was rolling, I turned back to Alain.

'Dr Parkes, can you summarise your conclusions for us, please?'

Which he did, as neatly as if he'd been speaking at a conference.

'It's interesting,' he said at the end. 'We have known that there were several breeds of sheep used for meat in early Australia, and this is good evidence that they were grazed together on the same properties, as at that time livestock were not usually taken far before being slaughtered. So we have a very interesting insight into the working methods of the early settlers.'

We wouldn't be able to use any of that—it was much too complicated for littlies.

'Could you say that again so a six-year-old could understand it?'

Alain blinked and smiled ruefully, as if only now remembering why we were there.

'We've found bones from cows and sheep, so we know that right on this spot was a butcher's, and people who lived around here came here to get their meat. And the animals would have lived around here, too, so we know that the area was a farming area.'

'Perfect. Will you need to do more investigation?' *Please say no.*

Alain hesitated. 'I'd like to see if we can find any post holes. For the block and tackle, you know.'

I signalled 'cut' to Terry. I understood what Alain was talking about, and I was pretty sure that the Year 1 teachers did not want their six-year-old students to hear about animals being strung up by their heels while their throats were cut.

'Will that take long?' Even I could hear that my voice was plaintive.

Alain patted my hand. 'No, no, we just need to survey what we can get at here. It's just for confirmation, really. We know how they used to butcher. A day or two at the most.'

Terry was puzzled about why we'd stopped filming, so I went over and explained. He and Dave laughed and started making bad jokes about slaughterhouses and blood and horror movies. Hah! Let them. Abattoirs held no fears for me. That particular smell of fresh blood in a cold room just makes me nostalgic, full of memories of going to work with Dad during the school holidays. I said so, and had the satisfaction of shutting them up.

In the quiet, we all looked at the bearer where Julieanne's head had hit, and jokes about slaughterhouses weren't funny any more. Mirha looked green, and the men solemn.

'We're done here,' I said. 'You can head back.'

'She's tougher than she looks,' I heard Terry mutter to Dave as they started to pack up.

Tol looked as though he was thinking the same thing.

I smiled tentatively at him. 'Coffee?' I asked. 'Before you get on with the survey?'

'Great idea!' Any reservations he had about my blood-thirsty streak disappeared, and he helped Alain out of the pit with enthusiasm.

We waited until the crew had left and then walked down to Graciella's and had coffee and her fabulous pistachio macaroons. Alain told me the story of his life. He was married to a journalist and was devoted to Middle Eastern archaeology, which meant that he disappeared to Jordan for at least six weeks every year to dig. He taught at university the rest of the year and occasionally took guided tours over the sights of Egypt. He told me about his family, his career, his hopes, the book he hadn't finished writing, the books he wanted to write, and the difficulty of a career in archaeology where 'not only do you study dead men's shoes, you have to wait to fill them if you want to advance'.

Tol teased him a little at various points, but mostly just sat and let him talk. On the way back to the house, he let Alain walk ahead and said quietly to me, 'I've never heard him talk that way to anyone apart from his wife.'

I shrugged. 'Happens to me all the time,' I said. 'People talk to me. I've just got that kind of face, I guess.'

He studied my face intently, and I wondered what he was seeing. Whatever it was, his eyes softened and he smiled. My breath came a little faster.

'Lucky Stuart,' he said, then quickened his pace to catch up with Alain. For some reason, that made me sad.

When we went back to the house they started on the dirt outside the central pit, seeing what they could find. I went upstairs, prompted by a need to make sure Julieanne hadn't left any other signs of her presence behind. Surely Detective Chloe would have taken anything away? The chipboard floors had always had stains—were there any new ones? I couldn't see any. But in the built-in wardrobe (the only modern thing in the house) I found a couple of bottles of wine in the bottom. Red. Jacob's Creek—a nice drop, but not too expensive. And not mine. I had reached out to pick one up then thought better of it. If they were Julieanne's …

I rang Stuart.

'You didn't leave any wine at the house, did you?'

'At *your* house?'

'Yes,' I said. 'As a surprise, maybe?'

'Was I supposed to?'

I sighed. 'No. But I found two bottles in the wardrobe.'

'Oh.'

'Julieanne, Stuart,' I said. 'Maybe they were Julieanne's.'

'Maybe they belong to the film crew.'

But I didn't think so. Red wine gave Terry migraines and Dave drank beer. And Mirha never drank alcohol.

'Um, I have to go,' Stuart said. He sounded distracted. I should have remembered he didn't like being called at work.

'Bye,' I said absently, thinking hard.

I decided to call my friend the police officer.

'They weren't yours?' Detective Chloe said suspiciously. 'They were with other things of yours that had your fingerprints on them.' Ah, yes. The yoga mat, the condoms—the accessories of sex that I couldn't keep at my parents'.

'What about the bottles? Whose fingerprints did they have?'

There was a pause. 'We didn't print everything. Once we found your prints and your boyfriend's prints on the other things, we assumed …'

I restrained myself from pointing out her mistake.

After a second, she said, 'Have you touched them?'

'I'm not that stupid!'

'Stay there. I'll send Martin over for them.'

'She was meeting someone here,' I said, a touch of complaint in my voice. 'Who, do you think? My money's on Carter.'

'Martin will be there within an hour,' Detective Chloe said. She hung up.

I obediently waited until Steve Martin arrived and let him go upstairs in his natty latex gloves before explaining to Tol and Alain what it was all about.

Tol looked grim, and too late I remembered that if Julieanne had been meeting someone, she'd been two-timing him. Not only was it a horrible thing to find out, it gave him a terrific motive for killing her.

It was clear that Detective Martin thought so too. When he came downstairs with the bottles inside a big evidence bag, he approached Tol.

'Lost your temper, eh?' he said. He lifted the bottles. 'Found out she was screwing someone else and lost it?' He nodded. 'I can understand that.'

He went on for some time, trying to be the good cop, *us blokes know how it goes, you can trust me I'm just like you, I understand* … a tactic that's supposed to be irresistible to someone racked with guilt.

And right then and there, I became completely convinced that Tol hadn't killed Julieanne. I don't know why, exactly. Something about the set of his mouth—a barely restrained impatience with Martin, irritation at being interrupted at his job. No guilt at all. I was filled with irrational happiness. It didn't matter, did it? But it did.

Tol let Constable Martin talk himself out and then said, in a calm, reasonable voice, 'I didn't know about it. I don't know who she was meeting. I didn't kill her.'

It infuriated Martin, but there was nothing he could do. He left grumpily.

Tol stood in the pit and looked up at me. His eyes were bleak. 'Do you think I killed her?'

'No,' I said.

He didn't smile, but his eyes warmed and the corners of his mouth unclenched a little.

'Good,' he said. He turned back to the floor of my house, searching between the uncovered beams for evidence of slaughter. I looked at the bearer where Julieanne's head had hit and shivered. Slaughterhouse, I thought, but I couldn't afford to think like that. I loved this house. So I pushed the images of Julieanne as a lamb to the slaughter out of my head. *More like a goat*, I told myself and somehow that image stayed with me. *A sacrificial goat*.

CHAPTER EIGHTEEN

That night, Stuart came over for tea for my sister Carol's birthday. A family birthday like that gathers in around twenty people, all of whom can carry on at least two conversations at once. It was just the usual family spread: roast lamb, turkey roll with stuffing, ham, roast vegetables, gravy, cauliflower with white sauce, my Aunty Samantha's crumbed pumpkin mash (fantastic!) and peas, as a vague concession to good health.

Everyone loved the fact that my house had been a butchery, especially Dad. My nephews (eight and ten) wanted to come over and dig for skeletons so they could take them to school.

'Any skulls?' Josh asked. 'A sheep skull would be cool.'

'I'll ask Tol to save you one if he finds any,' I promised.

'You were meant to get that house,' Aunty Mary declared. 'It's a sign.'

I thought so too.

We were in the middle of the meal, with Stuart advising on superannuation choices for my brother and another of my aunts, and everyone for once was listening in case he let fall some information that would make them rich, when the doorbell rang.

My nephews raced to answer it, and went silent.

'Who is it?' my mother called. 'Bill, you go and see.'

My father hoisted himself up and disappeared to the front door, then came back leading Detectives Chloe and Martin.

'Could we have a word with the two of you, in private?' Chloe asked me and Stuart.

The table of faces turned to stare at her, at me, at Stuart, and back at her. She remained stolid, but Detective Martin shifted from foot to foot.

'Are you going to jail? Cool!' Josh said.

'Course she's not!' his older brother said scornfully. 'Like she could kill anyone!'

'She could too!' Josh was defending my honour, I knew, but the timing was unfortunate.

The family was divided between laughing and shushing the boys. My cousin Mark, who was a police sergeant in Randwick, said, 'Hey, Steve,' to Martin, who nodded back warily. I grinned and winked at Josh and led the police into the kitchen, Stuart following.

'Hungry?' I asked, indicating the platters of ham and turkey.

Chloe looked momentarily rueful, as though she were very hungry but it was against regulations or something to take food from a suspect. I started to put food into the take-away containers Mum used to store leftovers.

'We don't appreciate having our time wasted,' Detective Chloe said.

'Sorry?' I asked, puzzled.

'Did you think it was funny, sending us on a wild goose chase after the wine?'

I just stared at her, not understanding at all. Next to me, Stuart moved his feet uneasily, and I glanced at him.

He looked at me and hissed, 'You told the *police*?'

'Of course I told the police!' I said. 'Why shouldn't I?' Then it dawned on me. '*Your* fingerprints were on the wine? You did put it there, didn't you?'

He winced. 'Um, well—'

'*When* did you put the wine there, Mr Douglas?' Chloe said with an edge to her voice.

Stuart floundered. 'Um, well, what happened was, you see, it was just a coincidence …'

'For God's sake, Stuart, just spit it out!' I snarled. He'd *lied* to me. Actually, reviewing our conversation about the wine, he hadn't exactly lied. He'd just avoided answering. Avoided it with great skill.

He flushed. 'I was coming over here,' he said defensively. 'And I walked past the house, because I was hoping that, er—well, that you'd be there, Poppy, and we could, um ... which was why I had the wine ... Anyway, I walked past the house and the light upstairs was on, so I knocked at the door, and that woman answered, like she was expecting someone.'

'This was Tuesday night?' Chloe specified. Stuart nodded, sweating.

'What time?'

'Seven o'clock. But nothing happened!' he protested. 'I just told her who I was and I wanted to put the wine in the bedroom for later and she—she let me.'

'She let a strange man into my house?' I asked.

'She knew me!' he said. 'She'd seen us together that first night they were digging there.'

I'd forgotten that.

'And then?' Chloe prompted. Martin was taking notes.

'Then I left,' Stuart said. He looked relieved, as though he'd finished something difficult, but it wasn't over yet, not by a long shot, and if he thought it was ... Not for the first time, I wondered just how bright Stuart was. At accountancy, obviously, but his people skills were a bit suss. 'I went home.'

'Why not come here?' I asked.

He ran his hand over his head, embarrassed. 'I just wasn't in the mood to socialise with your family.'

Softly, Detective Chloe said, 'That makes you the last person to see Julieanne Weaver alive.'

I couldn't resist it. I said, 'Except the person who killed her.'

'Let me tell you how we think it went, Stuart,' Martin cut in. 'We think you went in all ready for a bit of nooky and then Poppy wasn't there. But Julieanne was. Looking pretty good, too, eh? And maybe you thought, a bird in the hand … and tried it on. Put the wine upstairs and maybe suggested she share it with you. But she wasn't interested. Went downstairs. Asked you to leave, maybe. And then you got angry. Don't like being told no, do you? You're a big bloke, didn't take much, just a push. She was in those high heels, wasn't she? Just a little push. She went off balance and over she went, hit her head and it was too late.'

'We know you didn't mean to kill her,' Chloe said.

It sounded so plausible. The trouble with being a scriptwriter is that you see everything in terms of film scenes. I could imagine it. Low, noir lighting. Julieanne in her tight blue dress, Stuart looming over her, a push on her shoulder, a stumble … that all seemed just possible—but Stuart being pushy about sex? I couldn't imagine that.

Chloe seemed to read my mind.

'Maybe it wasn't about sex,' she said. 'Did she say something about Poppy? Julieanne didn't like her, did she? Were you defending her?'

I tried to imagine that, too, but somehow that was even less believable than Stuart trying it on with Julieanne. Which was a thought I put aside for later.

Stuart was shaking his head. 'No way! She was fine when I left. Anxious to get rid of me. I think she was waiting for someone.'

'Any idea who?' Martin pounced.

'A man. I'm pretty sure it was a man.'

'Why?'

Stuart hesitated. 'The way she opened the door … The way she stood … She smiled—and then she saw it was me. Her whole face changed. I don't know—she was expecting a man.'

There was a pause. Stuart couldn't resist filling the silence.

'She looked hot,' he said. 'And—triumphant, sort of. As though she was going to get something she really wanted.'

'A lover?' Chloe mused out loud.

'Preselection,' I said.

But Martin wasn't going to let go of Stuart that easily. 'Why didn't you tell us you were there?'

'You didn't ask,' Stuart said weakly.

Martin snorted.

'Why didn't you tell *me* you were there?' I asked. I felt vicious. I wanted to bitch-slap him. How dare he? How *dare* he lie to me about things that happened in *my* house?

He hung his head and looked like a sad beagle. 'I just didn't want to get involved in the—the—' he indicated Chloe and Martin.

'We'd like a DNA sample,' Martin said.

Stuart blinked. 'A DNA sample? What for? We didn't—I told you, nothing happened!'

'Then there's no reason not to give us a sample, is there?' Chloe said.

'I don't think I want to do that, or answer any more questions, without a solicitor present,' Stuart said suddenly.

He stood straighter, looking like someone at home in international boardrooms.

Chloe nodded, tucking a strand of brown hair behind her ear. 'Certainly, Mr Douglas,' she said. 'We'd like you to come into headquarters tomorrow and make a formal statement. By all means bring your solicitor.' She handed him her card. 'Ten o'clock would be convenient.'

Stuart took the card reluctantly, as though he hadn't expected that. 'I'll see you there,' he said.

'Might be a good time to go home, then,' I said. 'And ring your solicitor.'

He flinched at my tone, but one look at my face told him that it wasn't the right time to try to talk me out of it.

'Of course,' he said, quite formally. 'I'll go now.'

He left by the back door, wimping out on walking past the family, and let the door slam shut behind him. Rude pig! He could at least have said goodbye to Mum.

I hesitated. There was something Stuart had said that I just didn't believe. Should I tell Chloe? Again I felt like a stupid suspect in a murder mystery, the one who held back the vital piece of information. But he was my boyfriend … *Not any more*, part of me whispered. *Not on your life.*

'He was lying,' I blurted out.

Detective Chloe spun towards me, eyes intent. 'What?'

'He said it was seven o'clock.'

'So?'

'He never misses the seven o'clock news. Never.'

Martin humphed. 'He must—'

'*Never,*' I said. 'It's a ritual. I believe him about everything else, but I guarantee you it wasn't seven o'clock.'

They thought that through, and Martin smiled. I shivered.

'We'd prefer it,' Chloe said, 'if you didn't contact Mr Douglas again before his interview.'

'Hah!' I said. 'I may never contact *Mr Douglas* ever again.'

She smiled tightly. 'I don't blame you,' she said. It was the first sign of humanity in a while from her. 'You really didn't know about it, did you?'

I shook my head. 'I thought Julieanne had put the wine there herself. For whatever assignation she was there for.'

'And you nominate Carter?'

'Seems likely to me. Why else would he champion her for preselection? She didn't exactly fit the party image.'

'There's a problem with that theory,' Martin said. He looked to Chloe for permission, and she nodded. 'Carter has a cast-iron alibi. He was called to a meeting at the church to discuss the preselection. They were at it until one in the morning.'

I mulled that over. 'That doesn't mean she wasn't expecting him,' I said. 'Maybe someone else turned up instead.'

'Someone like Douglas,' Martin said with satisfaction. 'Innocent people don't ask for solicitors.'

I felt I had to say something in his defence. 'Stuart works with solicitors all the time. It would feel more natural to him than to most people.'

'Maybe,' Chloe said.

I had to know if Stuart really was a suspect, so I said, 'Was she really killed? Deliberately, I mean? Or could it have been an accident?' Please let it have been an accident.

Chloe paused, then shrugged. 'I can't tell you the details, but she was definitely murdered.'

I felt sick.

'Someone who hated her,' I said. 'Really hated her.'

'Or was angry. Or afraid,' Chloe said. 'Violence has a lot of causes.' That was the voice of an experienced cop, world-weary and full of distaste.

'Stuart barely knew her.'

Martin sneered down at me. 'Refused by a pretty woman? Doesn't take much to get a horny man angry. We see it all the time.'

Depressingly, I knew he was right, even though I had trouble seeing Stuart in that role.

Chloe glanced towards the dining room, which was full of eloquent silence. The family had heard the back door slam and were waiting for me to come back in. She smiled with real humour. 'We'll let you get back to your meal,' she said.

I put the lids on the takeaway containers and silently offered them to her. Chloe held my eyes for a moment, then took them.

'Thanks,' she said. 'Come on, Steve.'

They left through the back door, too, but they closed it quietly. I went into the dining room and spent the next ten minutes fielding questions. I told them all the truth (except about why Stuart might want to find me alone in the house). And why not? Discussing Stuart's perfidy was the perfect way to let off steam. I found that I didn't even want to defend him when my brothers started tearing him to shreds. He deserved it. And he was everything my brothers said he was: anal, weird, rigid.

My mother was trying hard to think the best of him. 'Perhaps it happened just the way he described.'

'Even if it did, Mum, he should have told me about it.'

Suddenly I felt like crying. Stuart hadn't been the love of my life, but we'd been close. I felt like I'd been deceived, betrayed, duped. How well did I really know him? I felt stupid and that, of course, made me angry.

'He's a wuss,' Josh said, summing it up with an eight-year-old's insight. 'He was scared of the police.'

Right on the money, Josh. But the question was, did Stuart have reason to be scared? Had I been sleeping with a murderer?

CHAPTER NINETEEN

Wednesday

Stuart tried to call me three times the next day. I ignored all the calls and finally blocked his number for both calls and texts. Then I spent a nice calm morning at work, dealing with lots of minor matters that had accumulated while I'd been out of the office, and viewing the rough cut of the Luna Park episode. Jennifer Jay wanted some archival footage of the park opening so I toddled over to Ultimo and had a pleasant afternoon spooling through footage from the opening in 1935, the re-opening in 1982 and the re-re-opening in 1995. I found the story of the park reassuring—in spite of all the machinations of big business, Sydneysiders' love of the place had kept it alive.

Then I came across the story of the Luna Park Ghost Train fire in 1979, which killed six people: a man and his two sons, and four other boys who were there together. The man and his sons had been on a family outing, and his wife wasn't on the train because she wanted an ice cream. She watched the ride burn and had to be dragged away from it by security guards, knowing her family was inside. I watched the news reports of the time, and then googled it. There were all sorts of explanations including rumours of gangland involvement and arson, but faulty electrical wiring was the official verdict. Forty years later, no one was sure what had happened. I sat in the viewing room and cried for the dead and the bereaved, and for Julieanne, remembering coming off the roller coaster and getting the phone call that had told me Julieanne was dead. Exhilaration and death, happiness and grief.

It was too dark a story for the little kids who would watch the program, for which I was glad. I wasn't sure I'd ever want to go back to Luna Park.

I went straight from Ultimo to my house, and opened the front door in time to find Detective Chloe asking Tol for a DNA sample.

Why would they be asking for DNA so long after the death? If Julieanne had had sex just before she was killed, they'd have known that straight away, wouldn't they? They wouldn't have needed a full autopsy to tell them that—

She'd been pregnant. They wanted Stuart's and Tol's DNA to see who the father was.

Julieanne, pregnant. I hoped, fervently, that it hadn't been Tol's baby, but I wasn't sure why.

Tol was still in the pit, although Alain had climbed out and was standing uncomfortably to one side. The fact that Tol wasn't showing his usual good manners made me uneasy. He was looking mutinous—much the same look as he'd had when I'd suggested interviewing him for the show.

Detective Chloe was playing the mild-mannered nice cop. I slid into the room and nodded at them all. Tol nodded back, but he still glowered at Chloe.

'I thought you said she didn't have sex with anyone that night,' he said.

'I don't think I said exactly that,' Detective Chloe answered calmly.

'But why now?' he said. 'Why didn't you ask me before?'

I sat on the edge of the pit, not quite next to Tol.

'I reckon it's because she was pregnant, and the autopsy showed it,' I said gently. His face went completely blank for a split second. I glanced at Detective Chloe. Apart from being cross with me, she wasn't showing anything, which meant I was right.

'You can have the DNA sample,' Tol said sharply, 'but the baby's not mine. I always use condoms.'

'I', I noticed. Not 'we'.

'A baby,' I said to Detective Chloe, 'would only be a motive for murder if the relationship was a secret.'

'Nice try, Poppy,' she said. 'But babies bring a lot of complications, even in a marriage. Easy for a man to get angry about having a baby sprung on him.' She held up a finger in warning. '*Not* that I have confirmed that Dr Weaver was pregnant.'

'Huh,' I said. 'So who got angry?' I turned to Tol. 'Since it couldn't have been yours—who got angry?'

'The baby might not have anything to do with her death,' he said, sounding as if he was hoping it did. I did, too. If he was so happy to give the DNA, that meant it really couldn't be his, and he would no longer be number one suspect.

'Or a man might get angry,' Chloe said softly, 'if he found out his girlfriend was pregnant by another man.'

Bugger. That hadn't occurred to me.

'I don't think so,' he said to Chloe, his expression one of pure disbelief. 'Not unless he was in love with her.'

'And you weren't?'

He flicked a look sideways at me, and I tried to pretend that I wasn't interested in the answer.

'No,' he said. 'I wasn't.'

But there was something in his voice.

Chloe heard it too. 'Was that a problem?' she asked.

He grimaced. 'She wanted to—she wanted the package, I think: marriage, husband, house in the suburbs. Not because she loved me; it was more politics than anything else. She wanted—she *needed* to seem normal to get what she wanted.'

'Normal? Wasn't she normal enough?'

Tol and I looked at each other, and we both shook our heads.

'Not the Australian Family Party kind of normal,' I said.

'Not any kind, really,' Tol added. 'She was an odd woman. Beautiful, but … very intense. Very *focussed*.'

'The sort to do anything to get what she wanted?' Chloe prompted. Like good puppets, we nodded agreement together.

'Hmm,' Chloe said. She took out a long specimen jar with a cotton bud in it and handed it to Tol. We've all seen the procedure on TV. He took it, rubbed the cotton bud on the inside of his cheek, hard, put it in the jar and handed it back.

She labelled the jar carefully across the seal and got him to initial the label. Then she tucked it into her bag and looked at the two of us. Alain had melted right into the background; out into the backyard, I thought.

'I wish you two had better alibis,' she said. 'If we had even a skerrick more evidence you'd both be under arrest for conspiracy to murder.'

'Come on, Chloe,' I said. 'You know we didn't do it. Think about it logically—if Tol cared about Julieanne enough to resent her being pregnant, he wouldn't be conspiring with me. If he didn't care enough, he's got no reason to kill her.'

'Except to be free to be with you,' Chloe said, as if that was obvious.

'Dr Lang,' I said, 'is going back to Jordan very shortly to take up his permanent position as the assistant head of the Australian Institute of Archaeology in Amman. He's hardly going to kill someone so he can have a holiday fling.' I avoided looking at Tol.

'Is that true?' Chloe asked him.

He nodded. 'Next month,' he said. 'I was just filling in time with this job.'

'So you had a very good reason to be angry if Julieanne deliberately got pregnant with your baby,' she said. 'Let's hope the DNA doesn't match. Or you might not be getting on that plane.'

She collected Martin with a nod of the head, and they left.

For a moment, we both stared at the floor of the pit, now free of bones.

'It's not my baby,' he stated.

'Good,' I said.

We looked at each other, but we didn't smile.

'You might have been a lot of things, but you wouldn't have been a holiday fling,' he said. His eyes were greener, today, reflecting his T-shirt, and the pupils were larger in the evening light. Or maybe just because he was looking at me.

He was leaving, so getting involved with him would be really, really stupid.

'I've broken up with Stuart,' I said. More or less true. I'd text him later, but I figured he'd already know I was pissed off with him.

Tol took a long breath and reached out a hand to my cheek. His fingers were dirty, but I didn't care. My heart was pounding and I felt warm from head to toe. Flamingly alive, as though each separate fingertip was an energy source that flooded me with heat. I turned my face into his hand, and he moved towards me.

Then the back door banged and Alain came back into the room, peering around the corner to make sure Detective Chloe was gone. He grinned when he saw us.

'Oops!' he said. 'Do you want me to go away?'

The moment was gone and I was sane again.

'No,' I said, scrambling up. 'I'll see you tomorrow. We need to redo the interview I did with Julieanne. I'll see you here in the morning.'

Tol nodded without looking at me and I left as quickly as I could without actually running. Six weeks, I reminded myself. He'd be gone in six weeks.

Detective Chloe was still standing by her car outside, talking on her phone. She saw me come out and waved at me to wait for her, so I leant against my picket fence, which needed new paint.

'Tomorrow,' she confirmed with whoever was on the other end. 'Early.' She put the phone back in her pocket. 'I don't want to hear a story about Weaver being pregnant on *The Daily Report*,' she said with a stern eye.

'Unconfirmed sources? That's not the way Tyler works. He likes hard evidence. It's the ABC, after all.'

She nodded. 'You think Carter was the father.'

I shrugged. 'It's a great motive for murder—and it doesn't even have to be Carter who killed her. Could be anyone in the church or the party. Carter getting a single woman pregnant and then promoting her for preselection? The radio talkbacks would go mad.' I hesitated. 'Off the record—has Carter given a DNA sample?'

'Haven't asked him yet. We have to exclude the obvious ones first—your Dr Lang, Mr Douglas, Paul Baume ...'

'Gerry Collonucci?'

'I thought they despised each other?'

'They did. But he was very smug about his alibi. I'd check those students of hers out, too. Especially the one with acne. He and Gerry are alibi-ing each other and it stinks to high heaven.'

Chloe looked at me with some exasperation. 'Anyone else?'

I thought it over. 'Ask Patience Carter,' I said at last. 'If there's been anyone at the church or the party, she'll have noticed. She's a smart girl.'

'I doubt Matthew Carter will let me talk to her alone.'

'Doesn't have to be alone,' I said. 'You're not asking her to implicate her father. He'll probably be glad if she can suggest someone else.'

It was a fine evening, and Chloe turned her face to the last rays of the sun as though seeking some benediction. 'I loathe cases like this,' she said. 'Most murders, you know who it is, or at least you have a good idea, even if you can't prove it. But this one—' She shook her head wearily.

I had the distinct impression that she didn't think I was the murderer any more. But I wasn't so sure about Tol.

'Do you suspect anyone in particular?' I asked quietly.

'You mean, do I think Lang did it?' She looked back at the house, where they'd turned on the light so that it shone through the window and we could see the men's shadows moving across the walls, huge and distorted. 'I learnt a long time ago, Poppy, that anyone can kill, given the right circumstances.'

It wasn't exactly comforting.

'How did Stuart go this morning?' I asked, more to break the silence than anything else.

'He gave us the sample and a statement,' she said. 'We're waiting on his phone records to confirm that he went home as he said.' She turned to look at me closely. 'How did you two meet?'

'Paul Baume introduced us at a museum exhibition opening,' I said. 'He and Stuart went to school together.' I paused. Detective Chloe's brown eyes were intent on my face. A thought was hitting both of us at the same time. 'He and Stuart went to school together. But ... Stuart never mentioned meeting Julieanne. Even before all this happened.'

'Odd.'

It was odd. Of course, Paul *was* odd. He didn't necessarily follow the normal rules of social behaviour. He might not have introduced Stuart to his girlfriend. But Detective Chloe looked like she might be planning to ask Stuart a few more questions.

'How do you think Stuart would have reacted to Julieanne being pregnant with his child?'

Badly. Very badly.

'It would have depended on what she wanted him to do,' I temporised.

'If she wanted marriage?'

I shook my head automatically. 'Stuart doesn't want to get married.'

Chloe smiled grimly. 'So here's a question for you—would you rather the killer was the man you've already slept with, or the man you'd like to sleep with?'

I was too experienced an interviewer to fall for that one. 'I would *rather*,' I said, 'that the killer was someone I don't know.'

She grimaced. 'Wouldn't we all? But it usually isn't, I'm afraid.'

And that was that. She drove off in that way cops have of accelerating immediately to the speed limit and I walked home slowly, half hoping that Tol would catch up with me, and half hoping he wouldn't.

He didn't. But I texted Stuart anyway. *Please stop calling me.* I know it's tacky to break up by text, but I was still so pissed off with him that I didn't care. And Detective Chloe's questions had made me realise that I didn't really know—or trust—Stuart at all. Besides, it was Wednesday. He wouldn't thank me for interrupting laundry night.

CHAPTER TWENTY

Thursday

I met the film crew at the house in the morning and we recreated the interview we'd done the first day with Julieanne, but this time with me asking Tol the questions. It was horrible—Banquo's ghost was with us the whole time, and Tol's answers were mechanical and short. I didn't blame him.

In the end, I said, 'Forget this, let's take the bones back to the museum and do it there.'

The team all greeted this suggestion with relief and we packed up. The camera crew headed out and Tol and I picked up the remaining specimens of bones and bagged and labelled them. As we went out the door a white council van drove up and the man who'd brought the heritage order over the day Julieanne had been found got out. What was his name? Fozina, that was it.

'Mr Fozina,' I said. 'What can we do for you?'

'Are you still working on this house?' he said suspiciously, brandishing a clipboard. 'The heritage order is still in force, you know!'

'This,' I said, indicating Tol, 'is Dr Lang, an archaeologist from the Museum of New South Wales, who has taken over following Dr Weaver's sad death. And you'll be pleased to know that he has proven conclusively that this was not the site of an early pastoral lease featuring fat-tailed sheep.'

At last, something's going right. I'd get this guy to sign off on the order and I could book in the electricians.

'Is this true?' Fozina demanded of Tol.

I'd never seen Tol try to be impressive before. He did a pretty good job. Being about six inches taller than Fozina probably helped.

'Certainly. There is no doubt at all. My colleague Dr Parkes from the University of Sydney has confirmed it beyond question. He is a world-renowned expert on animal bones.'

Fozina considered this, pushing his lips out so that he looked like a baby in a grump. 'Council is meeting on Friday night. If you want the order rescinded, you'll have to present your case then.' He looked at me and said, 'I'll get it put on the agenda.' Clearly thought he was doing me a favour, but I wasn't feeling grateful.

'Why can't you just accept Dr Lang's report?'

'Well,' he said, 'I can table the report, but there's a couple of councillors who are pretty gung-ho about heritage, so if you want to be sure the order is lifted …'

Bugger. I turned to Tol pleadingly.

He decided to be funny. 'Friday?' he said. 'Oh, I don't know. I might have other plans …'

I hit him on the arm. 'Tol!'

He grinned and tousled my hair. Despite my anxiety over the house, I noticed how natural it felt for him to tease me—as though we'd known each other for years. The way my friend Alex and I mucked around.

'What time?' he asked Fozina.

'Six o'clock sharp. And it helps if you have ten copies of the report.'

'If you write it, I'll print it,' I said to Tol.

'Who's paying me?' Another joke.

'The museum,' I said.

He grinned. What was he so happy about?

Then Fozina peered behind us to look inside the house.

'Are the police finished now?' he asked. 'I heard she was really beat up.'

Tol stopped smiling. 'I'll see you at the museum,' he said to me, and walked to his car.

'What's with him?' Fozina said.

'It was his girlfriend.'

'Oh. Oh, shit. Sorry.'

'Mmm. Can I have a copy of the heritage order?'

He detached it from his clipboard and handed it over. 'Word of advice? Keep it simple. Some of those councillors don't read so good.'

Wonderful. Democracy in action.

'Thanks,' I said. 'We will.'

At the museum, the crew had set up in front of an archaeological exhibit, with a circle of interested schoolkids whom
Mirha had warned to keep quiet. See how useful it is to
have an experienced crew? Tol was sombre, but he answered
the questions fluently and we got what we needed. The Tol
who had joked about skeletons was gone. After Terry and
the others left, I touched him on the arm.

'Are you all right?'

'Do you know how she died?' he asked abruptly. '*Was* she
beaten up? Was she—hurt badly?'

'I don't think so,' I said. 'From the questions Chloe's been
asking, it sounds like she fell—was pushed—backwards
and hit her head on the bearer.'

Some of the tension went out of his shoulders and he let
out a sigh.

'It doesn't seem real,' he said. 'I keep expecting her to
come around a corner.'

'I know.'

We stood there in the middle of the exhibition with the
kids yelling and bickering around us, and had nothing to say.

'I'll send you the report,' he said eventually. He walked
through the door that said STAFF ONLY and I went back to
Artarmon feeling depressed.

I found Paul Baume sitting in my visitor's chair.

'Paul?' Why was he here? Surely not to confess or talk
over his relationship with Julieanne?

He stood. 'Stuart asked me to talk to you.'

'And you *agreed*?'

'He's very upset. He thinks you don't really understand—'

'What I understand is that he *lied* to me. He saw Julieanne that night and he never mentioned it!'

Jennifer Jay perched on a nearby desk and listened unashamedly. So did Mirha and the other PAs. Fine by me. Stuart was dead meat as far as I was concerned.

'I know. He didn't want to get involved.'

'And now he's not involved. With me.'

Jennifer Jay and the girls applauded.

Paul shrugged. He'd done his job, and he wasn't going to push it. But he didn't leave. He glanced at Jennifer Jay and moved closer to me. 'Can I have a word in private?'

I led him into the viewing room where we watched the rushes and closed the door. He looked around and apparently found the available chairs unappealing. Too dirty, maybe. Unhygienic.

'Was Julieanne pregnant?' he blurted out.

'Why?'

'They asked me for a DNA sample. Stuart too. He thinks she might have been pregnant.'

'Detective Sergeant Prudhomme wouldn't confirm that.'

'But she didn't deny it?'

'No.'

He started pacing the tiny room. 'It wasn't Stuart,' he muttered. 'And it wasn't me. Could have been Lang, I suppose.'

'Paul?' I asked gently.

He whirled on me and I took a step back. In this small space I realised just how big he was. How strong. In a flash, the noir scene I had imagined between Stuart and Julieanne changed to a scene with Paul. He loomed much more believably than Stuart.

'What if I knew—thought I might know—the father?'

'You should tell Chloe,' I said promptly. 'Detective Prud-homme, I mean.'

He shook his head. 'I don't know …' He was pacing still, his hands picking at the sides of his trousers. 'I shouldn't have been watching her …'

I felt a prickle of excitement. 'You followed her? That night?'

'No, no, I knew where she was that night. But before …'

I could see it. She'd broken up with him, and he'd had to find out why. Who. So he followed her.

'Who did she meet, Paul?'

'She used to wait for him around the corner from that church,' he said, looking at the dark row of video screens as though looking back in time. As though he could see Julieanne again. 'He'd get in her car and they'd go—places.'

Motels, probably.

'Carter?' I prodded. 'Matthew Carter?'

'I don't know his name.'

'He's been on the news.'

'He was in that story you did for *The Daily Report*,' Paul said. 'Stuart and I watched that.'

'I thought that was laundry night?' I asked, exasperated.

'That's right,' he said. 'We do our laundry together on Wednesdays.'

Now if I'd known *that* I'd never have gone out with Stuart in the first place. The image of them ritually washing clothes and watching TV together was creeping me out.

So. Carter. Or Winchester? No, surely not, especially if Rick's gaydar was right. But I'd better check.

'Not the old guy? The pastor?'

'No, no.' Paul shook his head. 'Not him. The other one.'

That was a relief.

'She met the old guy a few times, but it was in a café,' he added.

'Amos Winchester?'

'The pastor guy.'

So she might not have been sleeping with Amos, but she could have been blackmailing him. 'Can I tell Detective Prudhomme this, Paul?'

'Don't mention me!'

'All right. I'll just say a source told me that Julieanne was having an affair with Carter.'

'With the guy from the church,' he amended. 'I don't know his name.'

Bloody curators. They need every i to be dotted and t crossed.

'The guy from the church,' I agreed. 'And that she met with Winchester.' Although that could have been purely party related.

He ran a hand through his hair. 'I suppose,' he said. He looked straight into my eyes, and I could see that he was haunted. 'I know she was ... not a good person. But we were close. I miss her.'

What could I say? I just nodded and stood there silently while he left.

Then I rang Chloe. She wanted to know my source, of course, but we got that out of the way and I repeated Paul's information word for word.

'A guy from the church who was in that story you did for *The Daily Report*,' she said thoughtfully.

'And *not* Winchester,' I added. 'I checked that.'

'God, I should hope not!' she said, then coughed to cover the lapse in correct form.

'She did meet Winchester several times, apparently, but only in a café.'

Chloe dismissed that. 'Probably just preselection business.'

Should I tell her Rick's assessment of the pastor? Something in me just refused to believe he was a killer. Despite the fact that I hated everything he preached. But because I hesitated, the moment was lost.

'Getting into a car clandestinely …' Chloe mused.

'Is it enough to ask for a DNA sample from Carter?' I asked hopefully.

'I doubt it. Anonymous tip-offs rarely convince a magistrate to issue a warrant.'

'You could just ask.'

'Mmm. Why are you being so helpful?'

'Because a couple of days ago you thought I did it. Another suspect sounds like a great idea to me. Especially Carter.'

She laughed. 'You really don't like him, huh?'

'He believes in submissive wives,' I said.

There was a short silence on the other end. 'Fair enough.'

She hung up. Not only no goodbye, no thanks either. But I was feeling much more cheerful. Chloe would arrest Carter—break that alibi of his, maybe—and the investigation would be over. Now, if we could just get the council to lift the heritage ban, I could get back to concentrating on my house. I badly wanted to call the electricians, but I didn't want to jinx the council meeting. All right, it was irrational, but better safe than sorry.

Out of nowhere, I was hit by a feeling that things were never going to go back to normal. That I'd never get my house finished. That I'd end up living forever at my parents, with my ex-boyfriend doing laundry with his school friend and my potential boyfriend digging up walls in Jordan while I never had sex again.

I went over to Jennifer Jay's desk.

'I think I'll take tomorrow off in lieu of that day I had to work for Tyler,' I said.

She looked me over and patted me on the arm, a thing she'd never done before. 'Good idea. You look like shit.'

Which about summed it up.

CHAPTER TWENTY-ONE

Friday

I spent a curiously soothing morning looking at kitchens. The kitchen-to-be in my house was small, which meant that proper planning was essential. That being so, my sister Theresa came with Mum and me. Theresa is my oldest sister, a solicitor, and an extremely organised person. She'd just renovated her kitchen, so she was full of experience and good advice. And questions.

'What's Matthew Carter like?'

'Smooth,' I said, opening soft-close drawers and letting them slide shut again. Easy to use, but expensive, and with all the mechanisms hidden. A bit like Carter.

'They're doing great work,' Theresa said.

'The church, she means, not the party,' Mum added, checking out a particularly clever corner cupboard that unfolded like a concertina.

'Radiant Joy?'

Theresa bridled at my tone. 'What's wrong with them?'

Oh dear. I should have known Theresa would like Radiant Joy. She is very conservative. More so even than Mum and Dad, although they wouldn't admit that.

'Prosperity gospel? I know you don't believe in that.'

'That's not all they believe in. At least they don't allow same-sex marriages!'

I just looked at her. We'd had that fight too many times before; I wasn't going to engage in it again, especially with Mum looking at me pleadingly from the other side of the display counter. Theresa huffed, and changed tack.

'They're getting all the young people in, and that's more than you can say for the Catholics!'

'That's true,' I admitted, and her ruffled feathers settled down. It *was* true, which made it all the more depressing. I've had lots of practice at deflecting arguments with Theresa, so I said, 'What do you think about induction cooktops?'

While Theresa went around gathering up brochures, my mother slid her arm through mine. 'She means well,' she said.

'She's a homophobic right-wing nutjob, Mum.'

Mum laughed as though I were joking and, reluctantly, I smiled.

'She just feels things very strongly.'

'I wish she'd pick her enthusiasms a bit more carefully.'

'Try to get along. She wants to be helpful.'

Which was true. Theresa loved being helpful.

We pondered pantries, benchtops, cupboards, deep drawers, narrow drawers, splashbacks and sinks, and then moved on to ovens, cooktops and grillers. Did I mention I like to cook? I wanted marble for the benchtop for when I made pastry. It was too expensive. Everything was too expensive.

'If you need a loan ...' Theresa said quietly, while Mum was checking out the engineered-stone benchtops. This is why I can't stay cross at her. She's so kind.

'Thanks, but I'd rather not get into any more debt. The ABC doesn't pay me enough!'

'You should get a proper job. With your research skills, you could walk into any law firm in the country and be earning twice what you're getting!'

'But would they let me get up at six o'clock in the morning to ride the roller coaster at Luna Park?' I grinned at her, and she reluctantly laughed.

'You'll never get Poppy to commit to nine to five,' Mum said over our shoulders. 'She always hated routine, even as a baby. I could never predict when she'd need a feed. Or do a poo. Not like you, Theresa. You were as regular as clockwork.'

Nothing like family, right? At least she hadn't said that in front of Tol.

Theresa went home and Mum and I rewarded ourselves with decadent hot chocolates and macarons at a nearby café.

'What's the matter?' Mum asked.

I realised that I'd been silently stirring my marshmallow into my hot chocolate for so long it had completely melted. 'Julieanne is dead. Someone I know, or at least have met, probably murdered her *in my house*. My renovations are stalled for who knows how long, and … Do you think that someone can be happy if they deny who they are?' I was still tussling with the enigma of Amos Winchester.

Mum sat back and went a little white. 'Oh my lord. Is this your coming out speech?'

'What? No! What?'

She went boneless. 'Oh, thank God. We've been worried.'

'I have a boyfriend!' My family are insane. I swear, they're insane. Or maybe this was what you got if you concealed your love life from them.

'But you're almost thirty and you're not married, and you must admit, it was a while before Stuart. And Stuart … there's not much spark there, is there?'

Spark. It always astonishes me that my mother puts so much stress on sex as the basis for a relationship. Tells me more than I need to know about why she and Dad got married.

'I'm not a lesbian, Mum.'

'Well, then …' She settled more comfortably in her chair, as if she hadn't just pole-axed me. 'Who were you talking about?'

'This is in confidence.'

'Of course.' Her curiosity was up now, but I had to be sure.

'Including Mary.'

'Oh, all right.'

'It's about Amos Winchester.' I took a sip of hot chocolate and watched her face carefully.

'Oh, no!' She looked very distressed. 'He isn't!' Her reaction would reflect that of anyone in the pastor's church. This was what he was risking.

'A friend suspects that he is. A gay friend. But he's never made a move or anything.'

'So it's just a nasty rumour!' Mum, when she's on the defensive, ruffles up like a hen and pecks. 'Someone's trying to bring him down because of all the good work he does. Because he condemns those unnatural practices!'

'No. Amos Winchester has never said that homosexuality is wrong.'

She opened her mouth and then closed it again. 'That's odd.' She pondered it for a while. 'That's *very* odd.' Pursing her lips, she shook her head with pity. 'Poor man. But he doesn't ... practise himself, you say?'

'Not as far as we know. And he says not. He says, "Not once."'

'You *asked* him? For Heaven's sake, Poppy, you can't go around asking men like Amos Winchester if they're gay!'

'Why not?' In that moment, I felt the gulf between us. I loved her to bits, but we shared almost no beliefs or opinions. Her God and mine were a long way apart.

'The church says that, as long as they don't *do* anything, gay people are welcome in Heaven. As long as they don't sin.' Her tone was hopeful. Winchester could sit at God's right hand, just like all the straights. So long as he never loved anyone.

'Good news for Amos,' I said, and sighed. 'Let's go.'

At home, I found that Tol still hadn't emailed me the report for that night's council meeting. I rang him.

He sounded harassed. 'I'll meet you at Graciella's,' he said, and hung up.

I considered writing to the newspaper about the decline of modern manners, but settled for putting on a nicer top and a skirt. It wasn't for Tol—if the report took too long to finish, we might have to go straight on to the council meeting, and I knew how important appearances could be for politicians, even local ones.

But I admit the lipstick was for Tol.

He didn't notice, of course. They never do when you want them to, unless your neckline is down around your waist. He was typing on a laptop and sipping—uh oh—an espresso. If he needed that much caffeine, things were bad.

I sat down opposite him and waited.

'There,' he said. He spun the laptop around so I could read the report. It was full of technical information. Very impressive. But the councillors would only understand one word in three.

'If you'll permit me,' I said. I typed in, right at the start, *Conclusion: There is no evidence of fat-tailed sheep at the site. The site is not of historical significance.*

I spun the laptop back to him and he read it. His brows contracted and I felt absurdly nervous. So many men hated being corrected in any way. Then his face relaxed and he laughed, so I saved the document to my dropbox.

'You don't think the mayor will get the gist?'

'Fozina warned me to keep it simple.'

He leant back in his chair and let out a long breath. 'Fair enough.' He took a sip from his espresso as if it were his life-blood, his long fingers curling around the tiny cup.

'Are you all right?'

'Didn't get much sleep.' He stretched. 'I was up late talk-ing to the director at the institute in Jordan. The time dif-ference is a real bitch.'

Ah. Walls. 'You'll be leaving soon, then?'

He shrugged. 'About six weeks. They've had to pay out long-service leave for the woman who's leaving and they can't afford to bring me on until that's over. Archaeology's always run on a shoestring. So I've told Annie I'll stay until she can find a replacement for Julieanne. If that's earlier than six weeks, I've got some contract work in London.'

Six weeks. Long enough for a fling, but I didn't want a fling.

'You're very serious,' he said. 'Are you all right?'

I found I couldn't withhold information from him. 'Paul Baume followed Julieanne and saw "the guy from the church" get into her car several times and go off with her.'

His eyes grew intent. 'Carter?'

'Who else?'

'I thought he had an alibi.'

'Alibis can be broken.'

He sat back and tapped his fingers on the table. 'Maybe. Or maybe he's not the only one with a stake in keeping the relationship quiet. Can you imagine what it would do to the party to have it made public? Religious MP gets preselection candidate pregnant? Twitter would go crazy.'

'That opens up the suspect list pretty wide.'

'Well, that's Detective Chloe's job.' I was startled to hear him use my private name for her. 'At least she won't be looking at us any more.'

'I don't think she's crossed anyone off the list.'

He finished his espresso. 'I need another coffee. Do you want one?'

We spent an hour or so just talking. He told me about Jordan, I told him about the ABC. It was pretty low-key; neither of us felt like making jokes or being too lively. But I relaxed for the first time in days.

We arranged to meet at the council, then I went home and printed out eleven copies of Tol's report.

I was at the council chambers in plenty of time, but Tol was nowhere to be seen. I spent a jittery hour waiting in the public section until my case was called, but there was no sign of him. When they finally called me, I presented the report and drew the council's attention to the conclusion.

The mayor was a middle-aged matron who, I remembered from the election, had used her Italian descent to tap into community support. She had that reddish-gold hair you get in the north of Italy, and her clothes undoubtedly came from Milan via the expensive shops in Leichhardt Plaza. She listened to my report with barely concealed scepticism, and I wondered if she was one of those women who secretly despise other women.

One of the male councillors, a fussy-looking man with a brown cardigan, tapped his finger on the report. 'They found sheep,' he said accusingly.

'The sheep they found were much later than the archaeologist suspected,' I said. 'And of a number of different breeds, but not fat-tailed sheep, which was what she was interested in.'

'Hmm.' He whispered something to the woman next to him, and they glared at me suspiciously. 'But there must have been *something* there.'

'They think it was a butcher's,' I said. What the hell. If Tol did turn up, that's what he'd say. I deliberately used the word 'butcher's', though, instead of slaughterhouse, because it sounded much less interesting or historical and there was a reporter from the local paper slouched on one of the chairs looking bored. Which was also why I hadn't used Julieanne's name. The last thing I wanted was an article headlined 'Murder in the slaughterhouse'.

'I'd like to hear from the archaeologist herself,' the mayor said in a dissatisfied voice. 'Why isn't she here?'

'Um … I'm afraid she's passed on,' I said in a hushed tone. The mayor blinked and flushed a little, embarrassed. 'Another archaeologist from the museum wrote up the findings for the council.'

Cardigan man checked the report. 'Dr Lang?'

'Yes.'

'Get him in. We'll hear from him at the next meeting.'

'That's a month away!' I protested. 'The report is quite clear.'

'I'm not prepared to sign away part of our local heritage if the archaeologist concerned isn't willing to report in person. Some respect for the traditions of this area—one of the oldest in Sydney ...'

He was off on a lecture and it was clear the other councillors tuned out immediately, leaning back in their seats or doodling on their notepads. They'd heard it all before.

'Let's put it to a vote, then,' the mayor interrupted when cardigan man paused to draw breath. They voted to wait until Tol could report in person.

My little house was doomed. In a month, Tol could be in London.

I left the council chambers fuming with anger—at brown cardigan man, at the mayor for not standing up to him, but mostly at Tol for failing to show up.

Bastard.

How could he?

I stood in the parking lot and fought the tears that surged to the surface. It wasn't fair. It really, really wasn't fair. I felt like he'd betrayed me. Not just let me down, but stabbed me in the back. He *knew* how important this was!

One of the things I most hate about myself is that I cry when I get angry—as though all the emotion is just too much and it has to come out. I hate it because when I get into an argument and start to cry it makes me seem weak. Girly. The problem is, I have a very bad temper and I have learnt to keep it under control—but the fight to do that is what generates the tears. So I have a choice of crying or hitting someone. Right then I'd gladly have hit Tol.

My mind flashed to Julieanne. Is this what the person who'd killed her had felt? This urge to smash whoever was closest—whoever had caused the distress?

They had my sympathies.

My phone rang.

'Yes?'

'I couldn't come because the police hauled me in for questioning,' Tol said. I had to admire the technique. Straight to the point before I had the chance to hang up on him. 'I'm sorry. I'm still at the police centre. How did it go?'

'They won't lift the order unless you appear in person and tell them to.'

He paused. I could hear shouting and swearing in the background. Just another night at the police centre. 'When?' he said cautiously.

'A month.'

'I'll be there if I'm in the country,' he said. 'Otherwise I'll get Alain to do it.'

What could I say? *You're a bastard and I hate you?* It wasn't his fault.

'What did the cops want?'

'I don't want to talk about it here,' he said. 'Can you pick me up and I'll fill you in? My car's back at your place.'

'Okay.' I hung up. Why not? Nobody else said goodbye.

When I got there, Tol was standing outside the police centre, leaning on a lamppost. He looked tired. He got in the car without a word and I pulled away.

'Have you eaten?' I asked.

He shook his head.

'Let's go to Bill and Toni's.'

'Good idea.'

I threaded through the Darlinghurst streets, keeping an eye out for a park. Bill and Toni's is a Sydney institution; one of the first Italian restaurants in the country and definitely Sydney's first coffee bar. It had great coffee, terrific gelato, reasonable pasta and primi and decent biscotti. I felt like I could do with all of them right then.

We didn't talk until the pasta came—arrabiata for me, puttanesca for him.

As he sprinkled the parmesan over his plate, Tol said, 'There was a baby.' His eyes were fixed on his plate. 'It wasn't mine. They seemed to think—Martin, at least—that that gave me a motive.'

'Did they say whose it was?'

He shook his head and looked up briefly. 'I don't think they know. But the questions … the questions they asked told me how she died.'

I waited.

He dug his fork into the pasta, then put it down again and leant back. 'Whoever it was,' he said, 'pushed her and she hit her head. Probably not intentional. It would be hard to calculate the angles on the spur of the moment.'

'So they pushed her and she fell.'

'They think she was unconscious. And then …' He picked a slice of bread to pieces, his head bent, then looked up, his eyes dark and unhappy. 'Then they squatted over her and banged her head against the bearer a few times, until she was dead.'

It was a horrible image. Disgusting. I shuddered. Someone I knew—the odds were it was someone I knew who'd done this. In my house. Someone I'd worked with, maybe, or someone from the church. Someone I'd interviewed.

The dark, violent act didn't fit with Carter. I could see him pushing her and running away when he knew she was dead. But I couldn't see him balancing on the beams and deliberately bashing her head in.

'They would have had to take her head in their hands,' I said slowly.

'Yes. That feels … intimate.'

'A real hatred, is what it feels like to me. Deep, abiding hatred.'

'That's intimate,' Tol said. He sounded exhausted.

'Eat something,' I said. 'Or have a drink.' The restaurant was BYO, but we'd ordered chinotto. Tol drank some and the colour in his face got better.

'The worst thing is …' Tol said. He paused.

I made a wordless sound of encouragement.

'The worst thing is that I can't help but think that she might still be alive if she'd been kinder.'

It was a terrible epitaph, but he was right. And yet …

'Men kill kind women all the time,' I said miserably. 'Being nice is no protection. One woman a week in this country alone.'

'By partners or ex-partners.' Tol rubbed his eyes. 'That's why the police are concentrating on me.'

There didn't seem much else to say. We ate. Tol insisted on paying. I drove him back to the house and pulled up next to his car. He sat for a moment before getting out.

'Poor Poppy,' he said. 'All this has just been dumped on you. It's not fair, is it?'

He was kind. Understanding. But if I didn't want to cry all over him, I couldn't tell him how low I felt.

'Oh, well,' I said. 'I guess another month will give me time to save up some more for my kitchen. I might be able to afford marble benchtops after all.'

He gave a small laugh and got out of the car. 'Good try,' he said. 'Wait a minute.' He fetched something from the back seat of his car and came around to my window. It was a thick manila folder. 'That's Julieanne's notes, with mine added. In case you need to brief Alain. You can give them back to Annie afterwards.' He touched my cheek. 'Take care, little one.' He bent and kissed the corner of my mouth. But that could have been a coincidence. He was aiming for my cheek, I think.

I managed to say, 'Goodnight,' before he got in his battered old car, and he waved acknowledgement as he drove away.

I parked my car where his had been and walked home through the windy dark, telling myself that I didn't—no, really, I *didn't*—want to fall in love with someone who was going away.

CHAPTER TWENTY-TWO

Saturday

In the morning, too early, I got a call from Annie.

'Julieanne Weaver,' she said, 'has gone and bloody made me executor of her will.'

I paused, taking that in. Julieanne had had no one she could trust with her estate except her boss.

'When you think about it,' I said, 'that's a bit sad.'

'I talked to the solicitor yesterday afternoon,' Annie said, a bit more quietly. 'She's left the museum most of what she had. Some to charity. Some to her old school. Her apartment has to be sorted out. I have to go through all her stuff.' Her voice was full of distaste. 'And you're helping me.'

I've been friends with Annie long enough to know when to give in without an argument.

'What's the address?'

Julieanne had lived in Elizabeth Bay, in a small, 1930s Art Deco block a few streets back from the water. It looked a bit shabby, but shabby chic—typical for the area, which was sandwiched between the red-light district of Kings Cross and some of the priciest real estate in Australia at Rushcutters Bay. Drug addicts and millionaires frequented the area; some residents were both.

Once Annie had buzzed me in through the inevitable security door and I was past the bit that could be seen from the street, the shabby disappeared and opulence took over: metallic wallpaper, leather seats, living plants, the quiet hush of expensive air conditioning. Even a lift, although the building was only two storeys high. Julieanne must have put everything she had into buying this place.

I took the stairs. As I approached the door, Tol opened it, and saw the surprise on my face.

'Annie conscripted me to go through her papers,' he said, 'and pull out anything that should go back to the museum.'

I walked into the entrance hall feeling a combination of voyeurism and unease. On the drive over I had speculated about what Julieanne had been like in her own space; I expected to get a glimpse of the real person. But following Tol through to the lounge room, I saw a space that was as bland and impersonal as one of those serviced apartments that caters to the travelling executive. The Art Deco touches the flat must have come with, like cornices and lintels, had been stripped away and replaced with modern minimalism, complete with new plate-glass windows that emphasised the water glimpses. Everything in good taste, everything high quality, nothing personal.

No, I was wrong—there was one thing: a photograph on the wall of that bloody stump-jump plough. I couldn't help but laugh.

Tol saw me looking.

'She got the plough after all,' I explained. 'That's the one we had the fight about.'

'I asked her about that photo when I first came here.' Tol straightened the frame with gentle fingers. 'She said she loved it because it never let anything stop it. When it came to an obstacle, it just jumped over it and went on.'

I guess that was inspirational, looked at a certain way. Unless the obstacle was another person. But it seemed both funny and sad that this was the only personal item on display.

'A stump-jump plough as personal mentor.'

Annie came through from the bedroom and swatted me on the back of the head like a mother cat reprimanding her kitten. 'Nothing to laugh about,' she said.

Organised as ever, she had brought in a pile of boxes and packing tape.

'We're boxing everything up for Vinnies. You and I in the bedroom, Tol in the study.'

'Yes, ma'am!'

She smiled reluctantly, but I could see that she found this task deeply unpleasant. Annie is a private person and likes to keep a certain distance. It takes time to get close to her. Ferreting through Julieanne's underwear went right against her grain. And while I was nosy, like all researchers, even I found the task eerie.

Julieanne's bedroom was as clean and impersonal as the lounge room. Annie was halfway through boxing up the clothes from Julieanne's chest of drawers. The undies were all beige—flesh coloured, so they wouldn't show under anything. I tried not to look at them—it seemed too intrusive.

I opened the door to the walk-in wardrobe. On one side were Julieanne's power suits, blouses, coats, arranged by colour. Shoes in boxes on the floor, stacked neatly. Shelves with jumpers, tops, T-shirts. A trouser hanger that slid out to reveal jeans at the back, and good pants at the front. I found it all a bit depressing. Julieanne tried so hard to keep everything under control.

Then I looked at the other side and, here at last, I thought, was the real Julieanne. I wouldn't call them sex toys; no dildoes or harnesses that I could see. But shelves of lingerie: black, red, sheer, lacy. High-heeled black shoes. Boots that were so tall they'd have come up to my crotch. And hanging up: a nurse's uniform; a schoolgirl's gym slip; some silk robes.

But the longer I looked, the less I thought this was really Julieanne, either. Those boots didn't look like the wholesome woman Paul had described. I picked one up and held it against me—it was longer than my entire leg. Sighing (because I'd always wanted to be taller, like my siblings), I started to roll it up, ready to pack.

But halfway down, it stuck. There was something inside. My heart sped up; this was like a real mystery. An actual clue? I'd better be careful of fingerprints. There were the black gloves right there, but I just couldn't do it. I went to the other side of her wardrobe and got a silk scarf instead, then I unrolled the boot and, with some distaste, slid my scarf-covered hand inside and pulled out the object.

An appointments diary. But it was an odd one—just a little week-to-a-view thing, like I used to have as a student. And inside, none of Julieanne's museum appointments. This was a record of her Australian Family Party encounters.

It was tricky turning the pages with the scarf covering my hand, but I managed. The most recent entry was the preselection meeting, which she'd marked with a big question mark. Going back, there were the meetings at Carter's house that Patience had told me about. Meetings at the party offices. A dinner at the Stephensons'. A lunch at the church. She'd marked a little x on each Sunday at ten am—the service at Radiant Joy. Although my imagination boggled at Julieanne worshipping anything (except maybe a stump-jump plough), it was clear she'd gone all-in on convincing the Carters and Winchester that she was committed to their values.

There were other little marks, too, but not on Sundays. Maybe prayer services? She used a wavy line for these, and they were irregular. A couple close together, and then maybe two weeks before the next. But they were there, and

I couldn't help but wonder if they represented encounters with Carter. I checked and, sure enough, there was a little wavy line on the night she was killed.

The earliest entry was an Australian Family fundraiser. Almost a year ago. It was the only place she'd written more than the bare minimum of description. In solid black letters, it read, 'The Beginning!' Underlined.

So she'd had a long-term plan; join the party and get preselection, probably assuming it wouldn't be until the next election. And then this by-election came up, and she saw her chance. I still thought Australian Family was an odd choice for her, but it was clearly one she'd made a while ago.

I had to hand it to her. She was focussed and determined and had been very likely to win ...

How did that woman, that determined and intelligent and sucessful woman, fit with the sexy clothes and the ridiculously long boots? Or with the costumes? I couldn't quite put them together in my head.

I wrapped the diary up in the scarf and put it aside for Detective Chloe, then walked out and into the study, which was white, organised and owed a lot to Ikea. Julieanne had economised here so she could spend money on the rooms that showed. Tol was sitting down, going through the file drawer at the bottom of the desk.

I hesitated. I really wanted to ask him, but there was no way I could pretend it was anything other than wanton curiosity. Still, maybe it had something to do with her death ...

'Um, Tol,' I said. How could I phrase it? There was no good way to say it. 'In Julieanne's wardrobe there's a lot of … stuff.'

He turned, his face showing nothing more than mild interest. 'What kind of stuff?'

'Um, sexy stuff.'

'Really?' The surprise seemed genuine. 'What kind—' He got up, then hesitated. 'Should I?'

'If you want …'

He stood for a moment, then shook his head. 'No. None of my business.'

And that convinced me more than anything else could that he hadn't been a part of any role-playing sex with Julieanne. If he had, he'd want to check for anything incriminating. So who was the gear for? Not Paul, not Tol. I couldn't shake the suspicion that it was there for whoever needed it. That Julieanne changed to suit the man she was with, and she had the equipment to do so. Wholesome for Paul, normal for Tol—what had she been for the father of her baby? I looked around the study. Were there any clues here as to who he had been?

For the first time, I felt a dreadful pity for her. It was as though she had been on show all the time, 24/7. I wondered who the unseen observer had been—who had convinced her, and when, that she had to meet other people's standards at every moment—even the most intimate moments?

Tol sat back down slowly and opened another file. He scanned the contents and whistled under his breath. 'Annie!'

he called. He half-turned in his chair and gestured to me. 'You'd better look at this.'

Annie came in and we both read over Tol's shoulder.

'Oh, shit,' Annie said, heartfelt.

'What are you going to do?' I asked.

'What do you reckon?' she said, frowning. 'Should I call ICAC?' The government watchdog. That was career suicide for Annie.

'This is a murder investigation,' I said. 'Call the police. Now.'

Detective Chloe had, it was clear, been playing tennis when she got Annie's call. She went for the matching top and socks option (orange) but I was glad to see she was in shorts instead of one of those flirty miniskirts with the frilly panties. She wasn't happy about being called when she was off duty.

'Well?' she demanded as soon as she stepped inside the flat. 'We've already been through everything here.'

'Have a look at this,' Annie said, and handed her Julieanne's file.

Detective Chloe opened it and began to read as she followed Annie into the lounge room. She flicked over the pages. 'So? We've seen this. It's just stuff about museum loans.'

The jargon was hard to interpret, I guess, if you weren't a museum person, but to Tol and Annie and me the import had been clear.

'Gerry Collonucci has been defrauding the museum by selling off artefacts to overseas collectors,' Annie said baldly.

'Julieanne found out,' I added.

Not to be left out, Tol said. 'She's documented it.'

Worst of all, although none of us said it aloud, they were Aboriginal artefacts. Not didgeridoos and boomerangs made for the tourist market, but pieces of pre-colonial art and culture which had had religious significance to the people they were stolen from. And still do to their descendants. The very fact that the museum had these items was controversial. The only reason they hadn't been returned to the traditional custodians was that no one was sure where they came from. They had been 'acquired' by a curator early in the museum's history, when 'Native artefact' was considered enough of a description in the catalogue.

I didn't understand why Gerry had picked them. They were hauled out every few years when someone thought they had figured out a way to decide what part of the country they were from—scanning for radioactive isotopes, or trying to prove artistic traditions, or analysing the wood or stone. We'd had some hope when DNA analysis became cheap enough for the museum to afford, but no usable DNA had survived, even in the belts of human hair.

Maybe that explained it. Gerry had figured that, with DNA a wash-out, no one would be checking on them for a while, because the agreement with the Advisory Committee for Indigenous Repatriation was that the items would be kept in sealed boxes until some other method of identification was developed. And this sort of artefact was increasingly rare and therefore very valuable.

'How much are we talking about here?' Detective Chloe asked Annie.

'Thousands for each piece. Maybe tens of thousands.'

A small smile curled Chloe's mouth. This was the kind of motive a jury would understand. 'He covered his tracks pretty well, according to this,' she said.

Annie nodded. She was pale, and she took a breath before she sat down on one of the immaculate cream sofas. 'He created false records of loans to other institutions—Indigenous ones, so no one would even think of asking for them back.'

'How did Julieanne twig to it?'

'It's on the next page,' I said. Chloe flipped and read, but I explained anyway, in case the jargon was impenetrable. 'She was collecting information about Gerry's management flaws, so she followed up on the fact that there weren't any formal letters from the other institutions requesting the items.'

'Probably thought he'd done a mate's loan,' Annie said. 'You know, "Oh, sure, mate, I'll organise that", and no paperwork was done because I wouldn't have approved it.'

'She wanted his job,' Chloe deduced. She looked at Annie, and then at Tol. 'But when she found out, Julieanne didn't come to you.'

'Probably figuring out how to best use the information,' Tol said sadly.

'And that got her killed?' Detective Chloe suggested.

'That's your department,' he said.

She hefted the file in her hand. 'This is evidence,' she said. 'I'll give you a receipt.'

'There's more,' I said, and handed over the diary.

'We searched this place!'

'It was stuck down one of her boots.'

'I'm going to kill Carmichael,' she muttered. 'He should have found this.'

'There's not much there,' I said. 'Except …' I pointed out the wavy lines, and especially the one on the night she died.

'Hmm,' Chloe said. 'Still, this museum stuff is a much better motive. And more urgent. I'll give you a receipt for both of these.'

Which she duly did, all official.

'No contact with Collonucci,' she warned, the little bobbles on her tennis socks flicking up and down as she strode out to surprise Gerry. 'I'll send Martin to go through this place again. Don't touch anything.'

'The next time I contact Gerry Collonucci,' Annie said fiercely to the closed door, 'he'd better be in police custody, or he won't walk away with his balls.' Then she paled. 'Oh, God, I have to call the Minister!'

The current Minister for the Arts and Environment, under whose authority the museum came, was a media groupie who lived for a twenty-second grab on the nightly news. His PR hacks would have to work hard to spin this one. Normally, Annie's boss, Tim, would have reported to him, but Tim was in Bruges at a conference and wouldn't be back for two weeks.

'Prompt and decisive action by the museum has brought this despicable criminal to justice,' I offered.

She smiled at me, but I could see the strain.

'They can't release anything yet, anyway,' I said. 'Or they risk derailing the investigation. When it's a fait accompli, they can spin it into an anti-corruption story.'

Tol put his arm around Annie's shoulder and gave her a companionable hug. Astonishingly, she didn't shrug it away.

She sighed. 'At least we can stop wondering who killed Julieanne.'

That was true. For the first time in days, I felt my stomach unclench.

'Gerry has an alibi,' Tol said.

'Not much of one,' I said. 'He faked it with what's-his-name, the one with acne.'

'Jake,' Annie and Tol said at the same time.

'How do you know?' Tol went on.

I shrugged. 'It was obvious.'

Tol and Annie smiled at each other, the indulgent smiles of parents with a clever child.

'What?' I asked.

'Never mind, possum,' Annie said. 'I'm going to the office to call the minister. You two stay and let Martin in.'

As she left, Tol said, 'Those marks in her diary … how far back do they go?'

'Almost a year,' I said reluctantly. 'Back to when she first targeted Australian Family.'

'So. The whole time we were seeing each other.' His face was a mixture of distaste and something else. Anger, disappointment, resignation? I couldn't tell. But at least it wasn't heartbreak.

'I'm sorry.'

He made a movement with his shoulders, as if resettling himself. 'Not your fault.'

He and I spent an uncomfortable half an hour perched on Julieanne's lounge waiting for Martin—or rather, I perched. Tol relaxed and watched the cricket on the large plasma TV he found hidden in a cabinet.

Cricket. And up until then I'd thought he was so civilised.

CHAPTER TWENTY-THREE

Sunday

On Sunday afternoon—early evening, really—my phone rang. Matthew Carter's number.

'Hi, Matthew!' I answered.

'We need to see you.' Abrupt. Not at all the smooth, conciliatory tone he'd used before.

'Why?'

There was a short silence. He hadn't expected me to question him. Really, that man was surrounded by sycophants.

'We need to discuss Amos.' Oh ho! Amos, indeed. For a moment, I was worried that Mum had let some of our talk slip and it had hit social media, but no. I would have heard about that; and I knew I could trust her.

'All right. Where do you want to meet? Should I bring a camera crew?'

'No! Definitely not. Can you come here?'

'Here being where?'

'My home.'

Hmm. On the one hand, I didn't feel inclined to obediently toddle out to Carter's place to suit his convenience. On the other hand, I really wanted to know why they wanted to talk and who 'they' were.

'Okay. In an hour or so.'

'Good.' And he hung up. Arrogant bastard.

I pulled on my jeans and a cotton top. No more dressing up for Mr Nice Church Man. But, because I'd seen an awful lot of cop shows, I called Annie before I left and told her where I was going. Because Mr Nice Church Man might be a murderer, although I didn't expect him to do anything to me at his own house.

'They' turned out to be Carter and Stephenson, in shortsleeved shirts and chinos. Eliza was nowhere in sight—it was Sunday, after all, she was probably doing something down at the church with Winchester. Was that why they'd chosen now to talk to me? Because they could be sure he was out of the way?

Carter showed me through to the lounge.

I sat on one of the Italian leather sofas and smiled until both of them gave up looming over me and sat down. My phone was in my pocket, recording everything. Now was the time to stop being the nice little girl who supported their goals. See how they liked that.

'Amos has had a talk to us about how you accosted him,' Carter said.

Stephenson just sat and glowered. It was odd, having one very handsome and one quite good-looking man scowl at you. I was conscious, suddenly, that I was alone in the house with them, and that one of them might well be a murderer. Or could it be both? I swallowed, and raised my chin.

'Accosted? I doubt very much that he used that word, because that would be a lie.'

'He was worried that you were about to, to—'

'To try to destroy us,' Stephenson cut in. 'Like the disgusting muckraker you are.'

I got up and began to walk to the door.

Both men sprang to their feet.

'Where are you going?' Carter demanded.

I just glared at him and kept walking.

He grabbed my arm.

Fear swept through me, cold and nauseating. 'Let go of me.'

He didn't. 'We have to talk about this.' He gave me a little shake, as though I were a recalcitrant child. Fury erupted in me but, unlike every other time in my life, I let it. There were no tears, only an icy rage.

'If you don't let go of my arm, I will charge you with assault.'

He let go and fell back, astonished.

I turned to face them. 'If I were going to defame Mr Winchester, I would have done it by now. I came in good faith. I have met with hostility and physical violence. Give me one good reason this shouldn't be on the news tonight.'

Stephenson laughed at me. 'You have no proof.'

My rage mounted, but I smiled. Just smiled.

His laughter faltered and he lunged forward. 'She's bloody recorded us!'

Carter swept an arm out, keeping Stephenson from me, but then advanced on me himself with deliberate menace. 'If you have been recording this conversation, you have to know that that's illegal.' He was attempting to go back to his normal smooth voice, but it wasn't working.

I smiled nastily at him. 'No, actually, it's not. If a person has a fear that they may be harmed in the course of the conversation, it's perfectly legal for them to record it. *Telecommunications Act 1997.*'

His face changed. The nostrils flared and whitened, and the lines connecting nose and mouth deepened. His eyes hardened, his fists clenched. For the first time, Matthew Carter looked like a dangerous man. Like someone who could have killed Julieanne.

'Give me the phone.'

My anger still buoyed me and stopped me from giving in to fear. I wanted to hit him. If I'd had a bat, I might have used it. But all I had were words.

'Mr Carter, you have two options here. You let me walk out of this house unimpeded, and hope I can't be bothered to send this recording to the police. Or you physically take my phone away from me, which will be a criminal act. I *will* report you. People know where I am, so if you have any intention of killing me the way you killed Julieanne—'

'How dare you!'

'—I'd think twice, if I were you.'

Carter was poised on the balls of his feet, ready to risk that assault charge. He took one step towards me and I turned to run—and there was Patience, in the doorway.

We all stopped dead.

'Dad?'

Carter was very still. His face struggled to find the right expression, moving between anger and sadness and a false jollity. Patience looked at him as if worried he was having a stroke.

'Let her go,' Stephenson said heavily. 'She's right. If she was going to take Amos down, she'd already have done it.'

'Amos?' Patience asked. Her gaze flicked from one of us to the other, seeking an explanation.

'Don't worry about Amos, Patience,' I said. 'Nothing bad is going to happen to him.'

Carter visibly relaxed and pulled himself together. 'Miss McGowan was just leaving.'

I smiled at Patience as I went by. 'Nice to see you.'

She smiled back uncertainly, and I winked at her.

'Remember? Not everyone likes your father. And your father, for one, doesn't like me.'

I closed the door very gently, because I wanted to slam it as loudly as I could. My hands shook with relief, and as I sat in my car seat, my legs started shaking too.

I'd thought of Carter as a possible murderer before, obviously, but that had been in a theoretical way. I rubbed my arm. Now, I absolutely believed he could have killed

Julieanne. And he had two possible motives: his own reputation and Winchester's. Maybe both. The church *and* the
party. Just how good *was* his alibi?

On my way home, I pulled into a park and called Chloe.
Played her the recording.

'Not much there for us, unfortunately,' she said. 'What's
all this about Amos?'

'He's gay.' If I'd had any doubts, their reaction had finished them. If Winchester were straight, that confrontation
would never have happened.

'No!'

'I have it on good authority. Gay, but celibate.' I still felt
obliged to be fair to the pastor. Possibly because he'd given
up so much to live by his beliefs.

'Well, well.' A pause. 'Did Julieanne know that?'

'I have no evidence that she did.'

'But they met a few times, just the two of them, right?'

'That's what my source told me.'

'He's got an alibi.' Chloe sighed. 'This case … it's drag-
ging on. Are you going to charge Carter with assault?'

I thought about it. It would probably hurt him politically. And could he still serve as an MP if he was convicted?
Probably—it would only be a misdemeanour assault, not
a felony (a felony would mean he was unfit to be an MP
and he'd lose his place in Parliament). And I would be a
target. The social media pile-on alone would be horrendous.
I could vividly imagine how that harridan from his office

would call up a Twitter mob on me. I'd get doxxed, and I was living at Mum and Dad's house …

'No,' I sighed. 'It's not worth it.'

'Probably wise, but annoying.'

'Yes.'

There was a small silence.

'Winchester, eh?' Chloe said. 'Thanks.' And hung up.

I needed to decompress, so I went lap swimming at Leichhardt Pool. To get all that lactic acid from the consuming rage out of me. From the consuming fear.

Carter. No matter what happened with Julieanne's death, I might well put some time into bringing him down. From behind the scenes. I tucked that thought away for later, and did a tumble turn to start another lap.

Afterwards, still unsettled, I went to my sister Carol's place and played with her kids.

Carol was the nice sister—where Theresa was quite prepared to fight with anyone in order to defend her beliefs, Carol just wanted everyone to be happy. She was as tough as Theresa, though. It just didn't show unless her kids were involved. I don't go to her house all that often because her husband and I don't get along, but he was out of town on a business trip.

Her eldest was twelve and in his first year of high school, having trouble with English, so I spent a half-hour explaining a couple of poems to him before dinner.

'You're good with kids. You'd make a great teacher,' Carol said as she served up homemade pizza. With peas. Carol had been a teacher before she had kids. Now she says she's 'just a housewife', which infuriates me. Her job is a lot harder than mine.

'I *am* a teacher,' I said, with a mock high-minded air. 'I teach through the new and innovative medium of television.'

'Aunty Poppy, can I have your peas?'

Emma, Carol's baby, was three, and obsessed with peas. Don't ask me why.

'What do you say?' Carol prompted.

'Please.'

'Sure, bub.' I transferred most of my peas to her plate and she ate them solemnly, one by one, with intense concentration.

'Why do you like peas, bub?'

Emma turned her cute little face up to me. All Carol's children are gorgeous. Emma has deep auburn hair and pale skin and warm brown eyes, like a Rossetti painting. 'They squish.'

Hard to argue with that.

'You were good on *The Daily Report*. You should do news.' Carol smiled at me. Sisters. Always trying to improve you.

'What's wrong with the job I do now?'

'You're so clever! Kids' TV isn't exactly rocket science. It seems a waste.'

This was the same attitude that believed that raising children was a 'just a housewife' job. But the trick to arguing with sisters is knowing the things they can't disagree with.

'There's nothing more important, though, than helping children grow up well.'

She shrugged and nodded and wiped the face of the second youngest, Jackson, who inevitably had cheese all over him.

The oldest girl, Mia, was sleeping over at a friend's and going to school from there.

'Next weekend,' I said, 'let Damon look after the kids and we'll go away. Or at least to the movies.'

Flustered, Carol cast a look at her kids as though I'd said something disturbing. 'Oh, I don't know … Damon doesn't like …' She couldn't finish that sentence without telling her children that their father didn't want to spend time with them. There's a reason I don't like Damon. I let her off the hook and dropped the subject.

It made me consider Julieanne's baby. Had anyone wanted that poor bub? Had Julieanne? It was possible.

But it was clear that, whoever the father was, he hadn't been grief-stricken enough to reveal himself. Was it the father of her child who'd killed her?

Emma crawled into my lap and I cuddled her thankfully. I couldn't stop worrying over Julieanne. Part of me, I was afraid, would never feel safe in that house unless her murderer was caught. And part of me just wanted justice for Julieanne, cast down into the pit.

Now that was a thought—could that have been a Biblical reference? A symbolic sending of her to Hell?

Everything I thought of led back to Radiant Joy Church.

CHAPTER TWENTY-FOUR

Monday

Fortunately for the Minister, the police decided not to publicise Gerry's arrest until Interpol had picked up all of his customers overseas. That was expected to take a couple of days, Annie told me early on Monday morning when she called to fill me in on the latest. But Gerry hadn't been arrested for Julieanne's murder. I debated telling Tyler everything and letting him run with the new angle before it became sub judice, but I decided that although my loyalty to the ABC was strong, my loyalty to Annie was stronger.

'Thanks, possum,' she said.

'Someone's going to leak it sometime today when Gerry doesn't show up for work,' I warned her. 'One of the students or staff at the museum, probably. I'll have to fill Tyler in then.'

'I'm having a meeting with the Fraud Squad and ICAC this morning,' she replied. 'If I can get through that and show that the museum was squeaky clean, it won't matter so much. The Minister can talk about us being partners in the investigation, blah blah blah.' She sighed. 'Keep your fingers crossed.'

I drove to Artarmon, barely noticing the beautiful clear skies or the shining sails of the Opera House. I put my head down and did some much-needed paperwork, made phone calls to set up interviews for the program after next—'People who help us: paramedics'—and worried about Annie.

Just after eleven, she rang.

'All clear,' she said, the relief plain in her voice. 'Your Detective Chloe was there, too, but she says that they haven't got enough evidence to arrest Gerry for murder. Yet.' She hesitated. 'The Minister's policy adviser wants us to take control of the media storm when the police announce the arrest tomorrow. I—er—I told him I could organise a friendly interview.'

I groaned, but quietly. 'I'll talk to Tyler,' I said. 'But I can't promise. Tomorrow, you reckon?'

'It turned out that Gerry only sold to a couple of dealers in Italy. They've got one and they expect to arrest the other tonight. So they'll be announcing a successful investigation tomorrow.'

I filled Jennifer Jay in and called Tyler. 'Want an exclusive?' I said. It was like offering meth to an addict.

So the next morning I had one of the most surreal experiences of my life: sitting in a TV studio interviewing one of my best friends. It felt like a joke; Annie and I had made films together as students, and I half-expected our old lecturer to pop out from behind the camera and correct my technique.

The ABC lawyer had briefed me about what questions I couldn't ask. Nothing that would prejudice a jury against Gerry. Difficult. Never make an assertion about his behaviour without putting 'alleged' in front. Be careful not to imply that he'd killed Julieanne, because that was defamation. Stick to the facts. I began to think that news journos really earned their money.

'Go hard,' Tyler said to me while I was being made up. 'Museum incompetence, lack of supervision, that kind of thing.'

'No,' I said.

He blinked. He really wasn't used to being told that.

'Annie's here only because she trusts me,' I said. 'This is not a story about museum incompetence. It's a story about a sleazy, opportunistic bastard who took advantage of the pure-minded but very competent people he worked with. And, incidentally, ripped off both the taxpayers of this country and the Indigenous population.'

Maybe I looked fierce. He backed down, waving his hands as though denying all responsibility.

'Go hard on Collonucci, then,' he instructed.

'Glad to.'

I started with easy ones.

'Dr Southey, what exactly have the police discovered about Gerry Collonucci's activities?'

We went through all the PR-sanctioned questions and answers and Annie came over as competent, thoughtful and thoroughly rehearsed. I went hard on Gerry and Annie abetted me. The Minister should be delighted. He even got a plug for funding a new security system. But then I thought I'd better give Tyler something for his cooperation.

'Is it true that the first person to discover Dr Collonucci's alleged criminal activities was Julieanne Weaver, who was murdered recently?'

'Yes, that's correct,' Annie said. She was a little white around the eyes, but she was performing like an old hand.

I smiled encouragingly. 'The police haven't made an arrest in that case, have they?'

'Not yet,' she said, implying that any second now, Gerry Collonucci was going to be charged with Julieanne's death.

'Was there a history of enmity between Dr Collonucci and Dr Weaver?'

I hadn't flagged that question with her because I wanted at least a couple that came over as unrehearsed.

Annie bit her lip. 'Well, I think anyone who worked with them at the museum would say that they didn't get on very well.'

'Dr Weaver criticised Dr Collonucci's management?' No matter how I phrased it, there was an implied 'And she was right, you weren't doing your job'. But I knew Annie had an answer.

'I had placed Dr Collonucci on notice that unless his performance improved, his contract would be not be renewed at the end of the financial year.'

I had to look as if that was news to me. 'So do you think that was what prompted him to this alleged illegal action?'

'I think he was feathering his nest while he had the opportunity,' Annie said bluntly. We were sailing close to the sub judice wind, so I changed tack.

'Do you know whether the police are continuing to investigate Julieanne Weaver's death?' Translation: Do they think Gerry did it?

'As far as I'm aware,' Annie said carefully, 'they are looking closely at Dr Collonucci's movements on the night in question.' Translation: Yes, they do.

'It's quite a scandal,' I said conversationally. 'Theft, fraud and murder.'

Annie was ready for that. She smiled. 'Poppy, the museum is one hundred and forty-two years old. It's seen worse scandals than this come and go, and it's survived because it has a special place in the hearts of the people of New South Wales. I'm sure they will understand that the actions of one dishonest man can't tarnish its reputation.'

She meant it, too, and that showed.

'Dr Southey, thank you,' I said.

The floor manager said, 'Thank you, everyone,' and the sound people rushed in to get our lapel mikes.

'Fantastic,' I said.

She was frowning.

'What?'

'If Gerry didn't do it, the real murderer is going to be pretty happy tonight,' she said.

That was a disquieting thought.

CHAPTER TWENTY-FIVE

Tuesday

Stuart turned up at Artarmon looking incredibly respectable in a three-piece suit. The receptionist, Cherie, knew all about my breakup with him and took some delight in keeping him waiting. She didn't even ask him to sit down, so by the time I got out there he was shifting from foot to foot and looking out the window onto the broken paving of the small and very dull courtyard.

I'd broken up with guys before—at my age, who hadn't?—and I'd always felt bad about it; either I hadn't wanted to lose him or I hadn't wanted to hurt him. So when I came out the security door that led to the back office, I delayed letting Stuart know I was there. But looking at his neatly tailored back I realised that I just didn't care. I didn't believe that he loved me, I guess, which meant no one was going to get hurt except for their pride—and Stuart's pride, I reckoned, was due for a fall. I felt a lightness, a freedom, that I hadn't expected.

'Yes?' I said as discouragingly as I could.

He turned around and frowned at me like a schoolmaster, then glanced significantly at Cherie. 'Can we talk privately?'

'No,' I said. I traded glances with Cherie and she nodded encouragement. Cherie's attitude to men veers wildly between complete infatuation and complete disdain, and we were in a disdain phase, so she was right behind me. She twirled her nose ring, which she tells me freaks suits out, and sure enough, Stuart winced and avoided looking at her. Which left him looking at me.

Even in this moment, I had to admit he cut a fine figure, but I was aware as I never had been of his small, pursed lips.

'It was tacky of you to break up with me in a text, Poppy,' he said, like a parody of Miss Manners.

'You knew we were over or you wouldn't have slammed the door at my parents' place on your way out,' I retorted. Attack, Poppy, I told myself. Don't let this jerk take the moral high ground. 'And you lied to the police!'

Cherie made a *tch tch* sound.

He was taken aback. 'No, I didn't!'

'Seven o'clock? You were walking down my street at seven o'clock? Did you expect me to believe that? You watch the news at seven o'clock. It's a bloody ritual!'

His face cleared and he pulled his iPhone out of his pocket and beamed. 'I stream it now!' he said proudly. 'So I can be anywhere and not miss it.'

That verged on obsessive. Then I thought it through. 'Do you mean to say,' I said slowly and dangerously, 'that you were planning to front up to my house and say, "Here's some wine, let's have sex but I just have to watch the news first"?'

'Um …'

'I have *so* broken up with you.'

'Unbelievable!' Cherie said.

'You keep out of this!' Stuart snarled at her.

'She can say anything she likes!' I retorted. '*She* belongs here. Unlike you.' I stood by Cherie's desk and crossed my arms. Cherie leant back in her chair and crossed her arms. We stared.

'I think you'll find you've made a very big mistake, Poppy,' Stuart said with an attempt at dignity.

'Do you know,' I said to Cherie, ignoring him, 'that Stuart and his old school friend meet on Wednesdays to do their laundry together? *Every* Wednesday. And not in a laundromat. In Stuart's flat.'

'Eughh. That is *so* weird,' Cherie responded obediently, although I could see by the widening of her eyes that she really thought it was.

Stuart stood there, reddening, as though he'd never even thought about it before. He was a lot more pathetic than he'd seemed. If I hadn't been staying at my parents I would have spent more time with him and found that out much sooner. So I guess it wasn't his fault he'd made me believe he was normal for so long.

'Go and get a life, Stuart,' I said, as kindly as I could.

He went out the door without another word.

'Well, he was cute, but really—*laundry?*' Cherie said and I thought she'd just about summed it up.

When I got home from work, I went around to my little house and worked in my garden. I couldn't do anything inside because of the council order, but I could mulch and prune and plant, so I did. It was lovely—a warm spring evening with the promise of better weather to come. I turned my phone off and just pottered. Then I posted before and after photos to social media and felt quietly smug at all the admiring comments.

That night, I watched Carmen Broadhurst trounce the independent candidate for North Hughes on a late-night political show. I hoped the big parties would get their acts together and put the boot in, or the Australian Family Party was going to hold the balance of power in State Parliament—which meant that Amos Winchester and Matthew Carter were going to be running things in my state. I didn't like that prospect at all.

On Wednesday night, I took my Aunty Mary to the hospital to see my cousin Stephanie, who'd just had a new baby girl. They were naming her Marie, and there was a big family fight going on over whether to pronounce it MAR-ree (traditional Aussie Catholic) or Ma-REE (French, 'foreign'). I hated both versions.

'Call her Mary,' I said, endearing myself to no one but my aunty.

The hospital room was full to bursting, and noisier than any new mother should be asked to bear. I shepherded them all to the coffee shop, stopped Aunty Mary giving a piece of her mind to Stephanie's mother-in-law (Italian, wanted 'Maria'), and zoned out. After all the tensions of the past week, a family squabble over a much-loved baby was curiously reassuring.

I drove Aunty Mary home and got her cross-examination about the case, my work, and 'Who is this Tol Lang your mother's told me about?'

Mary was an anomaly in the family. She had gone to England in her youth and then, influenced by Carnaby Street, she'd come back, opened up her own designer boutique, been picked up by David Jones and the major stores, then sold the label to a big company and retired on the proceeds. As far as I knew, she'd never sewn a stitch or picked up a sketch pad since, but she did always look fabulous. She'd married an older widower when she was in her forties, and lived all over the world with him as he advised developing countries how to breed better goats.

This varied life had worn away the sharp edges of the family tendency to judgement; she was far more accepting of difference than anyone else in the family, which made her one of the few relatives I could really talk to.

'He's going to Jordan in six weeks,' I said. 'Permanently.'

Maybe my tone said more than I thought, because she patted my leg. 'Nothing's permanent until it happens. If you want him, go for it. Who knows what might happen?'

That was the voice of long experience talking. It was tempting, but really not sensible.

'Until this murder thing is cleared up, though ...'

'Well, that's true. You don't want to get tied up to a murderer.'

Can't argue with that.

I dropped Aunty Mary at her retirement village and went back to my house to pick up Mum's secateurs, which I'd left there the day before.

But sitting on the front step was Patience Carter, dressed in jeans and a hoodie and carrying a big shoulder bag that bulged in all directions. She stood up uncertainly as I opened the gate.

'Patience?'

'I didn't know where else to come,' she said. She burst into tears.

You don't come from a family as big as mine without learning how to deal with crying. I patted her on the back, put tissues in her hands, murmured meaningless soothing sounds and steered her not into the house, but back to my car. If they suspected she had come to me, the house would be the first place they'd look.

Once she was in the car, hiccupping quietly, I drove down to the local harbourside park and stopped.

'How can I help?' I asked.

'I don't know what to do,' she said. Now that she'd let out the tears, she seemed dazed. Quietly despairing, which I didn't like. She looked out at Rozelle Bay, where the lights were reflecting from the Anzac Bridge in long streaks of gold.

'Tell me all about it.'

'I couldn't stay there!' she said.

'What happened?'

'After church, there was a women's Bible group. It meets once a month, you know? And they're trying to get more young women, so Mum asked me to come along.'

'Mmm,' I said encouragingly.

'She's such a hypocrite!' Patience flared. Ah, there it was. The one thing the young can't forgive.

'Why?'

'The text for the day was *The truth will set you free*. She got up and started talking about truth and how Jesus wants us to live honestly and justly and I couldn't take it any more! It was disgusting!'

'What did you do?'

She looked at me as though she didn't understand, and I realised that even disgusted and angry, Patience Carter wouldn't have done anything to disrupt a Bible class.

'I waited until we got home and then I put some clothes in a bag and—and I just left. I got the train to the city but then I didn't know what to do … so I came here.' She sounded uncertain and a little afraid.

'You did the right thing,' I said immediately. 'I'll do whatever I can to help.'

I was burning with curiosity about what made Eliza Carter a hypocrite, but I'd had enough to do with teenage nieces to know that it was really none of my business and Patience was more likely to tell me if I didn't ask.

'Thank you,' she said in a small voice, and relaxed.

There was a silence. She fiddled with the strap of her bag and I thought about what to do with her. Alex had a spare room, but was Alex the right choice? Despite Winchester's restraint on the issue, Patience had, without a doubt, been raised to be homophobic, and Alex and Rick would shock her to the core. Would that be good or bad at this stage? Bad, I decided. We didn't want to give her any reason to run back home until she'd confessed all.

'I could take you to my parents' place,' I said. 'But I'm living there at the moment, so if your family figure out you've come to me they'll go straight there. Seems to me you should stay with a friend of mine until you decide what you want to do.'

Pale as milk, she looked as if she was just realising that she'd walked out on everything. Family, school, friends. It had to be a pretty big betrayal to justify that. I pushed down my curiosity.

'My friend Fiona has a spare room,' I said. 'Do you like cats?'

Of course she liked cats. More than that, the idea of cats was reassuring. Homely. I rang Fiona and just said I had a young friend who needed a place to crash for a night or two, could I bring her over? Fiona is a Youth Officer with a local council, and what she doesn't know about kids isn't worth knowing. More importantly, she genuinely likes them, so she said, 'Sure.'

I took Patience over to Fiona's little house in Marrickville and stayed with them while she settled in. Patience blinked a couple of times over Fiona's spiked hair and pink gumboots, but her kindness and light touch soon allayed any worries.

Fiona's cats had avoided me ever since I bought my house because I always smelt of paint stripper or wood glue. But they wound around Patience's legs and Toby, the fat tabby, deigned to sit on her lap and be stroked, a rare sign of approval. Jughead, the thin calico, perched delicately on the arm of Fiona's chair and stared at Toby, trying to figure out if he was getting anything she wanted.

We ordered vegetarian pizza from the organic pizza place and ate in front of the television, two things I think Patience rarely got to do. Then a newsflash came on: A search for Patience Carter, believed abducted this afternoon from North Hughes. Patience's school photo came up on the screen and Toby squealed indignantly as she clutched him, then jumped off her lap, the bell around his neck jangling.

Fiona hit the mute button. 'You have to tell your parents you're all right,' she said firmly.

Patience panicked. 'I'm not calling them! They'll trace it or something and—and—and—' She started to cry, the jagged crying that comes with exhaustion.

'I'll ring the police,' I said.

Patience dragged in a great breath and started to object.

I put up a hand. 'I won't tell them where you are. Just that you haven't been abducted, you're safe, and you've made your own decision to leave home. You're sixteen, aren't you?'

She nodded.

'That means you have the right to live anywhere you like,' Fiona cut in. 'Your parents can't force you back.'

'Really?' Patience's eyes were saucers. It had never occurred to her that she had any rights at all.

I felt a stab of satisfaction. No matter what the outcome, Patience's life wasn't going to be the same after this.

I rang Detective Chloe, of course.

'Prudhomme.'

'This is Poppy McGowan. I thought you ought to know that Patience Carter hasn't been abducted.'

'Where is she?'

'She'd rather her parents didn't know that at the moment, but she is fine.'

'Let me talk to her.'

It was beginning to sound like those scenes in FBI shows where they try to negotiate with the kidnappers, so I handed the phone over to Patience. Time for her to speak for herself. She took it cautiously.

'Hello?'

I could imagine what Chloe was saying from the expressions on Patience's face.

'Yes. I'm fine. No. No, I don't want to talk to them!' Her voice was rising. 'No, I'm not going to tell you where I am! I don't want to talk to anyone!' She practically threw the phone back to me and ran off to her bedroom.

'Detective Sergeant Prudhomme?' I said sweetly. Calmly. Trying to sound like a responsible adult. 'Patience is fine, but she really doesn't want to go home. She is safe. She has somewhere suitable to live for the moment. She is over sixteen, so she has the right—'

'I know all about her rights, McGowan. The question is, what does she know?'

I hesitated, but I wanted Julieanne's killer caught as much as Detective Chloe did.

'I don't know. Something. If we leave her alone for a while, I think she'll tell us.'

'Tell you, you mean. There's no exclusive for the ABC on this one. If she knows anything, I need to find out.'

'I thought Gerry was chief suspect.'

Detective Chloe sighed. 'He's got an alibi,' she said.

'You can't trust Jake—'

'No, you can't, which is why he's been charged with interfering with a police investigation. He was lying. But Collonucci got him to lie because he was at home liaising with his Italian buyers—not an alibi he wanted to share with us. We've got computer logs, Skype records … one of the buyers even taped the conversation. So he's clean as far as Julieanne is concerned.'

I noticed, even through my disappointment, that 'Dr Weaver' had become 'Julieanne'. Because she'd been pregnant?

'So if Patience has information …' Detective Chloe prompted.

'I'll do my best,' I said. 'Don't tell the Carters who she's with.'

'Okay. You stick with her. If she wants to talk, she can ring me any time.'

'Good idea.'

She hung up. I turned my phone off immediately. I vaguely recalled giving Carter my card and I didn't want to be contactable.

Fifteen minutes later, a newsflash reported that Patience Carter had been found. The subtext from the news anchor was that there was some deep scandal waiting to be uncovered here. I thought he was right.

Then I thought about my position at the ABC and Tyler's expectations. I wasn't about to give him Patience, but maybe I could deflect him. Instead of calling Tyler, who would ask too many questions, I called Gina Kirikis, the police rounds reporter, and told her about Gerry's alibi.

Kirikis was grateful for the information.

'Guess that puts the spotlight back on the boyfriend,' she said cheerfully. 'Or it might turn out to be one of those ones where they never solve it—or at least never *prove* it.'

'Gee, that'd be great,' I said.

She remembered it happened in my house, but police reporters have hard noses and live by black humour. 'I know a good exorcist if you need her ghost laid to rest,' she said.

'So kind.'

She laughed and hung up.

I went to the spare room and tapped lightly on the door.

'Patience? Detective Chloe says you can ring her any time you want to talk to her. Just ask me.'

Leave it at that, I thought.

Sure enough, a minute later the door opened and Patience peered around the edge, eyes red.

'Do you think I should?' she whispered.

'If you know anything about how Julieanne Weaver died, you should.'

Her eyes filled again, and her breathing quickened. She was close to panicking. 'I *can't*,' she said.

Time to calm things down.

'You don't have to decide anything now,' I said. 'Get some sleep.'

A flicker of some other emotion went across her face. 'I suppose you think it'll all seem better in the morning?'

I had hopes for Patience. That kind of cynicism is what gets you through the tough spots.

'No,' I said. 'It'll seem just as shitty. But it's easier to deal with shit when you're not exhausted.'

It may have been the first time she'd ever heard an adult she knew use the word 'shit'. Her eyes widened and she half-smiled, then tucked the edges of her mouth in as if she was going to get in trouble for being amused. I grinned.

'I don't promise to be able to help you. I don't promise to keep secrets for you. But I promise not to bullshit you.'

She searched my face and whatever she was looking for, seemed to find it. She took a breath in and whispered, almost hissing, 'I think my mother killed her.'

CHAPTER TWENTY-SIX

Patience closed the door—closed it, not slammed it—and I heard the lock click.

Holy family, Batman! Eliza.

I stood there like a stunned mullet. I could hear the house settling around me and the Arabic music from next door. A plane went overhead. I reached out and touched the door, wishing I could see through it and into Patience's mind.

Carter had an alibi. But Eliza—she had all the motive Carter had, and more. Real hatred. Real zealotry. I was pretty sure she believed in Carter and the party a lot more than Carter himself did.

Fiona was making a cup of tea, which I badly needed.

'How's she going?'

'She's got the worst of it off her chest,' I said absently, taking the mug she handed me. 'But if she's right, she's facing some terrible stuff.'

'So many kids do.' Fiona sighed. 'Abuse?'

'No, no, not that. Unless you think that preaching the prosperity gospel to developing minds is abuse.'

'Comes close.' Fiona is anti-capitalist, anti-global and pro- just about any social cause you can name. She deals stoically with my meat eating, which is the real test of our friendship. She herself eats only fair trade, organically grown, fresh-from-the-farm vegetables. She won't even wear silk because they kill the silkworms to get the thread. Prosperity gospel to her was like communism to a McCarthyite.

I let her rant a bit. It was reassuring to hear someone else who hated the idea as much as I did. The familiar soothing anger in Fiona's voice washed over me. Should I ring Detective Chloe? I hadn't promised to keep secrets for Patience— in fact, I'd warned her I wouldn't. Didn't that mean she wanted me to pass it on?

I wrestled with the problem. And with the urge to call Tol and ask his advice. That was just stupid. Surely I could make up my own mind? So I asked Fiona instead.

'Find out why she thinks so first,' Fiona said with an air of having heard it all. 'Girls her age jump to conclusions like frogs in a fire pit.'

'Fair enough.' I had no idea where she got that metaphor from, and I didn't want to know. But I rang Mum and Dad and told them I'd be staying at Fiona's, in case Patience felt like talking in the middle of the night. I slept on the sofa, which was old and soft and smelt faintly of cat.

In the morning, Patience emerged tousle-haired and wary when she heard Fiona in the shower. I'm not that competent before I have my morning coffee—which I never got at Fiona's unless I brought my own fair-trade beans—but after a cup of organic tea I was alert enough to watch Patience assemble her own breakfast of toast and honey. She was used to doing it, that was clear. So, her mother didn't wait on her hand and foot. Too busy looking after the males in the household, no doubt.

The cats demanded to be fed, even though I happened to know that Fiona fed them at the crack of dawn when she got up for her morning walk and to let them out for the day.

'Don't do it,' I advised, but Patience gave them little nibbles of toast with butter.

Fiona left with a 'Close the door behind you, there's a spare key for Patience on the fridge.'

Patience sat at the kitchen table opposite me, but didn't meet my eyes.

What the hell. I could tiptoe around her all day and not get any further. Besides, I thought she wanted to talk.

'I haven't told the police what you said,' I started.

She looked up, shocked. 'Oh, no, don't do that!'

'But if you have evidence that proves your mother is the killer, the police need to know.'

'Oh, I don't have evidence,' she said with relief. 'I just—' She faltered to a stop, and took a bite out of the toast so she couldn't speak.

'You just think she did it.'

She swallowed with difficulty and looked at me earnestly. I could almost see the thoughts: Was I trustworthy? Was she betraying her mother?

'She lied to me,' she said eventually. She spoke as though reciting a lesson. 'She said she was going down to the church. I thought she was taking food down to the meeting Dad had gone to. She often did that. I put the boys to bed and did my homework and she still wasn't back. I went to bed. She didn't get home until after midnight. Dad wasn't back until three, but he's often out late. Mum never is.'

'Are you sure she wasn't with him?'

Her finger pushed the last triangle of toast around the plate. She nodded. Her hair fell forward and she tucked it behind her ear automatically. She was embarrassed about something.

'I—I checked. She used Dad's car because he'd taken the big one.' She stopped as though she'd explained something.

'So?'

'Um, well, Dad's car belongs to the electoral office. And you have to fill in a log book when you use it.'

'Your mother filled in the *log book*?' That was taking civic responsibility a bit far, I thought.

'No.' Her eyes were angry. 'No, she didn't. That's why I knew she'd been somewhere … else. But I looked at the distance meter thing and the log book had the kilometres from when she started and I worked out she'd driven forty-one kilometres.'

The round trip from Annandale to North Hughes was about that.

'And the next morning, she looked terrible. When the news came on that a body of a woman had been found in Annandale, she went so white. She *knew*. I know she did.' Patience's eyes filled with tears. 'And she was happy when that man was arrested. Relieved. I couldn't stop thinking about it. So yesterday, after service, I asked her where she'd been that night. She said she'd been to Aunty Sally's, but they only live two kilometres away. She *lied* to me!' It was clear that this was her mother's real sin. 'And I just couldn't take her getting up in front of the other women and preaching about honesty and kindness! I just couldn't!'

'But why would your mother kill Julieanne Weaver?'

'Dad … Dad looked at her a lot,' she whispered. 'I heard him on the phone, once, to someone, while Mum was giving the boys their bath. He said, "You know I only want to be with you."'

'You think he and Julieanne were having an affair?'

'He made me go to a purity ball and everything!' she said, grief-stricken. I realised that the last few weeks had undermined everything Patience had ever been taught. As for purity balls—how icky were they? Formals where fathers escorted their pre-pubescent daughters and promised to look after them forever—as long as they stayed 'pure'. Erk. Freud would have a field day.

'He's—he's—a whited sepulchre!' she almost shouted. Good. She should be angry.

'Yep,' I said. It stopped her as nothing else could.

'But—' Her mouth opened and closed, and opened again. 'He *tries* to do good, doesn't he? Maybe she tempted him.'

'I'm sure she did tempt him,' I said. 'But everyone gets tempted, Patience. Doesn't mean you have to give in.'

All the energy seemed to drain out of her and she slumped in her chair. 'They're all liars,' she said dully. 'The whole lot of them. I don't believe in anything any more.'

I was very, very glad that she was pulling away from Carter and his cronies, but I didn't want her completely demoralised. Completely bereft. Besides …

'Just because some humans have made mistakes and chosen badly,' I said carefully, 'doesn't mean that God is false.'

'My father's always talking about trust in God,' she said. Ah, that touch of cynicism again.

'Even liars say something true sometimes.'

The idea startled her so much that she laughed, and finished her toast. Confession may or may not be good for the soul, but it's great for the appetite.

'Chloe Prudhomme needs to know all this, Patience,' I said.

'Why not?' she said bitterly. 'I can't go home again. I might as well betray them completely.'

That adolescent sense of drama had returned full force, but I knew I had to take advantage of it straight away. I called Detective Chloe from the house phone.

'I think Patience would like to talk to you,' I said. 'But maybe not at the police centre.'

'Where, then?'

I suggested a nearby café.

'Too public. Clovelly Beach—at the kiosk.'

She hung up before I could respond.

I smiled at Patience. 'Time to get dressed, kid, we're going to the beach.'

It was still early, but I was going to be late, so as Patience got her things together I rang Jennifer Jay and told her I'd be working from home, setting up recces for the recycling episode we'd be shooting next. I would, too. Later.

I retrieved my emergency spare clothes from the car, took a quick shower and was ready to drive Patience to her appointment with betrayal. Poor little possum.

Clovelly Beach is twenty minutes from Marrickville, and is one of the curiosities of Sydney. I always think of it as 'the tame beach'. In the 1930s, when they were trying to make work for men on the dole, they essentially concreted the beach. There's a crescent of sand at the end, but the long inlet that leads to the sand has concrete banks on each side, with steps leading down to the water. The inlet itself is almost closed off by a breakwater. The result is one of the safest beaches in the world. It's very popular with Italian grandmothers, because no waves make it past the breakwater, but it's also popular with snorkellers and divers, because all the rocks piled up for the earthworks have made a fantastic artificial reef which teems with fish life. Most beginner scuba courses in Sydney happen there. There's also wheelchair access, so you often get groups of disabled kids there for an outing.

But at just past nine on a Thursday morning, it was deserted except for some dog walkers and a bunch of grey-haired women power-walking along the cliff track that led to Bondi. The kiosk was open and I bought coffee thankfully. Patience started to ask for a milkshake and then realised that she didn't have enough money. I saw panic hit her and jumped in before she could melt down and decide to run back home.

'I'll take you to Centrelink later and you can apply for youth allowance—until you decide what you're going to do.'

That was the way. Nothing final, nothing definitive. Just stopgap measures. If she was right and her mother had killed Julieanne, I suspected that her brothers would need her back home, but it wasn't the right time to say that.

She relaxed enough to accept a milkshake from me. Detective Chloe arrived soon after and I offered to leave them alone to talk. Patience hesitated, but Chloe had her kindest face on, so eventually she nodded. I went for a walk, savouring the sea air. I used to live at Coogee, the next beach over, and I missed the ocean a lot. The sense of space, the vastness of the sky. But I also wanted a house, and in terms of what I could afford, it was a choice between a flat near the beach or a little house with a garden in the inner west. The garden won. Somewhere to sit outside and drink my tea. Somewhere to plant roses.

I was lost in a dream of David Austin roses spilling over my narrow picket fence when Detective Chloe and Patience joined me. Chloe pulled me gently aside.

'Well. Interesting. This is all off the record, of course.'

'As if!' I said. 'For you, not a chance. For her ... okay.'

'Why did she come to you, do you think?'

'Because I was the only person she knew who doesn't like her father.'

Chloe laughed. 'Not the only one,' she said. 'Will she be all right at your friend's place for a few days?'

I nodded. 'Will it be over by then?'

'One way or another,' Chloe said grimly.

'It might not be Eliza. Carter was out until three, remember, but his meeting finished at one.'

'Time of death's earlier, we think,' she said absently, watching Patience watch the waves. The girl seemed calmer now she'd passed the point of no return.

'By the way,' Chloe said as she left, 'I tried to ring you to say I'd be a bit late. Your phone's still off.'

'Oh, bugger!' I pulled out my phone and turned it on. It started buzzing immediately. Tyler had called eleven times and left several messages, the gist of which was that I should get my arse into gear and go interview the Carters about their missing daughter.

I let Patience listen to the least profane of them.

'Are you going?' she asked.

'Do you want me to? I could take a message for you if you want.'

She shook her head. 'No. Don't let them know you know where I am. You'll get in trouble.'

She was finding it hard to understand that Matthew Carter wasn't in charge of the universe, but no doubt she'd learn in time.

My phone rang. I expected Tyler but it was my mother.

'There's a very unpleasant man here who wants to find you,' she said stiffly.

'What's his name?'

'Garry Monahan.'

Carter's private eye. Hah.

'Tell him he's on private property and you'll call the police if he doesn't leave,' I said. 'And tell him that I'm on my way to see his boss.' I turned to Patience. 'Sorry, but your dad is hassling my parents. I have to go see him and call his bluff. Otherwise Monahan will follow me and find you.'

She was pale. 'What should I do?'

'I'll drop you back in Marrickville and then—well, frankly, if I were you I'd have a sleep. Centrelink can wait.' I pulled out some money and gave it to her. 'Just a loan,' I said, forestalling her objections. 'Until you get yourself sorted out.'

'Okay,' she said. Suddenly she looked very young and very scared. I put an arm around her shoulders and hugged her.

'I can't tell you that it will all be all right,' I said. 'But I'll try my best to help.'

'Thanks.' She managed a watery smile.

I dropped Patience at Marrickville and watched her go inside before I called Tyler and agreed to meet Terry and Dave at the Carters' house. Carter himself was at the electoral office, trying to pretend nothing had happened, but I wanted to see Eliza.

'Carter is the story,' Tyler objected.

'Carter is as smooth a piece of work as you'll ever see,' I retorted. 'We won't get anything out of him. Eliza, on the other hand, is a worried mum.'

'Hmm. She won't talk to you.'

'Then we'll go beard Carter in his den. Let Jennifer Jay know where I am, will you?'

He grumbled, but it was the least he could do.

CHAPTER TWENTY-SEVEN

Terry, Dave and I rendezvoused down the road from the Carters' and went to the house in the ABC car. Detective Chloe's car was pulled up at the front door and they had private security guards at the entrance keeping the media out. I rang Eliza from the driveway. The answering machine picked up.

'Eliza, if you're there, it's Poppy McGowan.'

She snatched up the receiver. 'Poppy? Do you know where she is?'

'I think we'd better have a talk, Eliza. Tell your goons to let me in.'

I passed the phone over to the head goon, who looked barely old enough to shave but was full of self-importance and bravado. He grandly waved us through.

'Good job,' Terry said.

'She may not agree to talk to us,' I cautioned.

'I'm rolling,' he said. 'Either way, we get footage.'

Spoken like a true NewsCaffian.

Detective Constable Martin answered the door. 'Leave the camera crew outside,' he said.

Terry got what he could through the open door: Eliza, Chloe, Samuel Stephenson and his wife, and Amos Winchester, all looking up from their chairs and frowning.

'Out!' Martin said more forcefully.

I shrugged at Terry and went in and Martin shut the door behind me. Winchester looked up at me with a set jaw, as if he were afraid I'd start throwing accusations around. I nodded to him. A pact, a reassurance. His secret was safe with me. He nodded in return, fighting back some strong emotion which set a muscle in his cheek jumping. What would he do to protect the church? How far would he go? A man who could deny his sexuality for his entire life was a formidable person. But then he turned to Eliza and his face gentled. I was suddenly sure he would never hurt anyone. Not physically. Not deliberately.

Eliza was distraught. She ignored Winchester and Detective Chloe and came over to me, clutching at my arm.

'Where is she? That detective says she's all right, but she won't tell me where she is. Have you seen her?'

Chloe cut in. 'Why do you assume that Patience would go to Ms McGowan?'

'Where else would she go?' Eliza cried. 'None of her friends have heard from her. No one in the church. This woman has been a terrible influence on Patience! She would never have left otherwise.'

It wasn't the first time I'd been called a terrible influence. Mrs Dickens, the head of the altar society at my old parish church, had warned my friends about me in exactly the same terms when I was thirteen. I had the same reaction now as then: a mixture of outrage at the idea that I could be a bad influence on anyone, and a tinge of pride because of who was doing the accusing. I hadn't like Mrs Dickens's take on things any more than I liked Eliza's. Now that I thought about it, they agreed on a lot of things.

I looked at Chloe and she made a small shushing motion with her hand, so I didn't snap back at Eliza.

'I'm sure that, wherever she is, Patience is fine, Eliza,' I said soothingly. 'Isn't that so, detective?'

'She was when I spoke to her this morning,' Chloe said.

Eliza burst into tears. 'Why did she go? Why won't she come home?' she wailed.

The Stephenson sparrow woman patted her back ineffectually and Stephenson himself said, 'Now, Eliza,' in an intimidating tone, as if the woman was acting in bad taste by caring about her daughter.

Chloe and I exchanged glances, and she nodded at me. Apparently she wanted to let me put the boot in. Good.

'She doesn't want to come home because she thinks you killed Julieanne Weaver,' I said.

Eliza dragged air in with a kind of whoop that almost had me laughing. It was a reaction of total shock. Mrs Stephenson gasped, too. Even Winchester was startled. But not

Stephenson. He just watched Detective Chloe watch Eliza. That was the most interesting thing I'd seen in days.

Eliza sprang forward. 'Get out of my house! Get out of my house!' she shouted at me. She came at me with her fists raised. 'Jezebel! Whore! Handmaid of Satan! Out!' Her face contorted with hatred. Maroon with rage, mouth gaping— and the truly horrible part was that the rest of her was as neat as always, perfectly groomed, well shod, tidy. It seemed as though someone had CGIed this screaming fishwife face onto another body.

Chloe stepped in between the two of us. 'Out,' she said to me.

Martin took my arm and led me to the door, and it was only then that I realised I was shaking.

As Martin closed the door behind me, I heard Chloe ask, 'Is that why you killed Julieanne Weaver, Eliza? Was she a handmaid of Satan too?'

I so wanted to hear her answer. I met Martin's eyes and, bless him, he delayed closing the door long enough for me to hear. But Eliza didn't answer. She just burst into tears and sank to the ground.

Winchester bent over her and said something softly. That was all Martin was prepared to give me. He shut the door definitively, leaving me still shaking on the other side.

'What's happened?' Terry asked.

'I'm a whore and a handmaid of Satan,' I said, trying to sound flippant, 'and I'm no longer welcome.'

'Better get to Carter's office, then,' Terry said phlegmatically.

But Carter passed us on our way to the electoral office, driving fast and looking worried.

'They've called him home,' I said. 'Go to the party offices.'

Something was worrying me. There were two things I couldn't get out of my head. One was the fact that Carter had come home from his meeting two hours later than he said—but he couldn't have been with Julieanne, because Julieanne was dead by then. And Samuel Stephenson hadn't been at all surprised that Eliza might have killed Julieanne.

I struggled to remember what Paul Baume had said about the man who had been meeting Julieanne. 'The guy from the church,' he'd said. And that he was in the story I'd done for *The Daily Report*. It fitted Stephenson as well as Carter. There'd only been a couple of shots of Stephenson, which was why I hadn't immediately thought of him, but Paul could have seen him, even though Tyler had chosen not to use that revealing little moment in the car park.

Julieanne, Paul had said earlier, wanted to get married. Had implied that she had someone lined up, more important than Paul. Which didn't fit Tol at all. But Stephenson was already married, and even Julieanne couldn't have imagined that he would divorce his little sparrow wife to marry her. The scandal would have killed the party and any political aspirations either of them had. Julieanne was Psycho Woman, but she wasn't stupid.

So maybe I was being stupid. What was I missing?

Who was I missing?

If Carter wasn't sleeping with Julieanne … who was he with?

If Julieanne had planned to marry someone—who? Surely not Amos Winchester? That was just laughable, for all sorts of reasons. The only thing I was sure of was that Amos Winchester was proof against far more *fatale* femmes than Julieanne. And if she'd held his sexuality over his head like a sword of Damocles—no. She might have demanded preselection as the price of silence, but not marriage. So who? Who was the father of her child?

The party offices had a couple of camera crews and three print journalists waiting in the reception area. Terry, out of habit, shot a minute or so of footage of the receptionist, Samantha, who recognised me but was in full 'we will fight them on the beaches' mode.

'I'm afraid no one from the party is available to comment on anything at the moment,' she informed me, loudly enough for the others to hear. They rolled their eyes. One of the camera operators, who looked about fourteen, was playing his Switch and didn't take any notice. I heard Pokémon music. It was clearly irritating Samantha. She glared at him, but of course he didn't notice.

'Annoying, huh?' I said, leaning a little closer as if to speak over the music.

'He's been playing that for *two hours!*'

'I know Mr Stephenson's not here,' I said. 'I just saw him at the Carters'.' As if I was his best friend. 'Eliza's not coping well, is she?'

Samantha tried to put on the sympathetic friend face, but a flicker of contempt came first. Aha!

'Well … she's always been a bit high-strung,' she said. Non-committal tone, but 'high-strung' is polite-speak for 'neurotic as hell'.

'Really?' I asked. 'That must be hard for Matthew.'

'Oh, it is,' she said. 'But he's so loyal to her. He won't hear a word against her, you know.'

A tinge of bitterness there all right. Could Samantha be Carter's lover?

'Were you taking the minutes for the preselection meeting last Tuesday?' I asked, pulling out a notebook.

'Oh, I can't reveal anything that was said at the meeting!' she said immediately.

'So you were there?'

'I take the minutes at all confidential meetings.' Proud as a peacock.

'Matthew must trust you a great deal.' I positively purred it.

She sat a little straighter, as any trusted employee might at such a compliment, but the small smile on her mouth was full of private satisfaction. Yep, Samantha was my girl.

'What time did the meeting end?'

She hesitated. 'Around one, I think.'

'And what time did you and Matthew leave, Samantha?'

This time, I put all my secret knowledge into the question, leaning in and looking meaningful. My tone was spiced with just a little prurience. My smile was conspiratorial.

And God help me, it worked! She blushed fiery red, the tide sweeping up over her pale skin as though she was a bottle being filled with wine.

She fought it. 'Just after one,' she managed to say.

'Mmm. But he didn't get home until three, did he?'

She blinked at such intimate knowledge. 'How—'

I changed course. 'Mr Stephenson's wife—'

'What? What about her? You're not going to tell me *she* was killed? It was cancer!'

I backpedalled mentally. Stephenson's wife was dead? Then who was sparrow woman?

'Perhaps I misunderstood,' I said. 'The woman I saw with Mr Stephenson at service on Sunday?'

She relaxed. Off the hard subjects and onto something easy. 'His sister,' she said pityingly. 'Ruth.'

'Thanks, Samantha,' I said. I turned and signalled to Terry and Dave that we were leaving. They stopped an animated conversation with one of the other sound guys about Australia's chances in the World Cup and picked up their gear reluctantly.

'We going?' Terry said in surprise. 'We haven't got anything yet.'

'Oh, yes, we have,' I said, smiling sweetly at Samantha, who was white-faced, wondering whether she was going to be plastered all over the evening news as a home-wrecker, an adulteress, a handmaid of Satan.

I was seriously tempted. Seriously. But I had no evidence, and Australia has the most draconian defamation laws in the Western world. Making that accusation without proof was a shortcut to a lawsuit.

'You'll have to do another piece to camera,' Terry said as we left the building. He set up his tripod on the footpath so he could shoot me in front of the party headquarters sign.

Oh, shit. I hate pieces to camera. In education TV, you can avoid them almost entirely, but reporters lived and died by them. Well, if I did it badly enough, maybe Tyler wouldn't want to use me any more.

But when it came to it, I couldn't deliberately botch it. Just couldn't. And I wanted to be fair to Patience.

'Patience Carter, the daughter of Australian Family Party MP Matthew Carter, has been missing since Wednesday afternoon. The police say that she is safe and well, but will not reveal her whereabouts. She is clearly not prepared to come home. Party representatives are not commenting. Is this a simple case of a teenage runaway? Or is her absence linked to the death of Dr Julieanne Weaver last week? Dr Weaver was seeking preselection with the Australian Family Party in the seat of North Hughes, and was a friend of the Carters. Eliza and Matthew Carter are barricaded in their home with police questioning them and security guards excluding all media.' Tyler could sit Terry's footage from the Carters' house over that bit. The less they showed of me, the better. 'Poppy McGowan, for the ABC.' I finished off a little fast, maybe, but I couldn't think of anything else to say that Patience wouldn't read as a betrayal of her.

'Wonder where she is?' Terry mused. 'She seemed like a nice kid.'

'Yeah, she did,' I said shortly. I didn't like withholding information from my team, but if Tyler got the idea I knew where Patience was and hadn't interviewed her he'd have gone ballistic.

CHAPTER TWENTY-EIGHT

After the guys had dropped me at my car and taken the footage back to the ABC, I called Fiona's and left a message on the answering machine warning Patience that I might be on the news talking about her, but that I'd done my best to make it okay. I paused, hearing the buzz of the machine. 'Your mother's involved, but I think maybe she didn't kill Julieanne.'

Because if Carter was screwing Samantha, why would Eliza kill Julieanne? Unless, of course, she'd made the same mistake I'd made and assumed that Julieanne was the guilty party. But surely Julieanne would have set her straight?

I sighed, suddenly exhausted. All I wanted to do was go home and collapse. I couldn't believe it was only lunchtime.

I picked up a sandwich and went back to my little house to make phone calls to the various recyclers we were featuring in the next episode. I sat on the floor in the square of sunlight from the western window and brooded, phone in hand. I didn't have the mental energy to work. I couldn't be chatty and efficient with strangers. I just couldn't.

Instead, I rang Paul Baume, to check which 'guy from the church' he'd seen get into Julieanne's car. But he'd gone out into the field to assess some woman's collection of antique washing machines. And he refused to use a mobile phone because of the supposed health risks, so all I could do was leave a message.

I was sitting there in a stupor, not sure what to do next, when I heard the front door open and my dad say, 'There you go. Just shut the door when you leave.' Oh, no. I didn't have the energy to talk to Alain Parkes.

A moment later, Tol's voice floated up the stairs. 'Poppy? You there?'

Relief swept over me. Tol. He must have seen that I'd dropped my bag at the foot of the stairs. I felt reprieved, somehow.

'Up here,' I called.

He came up the stairs and appeared in the doorway, looking down at me enquiringly. I tried to smile but I don't think I did a very good job because his face changed and he sat down next to me.

'I heard about Patience Carter,' he said. 'Are you worried about her?'

'Not exactly,' I said. I needed to talk about all this, and Tol had arrived like a blessing from heaven. So it all came out: Patience. Eliza. Being a handmaid of Satan (he laughed at that), Samuel Stephenson, Samantha the receptionist, Paul's belief that Julieanne was planning to marry someone important …

He heard me out, head bent and eyes studying the floor as he took it all in.

'So you're torn between Eliza Carter pushing her into the pit because she thought Julieanne was having an affair with her husband, and Samuel Stephenson pushing her because Julieanne was blackmailing him into marrying her?' You've got to love a man who can actually think. Particularly when it was his girlfriend we were talking about.

For some reason I wanted to be fair to Julieanne. 'She might not have seen it as blackmail,' I said. 'Probably she thought he'd jump at it. She was twenty years younger than him, after all. And she may have been more interested in preselection than marriage.'

I pulled my phone out and called Chloe.

'Prudhomme,' she said, sounding harassed. I could hear Eliza Carter in the background, still crying. And the PA system from the police centre. So they'd arrested Eliza. Or at least taken her in for questioning.

'Get a DNA sample from Samuel Stephenson,' I said baldly. 'Carter wasn't screwing Julieanne. He's on with the receptionist. So Stephenson's the most likely guy from the church.'

'Not a chance in hell,' Chloe said. 'He's already refused.'
She hung up.

'I'm sorry, for the daughter's sake,' Tol said, 'but I have to
say I think Eliza's more likely. Carter could easily have been
having an affair with both the other girl and Julieanne.'

That was true. It didn't feel right, somehow, but it fit the
facts as well as any other theory. We talked it over a few
minutes more, but until we could talk to Paul, we had no
proof either way.

The doorbell rang.

'Probably Alain,' Tol said, getting to his feet and pulling
me up. 'Or maybe the councillors.'

'What?' I was so surprised I almost stumbled going down
the stairs. Tol put out a hand to steady me and smiled, a
little nervously.

'Er, this morning I called the permissions guy at the
council—what's his name?'

'Fozina?'

'Him, yes. And he told me the heritage subcommittee
was meeting this afternoon. So I invited them to inspect
the site personally and receive a report from Alain and me.'

I gaped at him. 'And they agreed on such short notice?'

He grimaced. 'I think they couldn't wait to get a look at
the crime scene.'

I was flooded with gratitude and maybe something
a bit stronger. Tol had gone out of his way to organise
this—I knew from Annie how busy he was trying to deal
with Julieanne's work as well as his own—to get me my
house back.

When he opened the door, there was not only Alain, there was Marco Fozina, the brown cardigan guy from the council (in a green cardie this time), the mayor, and two other councillors, who clutched their clipboards as though they expected to use them as defensive weapons. The mayor entered first, as if she never did anything else, and the others followed. I smiled hello at Alain and he smiled back, but the others were too busy looking at the pit to notice me.

'Is this where—' the mayor said delicately.

'Yes, that's right!' Tol said, loudly and cheerfully. 'That's the site. The bones have all been removed, of course, but we think we can still identify traces of where the killing took place.'

The subcommittee looked uneasy and shocked, not sure exactly which killing he was referring to, and I realised that Tol had done that deliberately. I won't say he was actually enjoying the situation, but by the gleam in his eye it did spark his sense of the absurd. More than likely, he was trying to distract himself from memories of Julieanne. I fought down a smile and addressed the mayor very seriously indeed.

'This is Dr Lang, mayor, from the Museum of New South Wales, who wrote the report, and this is Dr Parkes from the University of Sydney.' Introductions were made all around, and then I went on. 'Dr Lang—'

Someone knocked on the door lightly. Alain went to open it. It was Boris, beaming and flourishing his hammer.

'We's back in, eh, miss?' he said. 'I can put in the post, now?'

The mayor scowled at me. 'Have you arranged work to be done on this site in defiance of our order forbidding it?'

'Certainly not!' I said, in a shocked tone. 'That would be most improper.'

Boris was looking from me to her with some puzzlement. 'So, miss, what you want me to do?'

'Just wait a bit, Boris,' I said firmly. 'It's up to the subcommittee whether we can do the work.'

He subsided, the hammer falling to his side, and went to sit on the stairs. I took a deep breath. Calm, Poppy.

'Dr Lang and Dr Parkes are very sure that this site is not of historical significance,' I said.

'Historical interest,' Alain said judiciously, 'but not significance.'

'But we have so few sites of historical interest in this country!' cardigan man exclaimed. 'We should preserve all of them!'

I cast a look of entreaty at Tol.

'Do you live in the area, councillor?' he cut in smoothly.

Cardigan man nodded. 'Of course!'

'Well, I'm sure if we dug under your house—or yours, mayor—we'd find something of historical interest. That's the way with these inner-city sites. They've been in constant use since European occupation, and there's always *something* to find.'

They digested that and clearly didn't like the idea of someone digging up their floor.

Alain cleared his throat. 'It's just a few old mutton bones,' he said. 'The kind of thing you'd find at the back of any old butcher's shop. Early breeds, yes, but not so early as to be exciting.' His tone suggested that this was all a waste of their time, and the mayor nodded.

Marco Fozina, seizing the opportunity to get a piece of paperwork off his desk, stepped forward and presented her with his clipboard. 'If you'll just sign here,' he said, 'that'll cancel the heritage order.'

She reached out slowly and took the clipboard, looking at cardigan man for a kind of permission. He shrugged. The mayor took the pen Tol held and poised it over the paper just as someone thumped loudly on the door. The mayor jumped and dropped the clipboard.

I only just managed not to swear as I pushed past the mayor and yanked the door open. 'Yes?'

It was Samuel Stephenson.

'Matthew asked me to come,' he said.

I stood back and he strode in. He cast a quick look around, surprised at the number of people in the room, all spread out against the walls on the remnants of the chip-board floor. His gaze lingered for a moment on the bearer where Julieanne's blood had been. Which was interesting, because I had scrubbed it clean, the pit had been enlarged since then, and there shouldn't have been any reason he would know the exact spot where she had fallen.

I saw Tol follow his gaze and his lips tightened. He moved between me and Stephenson. It was a lovely, instinctive response, and it warmed me, but I couldn't see Stephenson's face, so I moved a little sideways. That brought his eyes back to me.

'Matthew thinks you know where Patience is,' he said. 'Do you?' No nice guy now. The round tones of the church elder were gone, and I could hear the accent of his youth underneath. He'd been born in Erskineville, I think, a working-class suburb at the time.

'*If* I knew where Patience is,' I said, 'I would probably have promised not to tell her family. Now, as you can see, we're a bit busy here.'

'You interfering little bitch,' he said.

Boris leapt up. 'You don't talk to her like that!' he said menacingly, hammer held high.

Stephenson looked at Boris as if he were a freak in a circus.

I wanted the mayor to sign that piece of paper, and out of the corner of my eye I saw Alain pick up the clipboard and give it back to her. But she was riveted by the conversation between me and Stephenson. I had to take him into the kitchen, give Alain and Tol a chance to close the deal, so to speak.

'It's all right, Boris.' I turned to Stephenson. 'Do you want a cup of tea?' It surprised everyone except Stephenson. It was what he expected women to say.

'No,' he barked.

'It won't take a minute,' I said, as though he were refusing out of politeness. 'Come on through.'

I edged past Fozina and the other councillors and led the way out to the space that would be the kitchen, where the kettle and tea-making paraphernalia perched on a milk crate. I filled the kettle from the bathroom tap and turned it on. Stephenson followed me and stood just inside the doorway.

'No milk, I'm afraid,' I said.

'Stop playing for time,' Stephenson said. 'Where is she?'

'According to the police,' I answered, 'she is safe, she is clean, she is warm, she is well fed. She is also over sixteen, which means that she doesn't have to come home if she doesn't want to.'

'That girl's a troublemaker!' he growled.

'Patience?' I said. 'Puh-leese.'

'You're all troublemakers.'

'Women?' Tol said, appearing in the doorway. He leant against the frame, somehow emphasising both his considerable youth and his height compared to Stephenson. 'I haven't heard that kind of talk since I came back from the Middle East.'

'Better be careful, Samuel,' I said. 'You don't want to sound like an Islamic fundamentalist.'

I looked a question at Tol and he raised his eyes skyward—the mayor hadn't signed yet. I made a shooing motion—*Get back in there and get her signing!*—but before he could, the others crowded—and I do mean crowded—into the doorway.

'Milk and two sugars,' said cardigan man.

'I take mine black,' the mayor said.

'I like strong,' Boris shouted from the back. 'Lots of milk.'

Now if I had a normal family, I wouldn't have had enough mugs to go around and I could explain that and make them all go away. But I have a large, tea-drinking family who like to inspect whatever is happening and have a cuppa while they do it. Which meant that about twelve mugs were lined up on the kitchen windowsill in full sight.

'There's no milk,' I said.

'I go get some,' Boris said helpfully, and headed out the door, leaving it open behind him.

I made tea and put sugar into one mug, stirred it, and handed it to Stephenson. He took it, but didn't drink.

I gave a mug to Tol. He slid down quickly and put it on the floor. Wanted his hands free. That was a good idea if Stephenson was a murderer, but I preferred to have a mugful of scalding water I could throw in his eyes.

'There are people in the church who will look after Patience,' he said, trying to sound reasonable, trying to ignore the spectators. 'If she'd turned to them in the first place—'

I made tea for the mayor and handed it to her, passing it over Stephenson's shoulder. He took a sip from his mug and frowned, but I don't think it was the quality of the tea that was bothering him.

'Her friends at the church—'

'Would have taken her straight back to her father,' I cut in. 'And her mother. Who, apparently, may be a murderer.'

A small smile curved the very edges of his mouth. He drank to cover it up, and I rejoiced. *Take another sip, Samuel*, I urged him silently. Leave lots of lovely DNA all over my nice clean mug which my mother, God bless her, had washed only the day before.

'Really?' the mayor said. 'That girl who was missing? Her mother's the murderer?'

All the councillors craned in, eyes agog.

'There's no evidence of that,' Stephenson said automatically. 'What are these people doing here, anyway?'

'I am the mayor of this municipality,' the mayor answered, icily. 'I have every right to inspect any work which may affect the historic heritage of this area.'

'*We* are the heritage subcommittee,' cardigan man added, wanting to claim some of the glory.

Someone came in the front door. Boris with the milk? That was fast.

'Poppy?' It was Chloe's voice.

Her natural authority worked wonders—the council party moved back into the dining alcove to let her come through to us. The mayor even smiled at her. Chloe summed them up with one glance and then ignored them. Stephenson took another swig of tea while they sorted themselves out, as though he needed strength.

It wasn't just Chloe. It was Chloe and Martin and Samuel Stephenson's sister, Ruth. I must have looked surprised, because Ruth jumped into speech with a flurry of breathy phrases.

'I went with Eliza. And Matthew said Samuel had come here. So instead of making the detectives take me all the way home, I thought Samuel could—I mean, I thought we could meet Samuel here. I didn't think you would mind. I saw you at the office …. You seemed like a nice young lady and ... It's such a long way out there and—and—oh, dear ...'

She ran out of steam in the face of her brother's glare, and only then seemed to see the others. She looked at them, bewildered. I felt sorry for her and irritated at the same time. But this was a great opportunity, and I couldn't pass it up.

'Were you at the meeting with Matthew Carter the night Julieanne was killed, Samuel?' I asked.

'Yes,' his sister squeaked.

'No,' he said at the same moment.

There was a silence in which Detective Chloe and Martin both turned slowly and looked at Stephenson.

'I *was* at the meeting,' he amended hastily, glaring at his sister. 'You can ask Matthew. But I left early.'

'Why?' Chloe asked.

In the same moment, Ruth said, 'But you weren't home until quite late, Samuel.'

Stephenson cast a quick look towards the pit. He seemed to weigh his options. 'If you *must* know,' he said, 'I followed Eliza Carter.'

So he was throwing Eliza to the wolves. But, of course, she might deserve it.

'Why?' I asked.

'She'd been ... agitated ... that day at the electoral office. I made my views clear to the others and then I went to talk to her. If they picked Weaver, I wanted Eliza to accept it with grace.'

'Because you were supporting her?' I asked. *Weaver*. Not *Julieanne*, not *Dr Weaver*.

Chloe said nothing, just watched.

'She was a good candidate,' he said defensively. 'She proved that in the TV debate.'

'What did Eliza say?' Martin asked.

'She didn't say anything!' Stephenson said, almost triumphantly. 'When I got to their house, she was just driving away. She looked upset. So I followed her.'

Of course he did. Such a normal thing to do.

'Why?'

'I didn't want her to get into trouble. I thought she might, um—'

'Kill Julieanne?'

'No! Of course not. I just thought any confrontation between them was best avoided.' The rounded tones were back in full. He'd rehearsed this, planned out his answers. He was also aware, as I was, of the interested faces at the open dining-room window, which, being at a right angle to the kitchen window, gave quite a good view in. I noticed that the mayor had secured prime position. She looked meaningfully at the closed kitchen window. What the hell, I thought, and opened it so they could hear properly.

'So what happened?' That was Martin.

I looked at Tol. He was staring at Stephenson with a peculiar intensity. His hands were clenched. I felt my stomach drop. He didn't look—safe.

'Eliza drove here.'

'And?'

'And nothing. I had no idea what this house was. I knew it wasn't Weaver's home. I assumed Eliza was here on church business. We do a lot of welfare work, you know. I waited. After a while, Eliza came out. She seemed upset. She sat in the car for a minute, then drove home. I—er, I made sure she got there safely, and then I went home.'

'And the next day?' Detective Chloe's voice was smooth. 'When Weaver's death was announced? It didn't occur to you to inform us?'

He hesitated, glancing at his sister as if for support. She was staring at him with a troubled frown. Not used to thinking of him as anything less than perfect.

'I confess—I thought that if I came forward and Eliza was arrested … I thought it would ruin the election.'

'So you protected a murderer for political gain,' Chloe said. 'That makes you an accessory after the fact.'

He didn't even blink. He'd thought this through and done his research. He smirked and crossed the kitchen, put his almost empty mug down on the milk crate and then moved back to stand next to his sister. I suppressed a smirk of my own.

'I don't think so, detective. I had no real knowledge of what happened in this house. I *still* have no real knowledge. All I know is that Eliza Carter visited here on the night in question. I hardly think that makes me an accessory.'

'We could charge you with hindering a police investigation,' Martin said.

From the dining room, a voice came from one of the councillors who hadn't spoken before: 'I'm a solicitor, Mr— er, and well, I'd be happy to represent you.'

Stephenson just glared.

'Of course, I don't do a great deal of criminal law, but I know the basics …' the solicitor trailed off.

Stuff this. He would never have just sat in that car and waited. He'd have had to know what she was doing in here. *If* he'd followed her, which I doubted. He'd come to meet Julieanne. Eliza was just a coincidence.

'It still makes a great story for the news,' I said. They all blinked, even Tol. They'd forgotten who I really was.

'You can't report this!' Stephenson said.

I laughed. 'Try and stop me! A conversation in my own house in which I participated? No one said "Off the record" that I heard. What about you, Tol? You hear anyone say "Off the record"?'

He shook his head, a grim smile on his face.

Chloe just watched.

Faintly, I heard the councillor talking again: 'She's well within her rights, you know …' and the mayor shushing him. I pushed down the desire to giggle. It was like a Gilbert and Sullivan show, with a little chorus.

'Nope. It's a great story,' Tol said. 'Not as good as the real one, but certainly newsworthy.'

There was a small silence. Go on, I thought. Someone has to ask.

It was Ruth.

'Real story? I don't understand.'

'The real story is a little more complicated,' I said. 'The *real* story is that Julieanne Weaver was having an affair with your brother. She got pregnant.'

There were gasps from the dining room and I took a deep breath. If I was wrong, Stephenson had a lot of witnesses to slander.

'Samuel?' Ruth asked, voice quavering.

'You'll never prove that!' he said.

I moved to the milk crate, picked his mug up and tossed the dregs out the back door onto the garden.

'No? Why, Detective Constable Martin, I think my coffee mug may have on it the DNA of someone who was in the house that night. You had better test it.'

From the dining room came the faint sound of clapping. Someone appreciated my sense of drama, anyway—probably Alain. I handed the mug to Martin, who accepted it blankly, then shot a glance at Stephenson and bit back a smile. He took an evidence bag out of his pocket and slid the mug into it carefully. For a minute, Stephenson looked as if he would grab it back, but he controlled himself. He was sweating a little now, and his composure seemed forced.

'Well, Mr Stephenson?' Chloe said. 'Will we find that Julieanne Weaver's baby was yours?'

'Who knows?' Stephenson snapped. 'She was a whore to her bones!'

'But the possibility is there.'

He looked at his sister. Ruth had taken a handkerchief from her cardigan pocket and pressed it to her mouth as though she felt sick. I didn't blame her.

'We have a witness who saw you getting into her car,' I added.

'All right!' he said. 'I had—relations with her.'

'Aha!' said the mayor.

'Samuel ...' Ruth whispered, not accusingly but with great sadness. 'How could you?'

'You wouldn't understand!' he said. 'Men have *needs*. After Gloria died I needed ... I knew better than to—to get involved with someone at the church. Weaver was ... convenient.' He was really sweating now, and interestingly, his explanation was all to Ruth, not to Chloe. His sister's opinion mattered to him, which I hadn't expected.

Convenient. It was a horrible word. Julieanne Weaver had been a lot of things, but she'd never been a convenience in her life.

'Convenient?' Tol asked, as if sharing my thoughts.

Stephenson looked at Tol for the first time, and I realised that he didn't know who Tol was.

'Dr Lang was Julieanne's *official* boyfriend,' I explained softly, and there was an intake of breath from our audience. For the first time Stephenson blanched. A man for him to answer to.

'She wasn't worth your concern,' he said earnestly to Tol. 'A loose woman is a blight on everyone she comes into contact with. She was shameless! Parading around the bedroom in those—outfits. Decent women don't own underwear like that. You're better off without her.'

Julieanne had been whatever men wanted her to be; it didn't surprise me, somehow, that Stephenson wanted a whore.

'Is that why you bashed her head in?' I asked. 'Because you were better off without her?'

He was thrown off balance by the accusation, not expecting it to come from me. His mouth opened and shut, but he didn't answer.

'Eliza Carter told us,' Chloe added, 'that she pushed Julieanne into the pit. She thinks that Julieanne died as soon as her head hit the beam. But she didn't, did she, Samuel?'

Now was Martin's moment. 'You didn't follow Eliza, did you, Sam? Eh? You came for a session of hot sex with Julieanne, and when you arrived, what? Eliza was coming out? Or did you arrive later? We know what you did. You took her head between your hands and you bashed her skull against that beam until she was dead, didn't you? Once, twice, three times … what did it sound like, Sam? Did you enjoy it? Was it as much fun as fucking her? Eh?'

Ruth rushed out the back door and we heard her being sick in the garden. We all looked towards the sound and Stephenson used the distraction to run. He sprinted down the narrow strip of chipboard that led to the front door with surprising speed, but Tol moved faster, reaching out a long arm to jerk him back. Stephenson teetered on the edge of the pit.

Time slowed. I saw—I swear I saw, even though it must have happened in a split second—Tol thinking through letting him fall, letting him die, maybe, and then rejecting the idea. He pulled Stephenson around by his expensive jacket so that instead of falling headfirst he sprawled half on and half off the chipboard, hands scraping for purchase, feet scrabbling in the dirt.

Chloe and Martin ran over and Martin grabbed him, hauling him up.

'She deserved it,' Stephenson said, looking at Tol. 'She said I had two options: I could marry her and be the MP's husband, the power behind the throne, or I could buy her silence and an abortion with preselection. She threatened that if I didn't make sure she was the candidate, she'd announce the affair to the media, and ruin the party. The church, too. I couldn't let a little whore destroy everything we'd built, Matthew and Amos and I.'

'When did she say that?' Chloe asked. 'That night?'

'Eliza only bruised her a little. I arrived just as she was coming out. I let Eliza leave and when I came in Weaver was sitting on the beam, there'—he pointed to the pit—'rubbing her head. She looked up at me and she laughed about Eliza. Thought it was funny that Eliza believed Matthew had been—had been intimate with her.'

It astounded me that after everything he'd done, he still couldn't say the word sex.

Ruth had come back in and was standing in the kitchen doorway, wiping her mouth. Her eyes were dark and burning. 'You are a murderer,' she said.

'I had to protect the church!' he said, pleading for her understanding. 'It's more important than a slut like her.'

'You killed your unborn child,' Ruth said. She raised her hand, finger extended, and pointed at him with steadfast condemnation. 'You are damned for all time.'

She was implacable, the voice of judgement, and Samuel bowed his head beneath it, his shoulders shaking as he began to cry.

'Ruth!' he cried, but she walked past him, shoulders straight, and went out the door without a backwards glance.

A second later Boris returned with a two-litre jug of milk, looking over his shoulder at Ruth as she walked down the street.

'I miss something?' he asked. He passed the milk to Fozina.

'Yes,' I answered. My head was spinning and I felt sick, but there was something I was determined to get done. I marched over to Fozina, picked up the clipboard which the mayor had dropped again in all the excitement, and handed it to him. He looked at it blankly, and then looked at the milk, so I took the milk away and pointed at the mayor. Obediently, he sidled around the edge of the room on the chipboard ledge and gave the clipboard to her.

She looked at me with a challenge in her eye.

'I'm a member of the media,' I said. 'Do you want to make an enemy of me?'

She signed, tore off the top copy and laid it carefully on the floor in the corner. Then she gathered her dignity and walked out, followed by her entourage, with Boris trailing behind, saying, 'Can I do the post now?'

I sighed and sat down on the edge of the pit, feeling boneless and curiously empty.

Detective Chloe and Martin did the whole process of telling Stephenson his rights while Boris enthusiastically dug the hole for the newel post, whistling. Chloe called for backup and when a patrol car arrived they handcuffed Stephenson, put him carefully in the back and watched as the uniformed officers drove him off. By that time, I'd pulled myself together, and went out to her.

'Um—have you actually arrested him?' I asked.

'You've got about an hour before he's formally charged. I guess you've earned an exclusive.'

'Fantastic!' I said. 'Thanks.'

I called Tyler and said, 'Tape this conversation *right now*.' I opened the camera app on my phone, handed it to Tol and said, 'Film us. Close up to get the audio.'

'Taping,' Tyler said.

'Okay,' Tol said, aiming the phone.

'This is Poppy McGowan for the ABC. I'm speaking to Detective Sergeant Chloe Prudhomme.' I turned to Chloe. 'Detective Sergeant, is it true that there has been a breakthrough in the investigation into the death of Julieanne Weaver?'

She looked at me with a long-suffering air, but she said, into the phone. 'Yes. We have taken a suspect in for questioning.'

'And are you expecting to make an arrest?'

'We expect to be charging the individual concerned with the murder of Dr Weaver.'

'Is that individual Samuel Stephenson, the treasurer of the Radiant Joy Church and one of the preselection committee for the Australian Family Party?'

She took a deep breath, protocol fighting with a sense of debt. 'Yes, it is.'

'Eliza Carter, the wife of MP Matthew Carter, was taken into police custody earlier today. Has she been cleared of any complicity in the murder?' I wanted Patience to hear it straight from the police, not just from me.

'Mrs Carter is no longer a person of interest in this investigation.' Chloe stared meaningfully at me. That was it.

'Thank you, detective sergeant.'

She waited until Tol lowered the phone.

'I want you and Lang to come in tomorrow and make a formal statement about that scene in there. And you'd better email me the names of everyone who was in the room. God help us, we'll have to take statements from all of them.'

She and Martin made their way to their car.

I went back to the phone. 'Tyler? I've filmed this as well. I'll send it to you via Dropbox. You've got about an hour before they charge Stephenson. The background is that he and Weaver were having an affair and she threatened to expose him if he didn't guarantee preselection.'

'Shit!' Tyler said. 'Are you sure?'

'Very sure. She was pregnant, but they haven't confirmed it was his yet, so maybe you'd better not use that.'

'We can say she was pregnant and leave it to the punters to draw their own conclusions,' he said. 'And play that grab of him in the car park we didn't use before.'

'Good. Show him as the hypocrite he is.'

'This is great stuff, sweetheart. You want a job with me?'

'No, thanks!' I said. And hung up. I felt a dark satisfaction. That was the end of Australian Family trying to take over the New South Wales parliament or any other. Carter might hang on, but he'd be gone at the next election. I ticked off the 'Take down Carter' item in my mental to-do list, sent the video file to Tyler's email, and that was that.

Tol was watching me from the open front door, a curious look on his face, half admiration and half distaste.

'I wanted Patience to hear it officially,' I said.

His expression cleared, and I felt just slightly guilty. It was true, I did want Patience to hear it. But it also felt good to get the story. To get Tyler's praise. I understood how news reporters got hooked on their job—but I preferred kids' TV.

I rang Mum and told her briefly what had happened and that I'd be home later. 'You look after yourself,' she said gently. It almost made me cry.

Tol and I walked slowly back into the house, past Boris in the pit, and went upstairs, retreating to the small private space of the second bedroom. Tol was silent until we reached it and sat down, leaning our backs against the wall.

The patch of sun had moved to high on the wall. It was getting late.

'She told me once that she wanted children,' Tol said.

From below, Boris called out, 'I go get the concrete, miss.' He shut the door firmly behind him. It was just the two of us in the house now, and I felt the tension go out of me. I resisted the impulse to lean my head on his shoulder.

'Julieanne saw everyone else as puppets to dance on her strings. I doubt she thought of the baby any differently.'

It was one of the most terrible things I'd ever said about anyone, and part of me wanted him to deny it, to argue me out of it. But he merely tucked the corners of his mouth in and then sighed.

'Now what?' he asked, half to himself.

'I have to see Patience. Help her sort out if she wants to go home now her mum's not a murderer. Want to come?'

'She doesn't know me. I'd be in the way.'

He was right, but I was reluctant to leave him. That moment when he'd almost let Stephenson fall came back to me with force. This was a good man. A truly gentle man, who would never knowingly hurt anyone, not even the man who'd killed his girlfriend. How many people could you say that about?

I wanted to hug him. Comfort him. Kiss him. Even if he was leaving in six weeks.

'Tol …' I said, not sure what else to say. He moved towards me and reached out to touch my cheek, as he'd done before. I shivered, and he moved nearer.

I looked at his changeable eyes, his beautiful hands, his mouth ... Six weeks was long enough to fall in love. Did I want to risk that?

Maybe.

I thought of Julieanne, vibrantly and viciously alive one minute, dead the next. Maybe six weeks of love—or at the very least, love-making—was a good choice when death was a possibility for each one of us every day.

So I kissed him, and he kissed me back, warm and human and comforting and then, abruptly, so much more than that.

Six weeks. Six minutes. Six seconds was long enough.

ACKNOWLEDGEMENTS

My friend Ron Serdiuk first egged me on to write this book, so my first acknowledgement must go to him. And then to the other friends who let me use them as templates for some of the other characters—especially my husband, the ex-archaeologist, who might bear more than a passing resemblance to someone in the story … Particular thanks to those who beta-read the ms—Vicki Northey, Peta McCartney, Kay Ramsbottom, and of course Ron.

I had great fun writing this, and want to give my thanks to my agent, Alex Adsett, and the original editor (at HQ Publishing), Nicola Robinson.

Many thanks also to the team at Level Best Books for taking a chance on an Australian author!

talk about it

Let's talk about books.

Join the conversation:

 facebook.com/harlequinaustralia

 @harlequinaus

 @harlequinaus

harpercollins.com.au/hq

If you love reading and want to know about our
authors and titles, then let's talk about it.

www.ingramcontent.com/pod-product-compliance
Lightning Source LLC
Chambersburg PA
CBHW021454110726
47899CB00001BA/155